THE MISSING WOMAN

BOOKS BY GEORGINA CROSS

The Stepdaughter

THE MISSING WOMAN

GEORGINA CROSS

bookouture

Published by Bookouture in 2021

An imprint of Storyfire Ltd.
Carmelite House
50 Victoria Embankment
London EC4Y 0DZ

www.bookouture.com

ISBN: 978-1-83888-942-5
eBook ISBN: 978-1-83888-941-8

To my mom, dad, and sister.
We're the four Pilgrims.

PROLOGUE

"*Sabine!*" The voice screams after me, a menacing threat hollering through the woods.

Branches tear at my arms, their sharp points ripping at my clothes and hair. If I stop to look at my body, I'll see blood.

But I can't stop, can't worry about the slashes in my skin because they're getting close—too close. They'll find me. They'll strike me down and then…

My heart hammers against my ribs, my tongue dry, until all I can taste is fear. I lunge forward but it's hard to see in the dark.

Another branch whacks my face, a painful slice to my cheek, and I twist around, stumbling, the ground rising and falling beneath my feet, every root threatening to upend me.

I slam into something hard—my ankle smashing against rock, a horrible crack, and I catapult forward, my body hurling through the air until I'm splayed flat on my stomach, my hands skidding through wet leaves and dirt gathering beneath my fingernails. A cry pitches from my mouth.

But that's not the only sound. Branches crack in the distance. The heavy footsteps of whoever's coming after me.

Somewhere above the trees, fireworks. I used to think fireworks were so pretty…

Get up! Stand! I scream at myself, struggling to rise to my feet. Fear is taking hold, exhaustion too, and my frantic breathing fills my ears. But I need to keep going.

Find help. Move forward. *Save yourself, Sabine.* My thoughts repeat inside my head.

Another look up at the night sky.

You are not going to die in the dark.

PART ONE: PRESENT

CHAPTER 1

Erica

Saturday, the pool

There they sit. On one side of the neighborhood pool, Sabine and her crew with their monogrammed towels and teal tumblers with initials emblazoned on the sides. Hers reads *SLM* for Sabine Lorelei Miller, on the off chance someone could accidentally pick up her wine spritzer. Everything monogrammed: the calling card of Southern women.

It's hard not to notice the three women lying side by side on their lounge chairs wearing matching green sun visors, their hair pulled back into ponytails: Monica's hair jet-black; Sabine, a honey-blonde; and Carol, a natural redhead. Even their personalities have corresponding hair colors.

Their street is called Honors Row. Not my street, theirs. We live in the same neighborhood but orbit in entirely different circles. Those *other women*, as we call them. They're beautiful, everything I look up to. And I used to want to be like them, to have their money and happiness, to live and laugh and play, enjoying perfect marriages. But not anymore.

My daughter closes the pool gate behind me, a metal clang that hits sharply against the post and my gaze snaps away from Sabine and back to the present, my family's Fourth of July celebration at the pool.

Our group squeezes onto the patio: me and my two kids, hot and sweaty from dragging our bags across the asphalt parking lot, and my best friend Tish with her five-year-old son, Charlie. Charlie's cheeks are blotchy pink from the heat with his arms shoved into a pair of swim floaties.

"Erica, grab this, will you?" Tish asks me, off-loading one of the kids' pool noodles so she can readjust her grip on the rolling cooler. One of the wheels is turned sideways against the pavement and I make a mental note to replace the cooler soon.

Jostling the noodle under my arm, I feel it slip, my hands loaded down with three canvas bags and car keys dangling from my fingertips, and nudge the noodle in the direction of my eleven-year-old daughter. Lydia takes it without saying a word; she's too busy scanning the pool for friends.

I look too. The pool is packed and who can blame everyone for coming out? There's a reason why July in Huntsville, Alabama is called Hell's Front Porch. Situated at the base of the Appalachian Mountains, our neighborhood takes shelter in the shadow of Monte Sano at night, our homes stretched across the sweeping valley. But during the day, and especially during the summer, nothing but heat.

Blinding sun beams off the concrete, the water glaring an electric blue, and I bob my head once to let my sunglasses drop from my forehead to cover my eyes. The oversized thermometer on the clubhouse wall shows the temperature holding steady at a heatstroke-inducing ninety-five degrees. It's five o'clock. Three more hours until sunset.

The main reason we're here is the fireworks show tonight. The July Fourth holiday where we can stay at the pool and watch Roman candles dazzle the night sky, our faces tilted upwards as we clap and cheer. Every year, our neighborhood pulls out all the stops and this summer will be no different. The fireworks are said to be bigger than the last spectacle with everyone invited to the party—so long as you've paid your membership dues. The membership fees, I admit, I've spent months saving up for.

A group of children line up to have their faces painted. They're donning American flag swimsuits and holding popsicles melting in the sun. The clubhouse manager strolls past wearing a blue-and-white sundress and she calls out, "Happy July Fourth!" as we tell her the same.

Everyone is so cheerful and I know I'll remember this moment. A freeze frame in time before the fireworks fill the sky.

Tish walks ahead, her long blonde hair hiked in a messy bun, tiny wisps curling around her forehead. We follow, and so begins the process for us to find a place to sit. A table would be best, lounge chairs even better, but so late in the day and with the fireworks show scheduled for this evening, we'll settle for a single chair if we're lucky.

Halfway around the deck, sweat is dripping behind my ears and Taylor, my youngest daughter, who's seven, pulls at her ponytail that's slick against her head. Our flip-flops beat a rhythmic rubber *thwack*ing sound across the concrete as we move steadily through the crowd.

Tish side-steps a crying child, swim diaper ready to bust. A man sunscreens his son from head to toe, the kid puffing out his cheeks to hold his breath. Music pumps from the club speakers, surround sound blasting a Today's Hits playlist while kids shoot down the water slide, each child hollering louder than the last as mothers at the bottom scoop away their paddling toddlers.

Tish spots a solitary chair and she rushes over, plunking down her bags as if planting a flag. I hurry to throw my stuff down too before surveying our area, the four by six patch of concrete we've commandeered for ourselves. More sweat pools along my hairline, and I reach back, twisting the knot at my neck tighter.

Another look at the towels littered at our feet. One chair. Five people.

But Tish is on the move. She's spotted a seat a family doesn't appear to be using anymore and asks in the polite voice I've heard her use during countless budget meetings at work if we can have it. The woman says yes, without so much as looking up from her magazine.

Tish drags the chair over. "Beer me," she says.

With a grin, I pull two Blue Moons from the cooler and slip them into koozies, tossing the twist caps into my bag as we take long, deep sips. But before us, our brood is growing antsy, ready to bolt, and I set aside the bottle and hand Tish a can of SPF 50.

We go to town, coating our children with sunscreen, paying extra attention to the tender skin below their eyes, especially Charlie's freckly nose. Lydia insists on doing her own and carefully runs a sunscreen stick up and down her face with the precision of someone who has been experimenting with my makeup at home. She snaps the cap back in place, done.

Tish and my two kids are close, just as I am with her son, Charlie. She's practically an aunt to my children, having known them since they were small with Tish being an almost constant fixture in our lives. She and Charlie live just around the corner and come around often. We're both divorced so we also have that turmoil in common. And we work at the same aerospace and defense contractor, jobs we fell into after years of government proposal work, even though these days, I find I'm growing increasingly bored. Something lately has left me distracted.

Taylor shimmies to escape my clutches, her arms covered with white-streaked sunscreen I'm attempting to rub in.

"You're good," I tell her and her shoulders relax, but then I apply one more blast to the back of her neck and she shrieks, "*Quit it!*" with a gap-toothed smile.

I swat my daughter playfully on the butt and smack the back of Charlie's legs too. "Get out of here. Go swim," I laugh.

The younger two scamper toward the shallow end, water toys clutched in their hands. Lydia runs in search of friends near the diving board.

And I sit back, letting out my breath, willing for the peace to come. But I didn't know how short-lived that would be.

CHAPTER 2

Sabine Miller stands up. That's not a big deal, everyone stands up from their chair now and again to go to the bathroom, buy something from the clubhouse café, walk around and talk to friends—but she's leaving before the fireworks. She's pulling her white coverup over her shoulders and slipping it down her waist, sliding one foot into her flip-flop and then another, collecting her magazine, drink cup, and car keys before saying something to Monica and Carol. Her friends motion for her to sit back down.

She gestures to the parking lot and then somewhere in the distance, maybe her home. The women scrunch their faces, but Sabine lifts her cooler as if assuring them she'll restock their drinks and will be right back. Carol shakes her tumbler—it's empty—and Monica cracks a joke that makes all three of them laugh.

Monica and Carol are wearing nearly identical two-pieces, the kind with a twisted bandeau top that shows off their toned stomachs and sculpted arms. They do enough Pilates and walk enough miles around Green Cove to earn their bodies, Sabine too. Most mornings, I see the three of them power walking toward the nature preserve while I'm on my way to work, their ponytails and green visors bobbing in unison. I'm lucky if I can squeeze in a jog on the weekends.

I look away and plop down beside Tish. She hikes her foot on the chair and frowns at the Dark Raven nail polish that's chipping on her toes.

The sun is boiling on our heads and since we aren't lucky enough to secure an umbrella, the sweat is spreading across my lower back and into the cotton of my coverup, the material sticking to my skin. But I know we're content to sit for a little while longer. We do this every time—get the kids in the pool first before finishing our beers and jumping in the water.

A deep-bellied laugh catches my attention and I look up. It's one of the dads, Tom Humphries, making a cannonball splash in the deep end. Tom sells enough real estate to keep a home on Honors Row, his immaculate front yard awarded the recent Garden of the Month with his wife, Genevieve, responsible for sending the Green Cove newsletter every Sunday with the precision of a schoolteacher. Her latest email announced an increase in homeowner's dues, the money supposedly essential for maintaining the grounds and all six miles of painted fence. But I'm almost positive it's paying for the upkeep of the waterfall entrance at Honors Row. Genevieve stretches out on a chair, her perfectly pedicured toes pointing in the sun.

I also spot Jeff Maddox, my neighbor from two streets over. He's kneeling at the edge of the pool helping his daughter with her float. When he sees me, he waves awkwardly and I wave awkwardly in return.

We went on a date once, Jeff and me. It fell flat, the highlight of the night being a shared plate of chicken curry at a local Thai place. Making conversation with Jeff was like trudging through mud. Talking about the weather might have been easier or perhaps lawn care, as I see him cutting his grass every weekend.

After that, I told Tish, no more dating neighbors. It's bad enough we might run into each other at the pool but driving past each other or bumping into one another at the grocery store too?

We started using dating apps instead and with much better success. Tish met someone who lives about twenty minutes away in Harvest. He's divorced with kids about the same age as Charlie.

But he freaked her out recently, talking about second chances and getting remarried. Tish assures me they're taking it slow. And I've just started seeing a guy named Terry. We messaged a little bit last week before going on our first date. I'm hoping we'll be able to meet up again next weekend. Terry is divorced with no kids and sells software for a tech company. At least he laughs at my jokes which is something Jeff Maddox couldn't manage to do.

I hear the bounce of the diving board and it's Lydia, ready to jump, fingers pinched against her nose with one arm raised above her head. She comes down with a splash and when she surfaces, she spins toward me, her eyes blinking away the water as she smiles. I cheer and Tish looks up, clapping too.

A shout from across the deep end—it's Carol. She's cupping a hand to her mouth and calling to her daughters to, "Flip off the swan!" before reaching for Sabine's arm and gripping it tightly, insisting she watches before she goes.

Carol's daughter hoists her body up and over the swan inflatable before rising to her feet, steadying herself for one moment, two, before pushing off to a front flip, the float shooting behind her and skimming across the water. The girl breaks free to the surface. "Good girl!" Carol shouts, and her youngest daughter scrambles for a turn.

Monica says something to Sabine which prompts both women to smile at Monica's sons floating lazily on nearby rafts, neither of them lifting their heads at the commotion. Sabine doesn't have children.

Sabine hikes the cooler bag higher on her arm and blows the women a kiss, her wrist showing off a slew of silver bangles, one with a bright blue charm. Sunlight beams off the charm with a flash. Her friends blow a kiss back but it's rushed. They're turning their heads to watch the next girl jump.

Sabine shifts where she stands. She wants to say something, her eyes pinched, lips parting, as if a thought is charging swiftly across her brain. But the moment passes and her face goes still. Her friends are no longer paying attention.

She looks down at her feet, at the water. Across the pool. Our eyes lock.

And I catch my breath, my body halting in position. But I don't look away.

It's a coincidence, that's what it is. I'm in her line of sight. She's staring at something in the distance, someone standing behind me or the new row of crape myrtles planted behind the gate.

But no, there's no mistaking it. We're across the deep end from one another, a short enough distance—less than twenty feet—for me to know her eyes are fixated on mine. Her smile is gone and replaced with something hard. Wincing. Pleading and pained.

And something else—am I imagining this—*does she look terrified?*

A chill tingles across my scalp, the moment slicing through time. The look only lasts a few seconds but it's long enough. An unsettled sensation races down my spine until all I want to do is break free from her gaze and look anywhere else.

We've just shared something—I have no idea what it is but it's there. She thought of something. She remembered something. And I'm the only one who saw the shadow fall across her face.

But what, Sabine?

What could possibly be wrong with your life? And why look *at me*? We orbit in entirely different worlds. You live on Honors Row, and I do not. We don't attend the same dinner parties. We only share this neighborhood pool.

But I don't get to ask because Sabine turns her head and she's gone, the pool gate slamming behind her.

And the truth is, if I'd called out to her, I'm not sure if she would have told me anyway. I'm not someone she would confide to. Despite the heat, I suddenly feel cold.

*

"Ladies, is she here? Have you seen her?"

I'm on the other side of the pool standing in line with the kids who have been begging the last hour to have their faces painted. Mark Miller, Sabine's husband, is heading directly to where Sabine's friends are sitting and when he reaches them, I can't help but lean to one side to listen. I'm unable to forget that look she gave me.

And something else, a bracelet I found near the gate. Silver with a bright blue charm and looking very much like the one she had been wearing on her wrist. Another strange coincidence—me finding this jewelry while a crowd rallied around the snow cone truck, the kids pleading with their parents for money.

How did it drop—the bangle? Did it get tangled when Sabine hoisted the cooler bag up her arm, the clasp coming loose? And in her hurry, did she not hear the bracelet drop to the ground?

The bracelet is shoved in my pool bag now. I'm thinking I can bring it to Sabine when she returns. I can hand it to her quickly or leave it on her chair when her friends aren't paying attention. We don't have to speak.

But Mark is perched on the side of Sabine's chair and looking sorely out of place from everyone else in his khaki pants, tie, and button-down shirt. An American flag button pinned to his chest, the man in constant campaign mode.

He lifts his shoes, an expensive-looking pair of brown leather loafers, when he realizes he's parked his feet in a puddle of water. He keeps a steady gaze on Sabine's best friends.

Mark Miller, our county commissioner, is running for a second term this fall with billboards lined up and down the parkway, his golden hair and brilliant white teeth smiling upon every commuter, his radio commercials promising *continued transparency for local government.* The election is this November and a slam dunk if you ask me. Many of our neighbors are voting for him.

He's intense but well-loved. A shining star in local politics who can do no wrong. The addition of the new surgery center at the hospital is his major coup, along with the economic growth he's secured the last few years. Several companies have also announced they're relocating their headquarters to North Alabama and bringing more jobs with them. Mark Miller is everything and more you would want in your county commissioner and it doesn't hurt he is also drop-dead gorgeous.

"Sabine?" Monica says as Mark waits for an answer.

"Yes. She's here, isn't she?"

"Yeah, but..." She leans over and taps Carol on the arm. "She went back to the house, right, Carol? Isn't that where she said she was going?"

Carol lolls her head to one side. "She went to get us more drinks." She glances at the time. "But that was like an hour ago."

He presses his phone to his ear. "She's not answering. I've called several times and nothing." Motioning at Monica, he asks, "Can you try?"

In front of me, two chairs open up and Taylor and Charlie leap forward as Taylor points at a picture and asks, "What about this?" or "What about a ladybug?" and I nod faintly, not sure if she's asking me or Charlie, or the teenage girls assigned to face paint, because my head is tilted, painfully aware I'm still eavesdropping.

Monica frowns. "She's not picking up for me either. Maybe she has it on silent."

Carol shrugs. "Or maybe she ran to the store and left it in the car."

"I thought you were supposed to be at work?" Monica says.

"I was but I finished early," he says. "Thought it'd be nice to join you all and surprise Sabine. Come up here and watch the fireworks."

"You're so good," Monica tells him. "So sweet. Frank's not bothering."

"Ted neither," Carol adds.

He picks up his phone and tries again. "Why won't she answer?" A long, heavy pause as he stares at the pool. "I think something's wrong."

The women don't respond, and something about their silence is eerie. Carol's shoulders stiffen. The hair on the back of my neck tingles with alarm.

"Last night," Mark begins. "She was spooked."

Monica whips her head. "We were all spooked." She rubs at something on her towel, her fingers pressing harder. "She'll be fine."

Mark stands up. "Something's not right. I'm going home. I need to check."

She reaches out to him but he pulls away, looking worried.

"They won't try it again," she says.

But Mark doesn't look so sure. His often confident-looking face now appears terrified. Almost in a whisper he says, "You know as well as I do she shouldn't have gone home by herself."

CHAPTER 3

My daughter Lydia's voice from the backseat: "What's happening?"

Less than a half mile from the pool, we're rounding the corner to Honors Row when we spot police cars lined up and down the street.

We don't normally take this route home; it's much faster to cut through the back of the neighborhood around the other side of the golf course. But with the fireworks show finished, the crowd *ooh*ing and *aah*ing at every pop, aerial, and bang, the kids begged us to drive past the waterfall, the multiple tiers of water splashing and cascading down the rocks. The kids reminded us how they light up the landscaping for the July Fourth celebrations.

But it looks like we won't be seeing the light show today.

Lydia leans forward, her face appearing between the front seats, her eyes wide and unblinking, as she asks, "Whose house is that?"

Tish stares out the window. "I think it's the Millers'."

I slow down, a soft churn in my stomach.

Tish puts a hand to her chest. "I hope everything's okay."

I count eight patrol cars in all, their blue-and-red lights strobing against the Millers' chateau-white walls. Just beyond their roof, the sky lights up with the flare of a neighbor's firework, the pop and sizzle making my hands flex against the steering wheel.

A police officer stands in the middle of the street and directs us to turn around. I do what he instructs but only after coming to a near crawl, my foot pressing gently on the brake, my speed dropping to five miles an hour. My head, along with every one of my passengers' heads, swiveling to get a better look.

The front door of the Millers' house opens revealing a chandelier the size of my kitchen table rippling light against the foyer, a vestibule of marble floors and a grand curved staircase with several police officers assembled inside. Someone steps onto the front porch and closes the door, the light shining behind them through a patchwork of diamond shapes cut in the glass. He's clutching an evidence bag and runs it down the sidewalk to a waiting patrol car. They drive off, and in their place, a news van pulls up, and then another.

I look for Mark, any signs of Sabine, but there are only police officers from what I can tell, the front sitting room filling with the outlines of black uniforms. An ambulance is parked out front with its doors shut—no indication it's racing to the hospital any time soon. My stomach churns again.

"This doesn't look good," Tish says, but she coughs lightly, covering her mouth as if she didn't mean to say the words out loud, doesn't want to scare the children, but everyone hears. There's not a sound from anyone else in the car.

In my rearview mirror, a minivan pulls in behind me, the driver forced to turn around too. They're slowing down, both of us rubbernecking and cruising for a better look, but they're too close and I wish they'd back off. Frustration riddles its way through my body and I push lightly on the gas to move ahead slowly. But what I really want is another thirty seconds to find out what's happened.

The thought comes to me from out of nowhere—but I know it, I can feel it. *Something's happened to Sabine.* And she knew it too.

That tormented look from across the pool. The way she walked out, the gate behind her swinging closed. I sat there for the longest time trying to make sense of it, not saying a thing about it to Tish. How could I explain a look?

Time passed. The kids emerged from the pool asking for snacks and Tish and I went for a swim. Mark's calls to Sabine went unanswered, and then, the moment when Mark feared for her too.

He knew something... but what?

She shouldn't have gone home by herself.

A chill washes over me again, an unrelenting tightness in my chest and I swallow it down, an electric jolt running through my belly.

In my bag, Sabine's bracelet remains shoved at the bottom. I never got a chance to return it.

With the car behind me, I speed up until I have no choice but to turn at the next street, the Millers' house disappearing behind us in a veil of blue-and-red patrol lights. The van turns away too.

Several neighbors leave their houses and make their way toward the Millers', most of them still wearing their bathing suits and T-shirts after returning from the pool. They walk slowly, pensive, several of them pausing on the corner to stare. But I don't stop to ask. By the looks on their faces, they have no clue what's going on either.

Tish twists around in her seat and faces the front, and the kids do the same. She pulls at the seat belt that moments earlier was stretched across her collarbone and rubs at the skin.

"You think someone broke into their house?" she asks me.

"I don't know."

"They'd have an alarm, wouldn't they, Mom?" Lydia asks.

"I'm sure."

"Or someone got hurt," Taylor pipes up. "Maybe Mr. Miller fell down the stairs."

"Why the stairs?" Lydia asks.

"I don't know. People fall down the stairs sometimes."

Tish looks at me. "Didn't we see Mark at the pool?"

"He was up there."

"I saw him too," Lydia says. "He was shaking hands with people."

"Was he there for the fireworks?" Tish asks.

"I don't think so…" She stops to think. "I don't remember. There were so many people."

Tish glances at me again. "Or could it be Sabine?"

"I saw her at the pool too," Lydia confirms.

"You think *she's* the one who got hurt?" Taylor asks, a crack in her voice. "She's too pretty to get hurt."

"That's ridiculous," Lydia tells her.

"I don't want anybody to get hurt," Charlie cries also.

"No one got hurt," Tish consoles him.

"But you said Mrs. Sabine."

"I didn't mean to. We don't know what happened."

"I don't want anyone to fall down the stairs."

"No one fell down the stairs," Lydia says, sighing.

Tish twists back around to look at each of the kids, hoping to calm them. "It will be all right. The police are taking care of everything, they always do. It's nothing serious." She shoots me a smile. "Besides, we live in one of the safest neighborhoods on the planet. Isn't that right, Erica? The safest?"

My hands remain locked on the steering wheel.

"The safest," I agree.

*

Our other best friend, Amanda, calls as we pull into the garage. I've known Amanda Kimbrough since Tish introduced me at the neighborhood block party shortly after we moved in.

"Yes, we heard," Tish answers. "We drove right by. Yes, we'll be here."

I throw the car into park. "Does she know anything?"

"She's coming over."

Everyone grabs their bags as I punch the code into the alarm keypad beside the door: 14-27, my kids' birthdays. The children rush into the house and the tightness in my chest starts to ease, the steady relief of knowing we have an alarm and we're safe at home. After seeing the police cars lined up outside the Millers', it's comforting knowing we can return without fear of someone leaping out. No boogie men here.

But then anxiety riddles my chest. Had Sabine thought she was safe too?

The kids scramble through the kitchen as Lydia flips on one overhead light, and then another. Tish helps me toss the pool bags and wet towels on the floor before wrangling Charlie into the shower. She calls for Taylor to shower in my master bathroom.

In the kitchen, I set aside the remaining food from the cooler. Carrot sticks. Juice boxes. A soggy sandwich in a Ziploc bag that's tossed in the trash. An unexciting dinner at the pool but at least it was cheaper than ordering from the club café.

At the counter, Lydia pushes aside a stack of Taylor's artwork, an assortment of watercolors my youngest daughter insists on keeping out on display, some of the corners curled from someone spilling juice earlier. "Why doesn't she move this stuff?" Lydia mumbles, knowing as well as I do there isn't enough space.

We live in Green Cove just like everyone else at the pool but our home is a far cry from the wealthier section of Honors Row. While I might long for a larger kitchen with a stainless-steel island and marble countertops, enough surface area for Taylor to lay out each watercolor and a large prep space to make our spaghetti-and-meatball dinners, I know I shouldn't complain. I should remember how lucky we are. Our home is more than sufficient for us, especially on my single income. My ex-husband, Derek, and I have joint custody of the kids and we split the costs right down the middle. But for my mortgage I'm on my own.

Up and down our street, and particularly on this end of the neighborhood, our house looks like the others on our block, similar cookie-cutter style with nearly identical layouts: arched windows, white-bleached sidewalks, matching black mailboxes with our house numbers listed on brass plates on one side. Each house evenly spaced apart.

The kids and I have been living here five years, since Derek found an apartment closer to work. Tish is the one who told me how tranquil Green Cove is, set apart from the rest of the city and nestled within this valley. And I love it here—the playground where the kids can play; the fishing pond where I've taught Taylor and Charlie how to set their own bait, my years of growing up in Louisiana and fishing with Granddad coming into their own. On the other side of the park, a lane for Lydia and me to ride our bicycles.

But on the flip side of the neighborhood is Honors Row with its multi-million-dollar McMansions and chandeliers as big as the one we saw in the Millers' home, with golf carts parked in their driveways. Movie rooms and landscaped gardens. Doctors' and lawyers' salaries with three-car garages to fit their matching Range Rovers. Not a glimpse of that wealth in my humble cul-de-sac. Although I've seen Sabine on multiple occasions taking evening strolls along our same bike lane, we've never waved. We barely know each other.

The developers planned our subdivision twenty years ago with a vision this would be a place where all income levels could come together and share in the same space: same parks, same schools, the same grocery store. All of us sharing neighborhood amenities including the junior Olympic-size pool and our local church. But something the developers overlooked: the miles of differences in between. Especially when they put in that golf course and it cut through our neighborhood straight down the middle. A line drawn in the sand. Two distinct halves. Us vs. Them.

I've tried to ignore it, I really have. The feeling of inadequacy. My jealousy too, not wanting to let it get to me. But it's hard.

Working full-time and raising the kids while most everyone on Honors Row is still married with a nanny to boot. No one here to help me clear out the gutters or fix a pipe if it bursts. Certainly not a husband to help me landscape the garden, even though it was my idea to leave Derek. Sometimes a neighbor comes over and helps me pressure-wash the patio.

Lydia removes a Coke from the fridge, her hair pulled back in a scrunchie, her face pinched tight with worry. She's toggling the soda can tab back and forth while glancing nervously out the window.

"People wouldn't break into our house, would they, Mom?" she asks.

I shake the ice chips from the cooler. "They wouldn't dare."

"No, seriously. They wouldn't, right?"

"No one's going to break into our house, honey."

"How do you know?"

"They wouldn't."

"But what about the Millers?"

"The Millers have about eight thousand more things than us."

"We have stuff too."

"The Millers have nicer stuff."

"Well, I thought we had a Neighborhood Watch."

"We do."

"And the Millers would have an alarm."

"Yes, I'm sure."

"Unless they were home when something happened."

"They were at the pool."

"Or when they got back?"

Or when Sabine stopped at the house first…

I shake the thoughts away, hoping she doesn't catch my hesitation. Instead I tell her, "I bet whatever happened took place before they got home. They're filling out the police report right now."

"But why an ambulance?"

"It's protocol."

Her eyes light up. "So no one got hurt if no one was in the ambulance, right, Mom? I mean, it was empty. You saw that too? That's a good sign?"

My heart goes out to my daughter. Her frightened thoughts battling with the need to think everything is going to be okay.

"I think that's a very good sign," I tell her, and add, "You know, when things like this happen, a lot of things get safer afterwards. More cops, more patrol, more Neighborhood Watch. People won't go after the same neighborhood twice, and not so soon."

"Like a grace period."

I nod. "Yeah, like a grace period."

She fiddles with the Coke tab again. Another glance out the window as she chews nervously on the inside of her cheek. "Will you tell me if you hear anything?"

"Absolutely."

Lydia has been this way since she was a toddler, always the more anxious of my children. If I let her, she'd sit right here at the kitchen counter and wait on Amanda, listening to our entire conversation, but I won't.

"It'll be okay," I tell her.

She smiles meekly before crossing the room, her turn for the shower next. And I'm glad she's stepped away and out of earshot because the door from the garage swings open. It's Amanda, her brown curly hair shoved beneath a baseball cap and wearing a baggy T-shirt that hangs loose over track pants.

She tosses a bag of potato chips and several packets of M&Ms on the kitchen counter, her motions frenetic. The snacks are her way of saying *we're going to be up for a while*. It's nearly ten but there's no way anyone is going to sleep soon.

Amanda settles herself on a bar stool and Tish, finishing with the kids' showers and encouraging them to stay in Taylor's room and play, slides onto the stool beside her.

I stand opposite the counter from them, my hands gripping the edge of the sink, waiting to hear what she has to say.

"I heard it's Sabine," Amanda tells us. She looks buzzed. Excited. Her fear mixed with adrenaline.

My heart lurches—I was right.

Tish stares at her. "What do you mean it's Sabine? What happened?"

Amanda scrolls through her phone looking for updates or messages or both. "Whatever happened, it was at the house." Her eyes skate back and forth across the screen.

Tish leans over. "What are you looking at? The Nextdoor app?"

"Yes. All anyone in the neighborhood group is talking about is the Millers. Neighbors said they walked over but were told to turn around."

Tish nods. "We got turned around too."

"Mark is there, but not Sabine." Amanda taps with her thumbs. She clicks on something else. "Mark is frantic."

"How do they know that?" Tish asks. "Are the police saying anything?"

Amanda looks up. "It's all speculation right now but someone approached a cop and that's what he told them. They're out now looking for Sabine."

I spin on my heel and open the fridge with a yank. Forget the junk food; this Fourth of July is going to require more alcohol. I grab three beers and place them in front of the girls with Tish and Amanda barely acknowledging.

Tish's eyes grow wide. "Out looking for Sabine? Like she didn't come home or they think someone took her from the house?"

"They don't know."

"What do they think happened to her?"

"I don't know," Amanda says again.

Tish whips out her phone and says she's checking Facebook.

I take a long sip of my beer, the bubbles coating my throat, trying to calm the steady pang inside my chest.

"What about Ring?" Amanda asks. Ring is the video doorbell system that connects with an app on your phone allowing you to watch video of who is approaching or leaving your house.

"I don't have it." Tish glances at me. "You?"

"Nope."

"I do," Amanda says. "It's the one thing my ex did for me before he split. Putting up those cameras now that I'm living alone."

Tish rolls her eyes. "I'm convinced he's using them to spy on you."

Amanda's ex-husband, Connor, is one of the IT leads for a government defense contractor. If he could find a way to tap into her video cameras, he would.

"Even if he wanted to—which he can't." Amanda cuts her eyes at us. "My Ring cameras are only set up at my front and back doors. That's about as exciting as it gets."

Tish smirks. "He can still see who you've got coming over..."

Amanda smirks too. "Maybe I don't care if he sees that."

My unease rolls gently beneath the surface—unease or fear, or both.

"Okay," I say, cutting through their chatter. "What does Ring have to do with anything? It's not like we can see into the Millers' camera at their door. Only the cops will be able to do that."

"There's also a way for people to post info," Amanda says. "People can post alerts or videos in the app saying, *watch out for this.* Or *have you seen this person stealing packages from my front porch?* That sort of thing." She turns her phone toward me. "See?"

I look at a couple of hazy screen captures with videos and captions underneath. People posting about dogs or raccoons or coyotes getting into their trash, the cameras recording any movement in their driveway.

"I don't see anything about the Millers."

Amanda brings the phone back to her face. "Not yet, but I bet people will be posting stuff soon. Front porch views. Cars driving by. People returning from the pool. Video cameras showing anyone going up and down that street." She continues to scroll, her eyes locked in on anything that might be related to Honors Row.

"I'll check the news sites," Tish offers. "We saw a couple of vans pull up when we turned around."

"Good idea," Amanda says.

Tish clicks from one website to another. "Nothing yet. Maybe when we get closer to the ten o'clock news."

Amanda's phone dings, and she sucks in her breath. "They found blood."

My head snaps up with a jerk.

"Blood on the floor," Amanda says, each message lighting up her screen and shining a glint in her eyes.

Frantic, Tish says, "Whose blood? *Where?* Was it Sabine's?"

My heart races, a sickening swell rising through my chest and spreading to my body.

Amanda has a hard time meeting our stares. "The door was smashed in with blood on the floor."

CHAPTER 4

Tish rips the phone from Amanda's hands. "Who's saying that? The news isn't even reporting those details yet."

Amanda pulls back her phone. "One of the guys I work with."

Of course. Amanda works for city hall. With colleagues in both the mayor's office and friends in the sheriff's department, someone is bound to hear something and share that information with her, especially when it involves someone living in her neighborhood—not to mention someone as high-profile as County Commissioner Mark Miller and his wife.

"Someone hurt Sabine?" Tish asks. "Why?"

"How do we know the blood is hers?" Amanda asks. "It could be Mark's."

"Like he was trying to stop them?"

"Or they were going after Mark instead."

I hear them, but I'm not hearing them. The panic in my chest rises higher.

"And Sabine got in the way and they hurt her? *They took her?* Oh my God…" Tish settles against the bar stool, her shoulders sinking. She watches as Amanda's thumbs move rapid-fire across her screen. "What else do they know?"

"Not sure yet."

She rubs her arms. "This is crazy."

A loud noise rumbles inside my ears.

"Guys," I say.

But Tish doesn't hear me. "If there's blood, there was an altercation. And if Sabine is missing then whoever's got her could hurt her too."

"Or she could already be dead."

Tish smacks her on the arm. "Don't say that! Why kill her? Why not ask for a ransom?"

Amanda says, "Okay, fine. Or ask for a ransom."

"*Guys*," I say again. This time, louder.

Tish's eyes slide toward me.

"Something happened at the pool."

Amanda raises her eyebrows.

"I know something's wrong."

"Well, of course something's wrong," she quips, "or there wouldn't be a bunch of cops and Sabine missing with blood at the house."

"But what do you mean *at the pool*?" Tish asks.

I pause, my words slowing, not knowing exactly where to start. "Sabine… she was there. We shared this look…" I grip my beer bottle, my hands grasped tightly around the glass.

Tish eyes me. "Are you okay?"

I look at the blood that is leaving my hands and turning my fingertips white, and let go of the bottle, shaking my head. But it's not an answer to her question; it's more like confusion, my head spinning with a million dark thoughts whipping in every direction.

Amanda's eyes peer over the top of her screen. "She looked at you?" she says, in a way that means to imply, *that's it?*

"Yes." I feel silly now that I've said it out loud, but I've got to tell them. "It was odd. It felt… purposeful."

Amanda continues to stare. "Did she say anything to you?"

"No. Just this look from across the deep end. She…" I'm stumbling for the right words. "… she looked frightened."

"Why would she look frightened?"

"I have no idea."

"I saw her at the pool and she looked fine to me," Tish says.

"She *was* fine, and then she wasn't. Right as she was leaving. It was like something came over her, this fear from out of nowhere. And she looked at me." I nervously peel at the label wrapped around the bottle, my fingernail scratching at the foil until it's coming off in strips.

Should I also tell them I have her bracelet? That I'm weird for keeping it—that my intent is to return it to her?

"I know it sounds crazy but it was like she *knew* something was going to happen. To her. Tonight." I meet their eyes again.

"What do you mean she *knew* something was going to happen?" Amanda says. "How would she know?"

I shrug, confident I sound like a fool.

"And why you?" Amanda asks. "I mean, no offense, Erica, but you guys aren't friends. There was that thing that happened—"

A heat flushes down the back of my neck. "That has nothing to do with this."

"That thing at the auction last year," Amanda presses, and my stomach twists. "It was pretty intense. Maybe she never got over it?"

"It was stupid," I tell her. "It's over. Tonight, this was different." It's still difficult to explain. "She didn't seem angry—"

"*You're* the one who should be angry," Tish says resolutely.

I drop my gaze.

I don't want to talk about it. Not about that night. Not about the argument that seemed to come from out of nowhere between Sabine and myself. It was embarrassing and in front of all those people at the school fundraiser. An ordeal that lasted only minutes with Sabine storming out of the room. After that, we returned to our separate sides of the neighborhood.

"It's been a year," Tish continues. "So why would Sabine give you this weird look but not say anything to Monica and Carol? If something was upsetting her, that's who she'd tell."

Amanda asks, "Were they with her at the pool?"

"Always."

Amanda turns to me and waits for more of an explanation. I hesitate—I honestly don't know. "Maybe she already told them. Or maybe it was something else."

"Something else?" She sets down her phone.

"I heard Mark. He thought she was there. He wanted to surprise her."

"How do you know that?"

"I was eavesdropping. Over by the face-painting table, they were close by. And after Sabine gave me that look, I couldn't help myself." I pause, trying to remember his exact words. "He said she shouldn't have gone home by herself."

Tish's eyes bolt open.

"Monica said something weird too. She said, *they won't try it again.*" Worry crawls across my chest, my insides tightening.

"*They?*" Amanda says. "*Who* won't try it again?"

"I have no clue."

"And try what?" Tish asks. Just like Mark described and the way Monica said they all felt that night, Tish looks spooked too—the word coming back to haunt me.

A paleness spreads through her cheeks. "She knew something was going to happen to her?" Tish's words send goosebumps up and down my body.

"Erica"—Amanda looks at me—"you have to tell the police."

Panic seizes my chest. "Right now?"

"You need to tell them what you heard."

Tish's eyes bounce between us. "But won't Mark Miller tell them? Won't Monica? Erica doesn't have to get involved. If they've been having trouble, if someone's been stalking them or harassing them, or they think someone's tried breaking in before, they would have already told the cops. Wouldn't they?"

"I hope so," Amanda says. She looks at me intently. "But you need to tell the police too. Every piece of information is important.

They're out there looking for her and every hour is critical, you know this. We hear those same statistics."

I drop away from the counter, anxiety running through my head.

The cops. Getting involved. Cops at my house with kids who need to be going to bed soon. Lydia, who's already rattled and will ask a hundred questions when Amanda and Tish leave—she won't be able to sleep. I'm not sure how the younger kids will respond when police officers show up at our door.

I back against the fridge, noting the intense stares from my friends. Swallowing down my fear, I shake my hands. "You're right."

But Tish is still trying to find a way to get me off the hook. She knows I'd rather not get mixed up in all this—*who would?* The likes of us getting mixed up with the people on Honors Row.

Tish also knows about my daughter. She knows the crippling anxiety that can take root in Lydia—we saw it forming tonight; Tish has been with us before I don't know how many times when Lydia has cried herself to sleep or clung to us with the slightest shake of a thunderstorm. She'll worry we've left the house with the oven still on.

Tish says, "Mark's wife is missing. If someone broke into their house and took her and he knows there's been an issue before, he'll tell them who's done it. He'll tell the cops immediately. Her friends too. Erica doesn't have to say anything. She doesn't need to get pulled into their ordeal."

"And what if they don't?" Amanda asks. "What if they don't say anything?"

"Why wouldn't they?" Tish asks.

"But what if they don't know who it is?"

"Monica said *they*, right? She has to know something. She's already told the police too, I'm sure of it."

"I'll tell the cops," I interrupt them. "I just need to calm myself down first." I take another sip of my beer before setting down the bottle. The three of us grow quiet, my thoughts ricocheting until I'm squeezing the sides of my head; it hurts.

"Who would want to do this to the Millers?" I ask, finally. "It's so horrible. Who would go after Mark and Sabine?"

"Maybe someone who doesn't want Mark to be county commissioner," Amanda suggests. "Or someone who hates him and sees Sabine as collateral damage."

"No one hates Mark Miller," Tish says.

I nod. "He's everyone's golden boy."

But Amanda rolls her eyes. "He can't be that much of a saint."

It's frustrating sometimes to hear Amanda speak this way, her constant doubting of someone else's character especially if they're an elected official. But after years of working at city hall, her views have become jaded.

She's explained to us several times how her once-perceived notions of heroes in suits and ties, silk scarves and ruby brooches with plans for effective action, idealistic dreams and altruistic intentions, have fallen painfully short. Many of the politicians, she claims, only give podium speak—it's what we want to hear. They're full of hot air. Inaction. Or worse, they take advantage of their position. She's reminded us more than once how the wool has been pulled away from her eyes and it's hard for her to take them seriously anymore, even when it's someone like Mark Miller who's done so much for our community.

Tish shakes her head. "That poor family, that poor woman." Her eyes redden. "Do you remember when she helped the school build a new library?" She grabs a napkin and wipes at her cheek. "She doesn't have kids but she's always there, tutoring in the afternoons. She's read to Charlie several times. He thinks she's a princess because he says she's so beautiful."

My eyes redden too, my girls often having described story time with Mrs. Miller also, how she'll dress in character and wear the most elaborate costumes, often bringing the kids treats from the donut shop. "She's straight out of a fairytale," Taylor has whispered to me, and in her hands, she'll be clutching a book Sabine gifted every child.

Shame spreads through my chest. I should have thanked her. That stupid fight last year should have never happened. Instead, I should have told her what an amazing service she is doing for our children. Giving so much of her time when she doesn't have kids of her own.

I close my eyes. But she'd gotten in my face that night. She's the one who yelled.

"I can't imagine what Sabine must be going through," Tish says and my eyes blink back open. "Mark too. He must be out of his mind wondering what's happened to her, where she could be. How far they've taken her. If she's hurt or not." She clutches her arms, her fingers pressing tight.

At the counter, Amanda is reading the next set of messages. A ding, followed by another.

She looks at us. "Word is getting out fast. More details." Her eyes widen. "Back door smashed in. Sabine's car left in the garage. Her purse in the front seat. Blood trailing out the back door."

Tish stares at her phone. "It's all over Facebook too."

Nausea rises through my stomach.

Blood trailing out the back door…

The image of Sabine at the pool with that tormented look in her eyes. The countdown in her face as she carried her things.

I knew it—she was afraid something was going to happen to her. The fear she must have felt as she blew kisses to her friends, pretending to be brave and acting as if everything was fine when deep down, she had the notion that was far from the truth. Her one glitch—that look she gave me. The only clue about what she might have been thinking.

A frightening thought pulses through my body: *Then why in the world did you go home, Sabine?*

FACEBOOK GROUP POST

Praying for Sabine Miller (Private Facebook Group)

Saturday night

Alice Chin

July 4 at 9:58 p.m.

Bring Sabine Miller home safely! #SaveSabine

Eric Nichols

July 4 at 9:59 p.m.

We're joining the search team. Meet us at the corner of Chandler and Smoke Rise.

Heather Stephenson

July 4 at 10:02 p.m.

If anyone saw anything tonight, please contact police immediately.

Jennifer Krel

July 4 at 10:02 p.m.

This can't be happening! Not to that amazing woman. Not this amazing family.

> **Tamyra Meeks** My heart is breaking.
>
> **Alice Chin** We just saw her at the pool! She was dancing with the kids and buying ice cream.

Carolyn Castillo

July 4 at 10:03 p.m.

Any leads?

> **Heather Stephenson** Sabine Miller left the clubhouse around 6:45 p.m. and went home. Mark Miller went home around 7:40 p.m. He called the police.
>
> **Scott Wooley** Is Mark Miller a suspect?
>
> **Heather Stephenson** They've cleared him. He wasn't there.

Anthony Castillo

July 4 at 10:05 p.m.

What about Jacob Andrews? That guy running against Mark. Has anyone talked to him?

> **Hillary Danners** Anthony, you can't go around accusing people.
>
> **Lamar Jackson** You think he broke into Mark Miller's home and took the man's wife? Why would he do that?
>
> **Carolyn Castillo** Maybe to throw Mark Miller off his campaign trail.

Anthony Castillo Hillary, I didn't accuse anyone. I'm just asking.

Heather Stephenson If you have any specific information you need to contact the police.

Tish Abbott

July 4 at 10:11 p.m.

Really hoping Sabine Miller is okay. Thinking about her and Mark. #SaveSabine

Amanda Kimbrough

July 4 at 10:12 p.m.

Something tells me this wasn't a random break-in.

Scott Wooley Amanda, what do you know??

Carolyn Castillo I bet it's not random either. Amanda, spill it!!

Eric Nichols Instead of sitting around posting on Facebook, please join the search team.

CHAPTER 5

Amanda takes hold of the potato chip bag and yanks it open with a loud pop. So far, she's disregarded her beer, Tish too, and I pick up one of their bottles, claiming it for my own.

Tish holds up her phone. "Who started this Facebook group?"

"I don't know." Amanda crams potato chips in her mouth. "But you posted in there."

Tish gives her a look. "You did too."

I move to their side of the counter. "What group?"

Tish leans in close so I can read the heading: *Praying for Sabine.*

"That was fast," I say, reading through the messages.

Several more posts are coming in every minute. Carolyn Castillo. Paul Tomlinson. Heather Stephenson. All neighbors of ours in Green Cove.

"They're already talking about Jacob Andrews," Amanda points out.

Tish's eyes jolt. "The other guy running for county commissioner? Why on earth would he do something like this?"

"Who knows?" Amanda shrugs. "People get real desperate, especially when they're losing on the campaign trail. And from what I hear, he's losing badly."

"But this would be way more than desperate," Tish says. "Why go after your own opponent and kidnap his wife? Way too obvious."

Just like Mark, Jacob Andrews has billboards plastered around town too. Group photos at events and filling the pages of community business magazines. But instead of the golden looks and high-profile accolades like Mark, Jacob is considered the dark horse. A shark. I've never found him approachable, even when Tish drags me to Chamber of Commerce events to hear the latest news. The man is standing in the corner with a kind of abbreviated smile on his face, something that makes me think he's already considering his next move. The kind of guy who looks over your shoulder when he's talking to you, looking for a far more interesting person. A string of controversial business deals in his past haven't helped either, leaving bumps and bruises for investors along the way.

But this—this would be crazy.

"If I were Andrews," Amanda says, "I'd want a strong alibi right about now."

"You don't know it's him," Tish says. "Why would he do this?"

"Crazier things have happened."

"Maybe Mark pissed somebody off in the past," Tish says. "Some massive disagreement and this is someone else's drastic form of revenge."

"This would certainly be drastic." Amanda cocks an eyebrow. "The news outlets are going to have a field day."

I'm scrolling through the rest of the Facebook group, the prayer requests and calls for a search team with neighbors adding #SaveSabine to their posts, when halfway through, I recognize a name and the tension runs to the back of my neck. "Amanda!"

She raises her hands. "I didn't do anything."

I read her words back to her. "*Something tells me this wasn't a random break-in.*" I glare. "And now Scott Wooley is asking what you know."

Tish glares at her too.

"Carolyn thinks the same thing—a lot of people are going to. It's fine." She rolls up the potato chip bag. "They don't have to tie it back to me, or you, and think it's something that you heard."

"Amanda, I said I would tell the police."

"I know you will."

"Don't say anything to them, okay? And especially Scott. He has a huge mouth. He'll blab to everyone."

Tish scrunches her face. "That guy's a creep. Remember when he went around telling people the Barbs shouldn't use the pool until they paid their dues? They got banned from the club last summer."

Another time Scott complained about Lydia's fourth-grade teacher and almost had her fired. Turns out, the teacher was missing school for chemo treatments and didn't want anyone to know. The next time I saw him at the school parking lot I flipped him off out my car window.

With Sabine Miller missing and me overhearing something that Mark Miller may or may not have told the police yet, Scott is exactly the sort of person who would take this kind of information and run. It would be all over Facebook in minutes.

"I'll tell the police," I say again to Amanda.

"I sure hope so." She pushes the potato chip bag away. "We wouldn't want Mark or Monica hiding something, now would we?"

*

More calls come for people to join the search team and not just in the Facebook group but text messages too. I'm looking at my phone for the first time since we returned home, scrolling through the dozen or more alerts lined up on my screen, the same group texts that are buzzing for Amanda and Tish.

Tish says, "Jeff Maddox is joining the search. Eric Nichols is calling for more people too."

"Right. That does it." Amanda slides off the stool. "I'm going. You guys stay here with the kids. There are plenty of us who can go out and look."

Amanda doesn't have children, she and Connor having decided early in their marriage to remain happily child free with that decision making life much easier when their divorce became final.

I spin my eyes to Tish. "I can keep the kids if you want."

But she shakes her head. "It will freak Charlie out. It's best if I stay here too."

Amanda packs up the snack food she brought, taking plastic bags from my pantry and adding bottles of water and Gatorades she finds in the fridge, saying they'll want to have plenty of these while searching for Sabine. The Green Cove neighborhood is at least three miles across with hundreds more acres once the team heads into the nature preserve.

She hustles to the garage with Tish and I following, quick on her heels. The movement, the rush of it all, makes my heart pound. The action that is taking place. It's well after ten; Amanda will be out there past midnight.

Cold wings of fear propel us from the safety of my house and into the darkness of the garage. I flip the floodlight on, finding myself looking in every corner to chase away the shadows.

Tish's voice cracks. "What makes them think she's in the neighborhood? If someone took her, wouldn't they be miles from here at this point? They'd be long gone, right?"

"Unless someone thinks she ran from the house," Amanda says.

My eyes stretch wide. "She ran?"

"Blood trailing out the back door," Amanda repeats. "It's a possibility." She throws one plastic bag after another into her backseat. "Until someone comes forward saying they saw a car or there's video of a car taking off with Sabine, there's a chance she bolted from the house. And whoever was trying to hurt her might have gone after her too." She glances at the woods.

I think about the layout of Green Cove, the streets winding around the golf course, the front nine and back, with clear open views of the ponds and wide spaces for playgrounds. On this end of our neighborhood, our houses are close together with very few trees. But on the other side of Green Cove, a thick grove of pines provides the residents of Honors Row with plenty of privacy. And during this crisis, a place to search for Sabine.

I consider what's behind my house too, the narrow patch of grass leading to the shed at the end of my garden and a culvert that runs from the back of the hill. Beyond the hill, the golf course.

So much of our neighborhood is cleared and well-kept, but the woods stretching to Honors Row are a whole other matter: a labyrinth of roots and vines and boulders the size of Volkswagen Beetles with rocks sticking up from the earth with just enough jagged areas to trip you. I've often wondered if the developers left it that way to deter people from wandering around and ending up in the wealthier residents' backyards. It hasn't stopped a few trespassers: kids going out there to horse around, the younger ones building forts, while at night, older teens circle around with beer. One or two have wandered off and not looked where they're going, falling into a ravine. The ravine, not enough of a sharp drop to hurt anyone seriously, but enough to cause alarm.

It would be hell on earth running for your life through that.

"So you could be out there too?" I ask Amanda. "Digging around in those woods?"

"Possibly." Amanda stares into the dark, and for the first time, her brave resolve weakens ever so slightly, the weight of the night and what is happening, the information that is coming out. What she's about to go do.

The reality that a woman could be bloodied and huddled in a heap somewhere, her body sprawled in the middle of a field or wounded propped up against a tree, any member of the search team being the one to stumble upon her—including Amanda—is finally hitting her. She stands still for a moment, her jaw running slack. The look of someone with a million thoughts racing through her head.

But, just like that, Amanda blinks and her eyes snap to attention.

"Or the ponds," she says. "God knows we have enough of those around here too."

Tish's voice cracks again. "My God… the ponds. I can't even imagine."

"We'll have to check ditches. Those drains that run off the golf course. I bet they'll have us checking everything." Amanda looks up and down my street. It's quiet for now. "I heard the cops are going door-to-door asking people what they saw."

"Will they come here?"

"They're checking the neighbors on Honors Row first. Anyone who might have seen someone traveling in and out." She frowns.

Tish spots the look on her face and the realization hits us at the same time.

"But most everyone was at the pool," Tish says. "The fireworks."

"Exactly."

"A whole neighborhood waiting for fireworks," I repeat.

"I was in my backyard. Lawn chair out."

I slide my eyes to Amanda, a curious thought reaching me suddenly. "Hey, why didn't you join us at the pool?"

"Too crowded."

"You could have sat with us."

"I know. But sometimes it's nice not to have a hundred people around you." She tilts her head. "You know?"

"Well, maybe there will be others like you," Tish says. "Other people who stayed home and saw something."

"I hope so." Amanda turns and steps into the car.

But Tish stops her. Taking a good look at her baggy T-shirt and flip-flops, she says, "Do you want boots? Or a flashlight?"

Amanda stares down at her feet and releases a nervous laugh. "Yes, that would be smart, wouldn't it?" She hauls a deep breath. "I should take one step at a time and calm down. I'll run home and get boots."

"I've got flashlights." I move quickly to a shelf in my garage and pull a pair of flashlights, clicking each one to check the beams, the lights shining golden arcs across Amanda's car, my driveway too. "This one's good." I hand her an orange lantern, one of the larger L.L. Bean types the kids and I used on our last camping trip.

Amanda takes the lantern and flips it on, the light illuminating half my front yard, the crape myrtles looking like white spindly candlesticks sticking out from the edges of my sidewalk.

"That'll do the trick." She shuts off the light.

Amanda settles in the driver's seat. She peeks in the rearview mirror and adjusts the baseball cap on her head, tucking a curly lock of hair behind her ear before cranking the engine.

"Keep us updated," Tish calls to her.

"I'll let you know what I hear." Amanda sounds so confident and I'm thinking, *Sabine will be home in no time.*

We follow her car to the end of the driveway, Amanda on a mission with her phone lighting up again, an onslaught of new messages as she reverses the car, the glow casting a harsh white light against her skin, a lightning spark in her eyes as she pauses to read each one. I'm wondering what else she's hearing from her colleagues at city hall.

Amanda kicks the car into drive and she's gone.

I feel helpless, standing there with Tish, Sabine out there, somewhere, and numerous neighbors joining the search. Despite our differences, I'm scared for Sabine, I really am. I only wish things had been left better between us. They must find her safe and bring her home.

I scan the length of the street, my neighbors' houses on either side and across the way on the cul-de-sac, noticing that doors are closed, garage doors too, with lights blazing from every front porch. Everyone's doors are triple-locked tonight, I'm sure.

In a couple of the windows, shadows move against the drapes. I see the Simmons family finishing up what must be a late dinner since it's past ten o'clock—the fireworks and news about Sabine Miller's disappearance flipping everyone's schedule upside down.

Tabitha Simmons orders her kids to bring their dishes to the sink. Like us, she's staying home with her children.

Next door, the young couple, the Wilsons, who I'm almost positive will be staying in—Rebecca gave birth to twin boys less than four months ago. Mrs. Ferrington lives on the other side, her beige Cadillac parked outside. The woman, nearing seventy, will be staying put too, the newscast most likely still on, her eyes simultaneously glued to social media. I think back to who I saw posting in the Facebook group and can't remember if I saw her commenting in there also.

But at the end of the cul-de-sac, Todd Hampton's truck is missing. And so is the Atkins' vehicle, their house lit up like a Christmas tree. The TV that's normally glowing a washed-out blue in the front living room is switched off and I can only imagine they've joined the search team.

My eyes sweep one street over, a row of slate-gray rooftops outlined against an ink-black sky. The smell of freshly mowed grass still lingers, sweet and damp from someone having run their sprinklers earlier. The scent of honeysuckle and jasmine. The night air, still.

I fold my arms across my chest. It's not cold but with my worries gnawing the edges of my brain, I rub my elbows to bring me comfort. But it doesn't work. With night falling across the valley, the temperature has dropped to a more tolerable seventy-five degrees, and despite it being a summer evening, a deep chill settles inside my bones.

Sabine... out there... somewhere...

I think about Amanda, how she'll be lacing up her boots soon, her heart pounding, her feet hitting the pavement when she meets up with the search team. She'll be handing out flashlights. She'll tell them she brought bottled water. Her phone, no doubt, will continue to ping.

I look toward the hill. She'll be joining the countless neighbors and police officers who are already combing the woods and searching the grounds behind the Millers' home, their flashlights cutting this way and that, shining wide bands of light against the trees. The police will be trying to keep up with their search dogs, their howling and urgent tugging at leashes pulling the officers forward.

I prick my ears and listen for anything that resembles the search—any shouts for Sabine or barks from search dogs. Will their noises carry through the woods to where we're standing now? Will we hear repeated calls for Sabine with repeated pleas for her to answer?

Sabine! Where are you? One voice, and then another. Ten more. A whole mob shouting one on top of the other, their voices rising as a different search group calls from one street over. Updates blaring in from police walkie-talkies. Everyone's voices getting louder, their pitches higher. Then, strained. Exhaustion sinking in with each passing minute. The hours tumbling by.

But an adrenaline boost. The screech of a bullhorn, the blow of a whistle, or a cop busting a U-turn in the middle of the street. A tip coming in—*Have they heard anything? Do they know something?* More patrol cars racing down the street.

In the distance, the sound of something—a police siren? But no, they're too far off. I'm only imagining things as the police won't have made it to this end of Green Cove yet. For now, only the sounds of my air conditioning unit and every one of my neighbors' air conditioning units buzzing loudly around me, each machine revving a constant hum. The rattle and click as another one turns on. The deep *ribbit* of a bullfrog. The *tic-tic-fizz* of a sprinkler that someone's forgotten to turn off. Crickets. And the steady pounding of my heart.

I stare at the woods in the distance. Once they fan out from the Millers' home, will the search team spread through the cluster of trees next, the grove thinning out before they find themselves on the flattened turf of the golf course? Another row of houses around the corner?

I wonder when they'll make it across that hill. Will they carry long sticks and poke at the grass, checking every square inch? Will the police hand out whistles in case they spot something?

I hope Amanda has taken the lantern I gave her. She can shine a thirty-foot wall of light around her in every direction so she won't trip over anything. Most of all, so she doesn't get scared.

Like she said, they'll be checking each drain, every pond, and moving from one cul-de-sac to the next, searching through playgrounds and gazebos too. I assume they'll look for pieces of clothing—she was wearing a white bathing suit coverup, I remember that now. I see her standing at the pool: a white coverup with her hair pulled into a ponytail. Several bangles on her arm.

One of her bracelets that's shoved in my bag.

My gaze rips toward the hill. Somewhere on the other side, the search team will keep their eyes pinned down. Looking to see if she dropped anything, if anything was torn from her body—more proof she'd been chased and there had been a struggle. As she ran for her life, heart in throat, breath gasping in shocked, rattled waves, her lungs desperate for air, would she have experienced a fear so sharp and painful, would it have felt as if her chest was being sliced open, a hot searing burn until she was terrified her lungs would burst and she didn't know if she could take it anymore?

Or would she have been debilitated with fear? After sprinting from her house, bleeding and shaken, did she succumb and buckle behind a tree, eventually giving herself away with a muffled sob, a hiccup of breath, until they found her and struck her down? Did they haul her somewhere and hope she would never be found?

Will they find her blonde hair, pulled from the roots, wispy and left clinging to a branch and find blood on the ground too?

A handprint across a tree trunk. Or a bloody smear. Another splattering of drops against the leaves.

I shudder with another horrifying thought—or will they stumble upon her actual body? Will they realize she's gravely hurt… or worse… that she's dead?

Whoever chased her, there's a chance they may have dropped something too. Something torn from them in the process, a valiant fight from Sabine where she could have ripped a piece of their shirt or pulled off one of their gloves. Shoeprints could be left behind in the dirt—a rapid chase. Or crushed branches and broken limbs where the assailant plowed through the woods, not slowing down until they caught up with her.

My arms tighten around my shoulders. I know I'm freaking myself out. My mind is racing, my brain in overdrive just like Amanda's was earlier; I'm letting my thoughts consume me. I've got to take a deep breath to keep my hands from trembling.

A dog barks, and I jump. But it's the neighbor's dog and a single bark, not like one that would come from a pack of search hounds. *Get a grip, Erica.*

In the sky, a bright light. A crack and a discernible pop, a green sizzle followed by a blast of white, its embers showering down to earth.

For a second, I think it could be a police flare—*they've found something*—and I hold my breath. But it's not. A bottle rocket pops next accompanied by muffled laughter in the distance, maybe two streets over, and it's unsettling. The idea a group of teenagers are lighting fireworks and having fun, their attempt at clinging to their July Fourth celebration, while for everyone else the evening has turned into a nightmare.

Somewhere, a door slams and the fireworks stop.

I look up again, and for the first time notice the near full moon. Another two or three days before the moon will wax full, and for tonight, plenty of light to cast a glow against the hillside. That same light helping to illuminate the woods of Green Cove too.

The neighbor's dog barks again and I wish they'd bring it inside. Its low howl ratchets my nerves until I'm squeezing my shoulders again.

Standing beside me, Tish is grinding her teeth, her thoughts clearly churning in the same jittery ways as mine. She stares in the direction of a bottle rocket but doesn't say a word.

Finally, she says quietly, "It can't be Jacob Andrews."

I remain looking ahead.

"People can't possibly think he's behind this."

"It would be insane, wouldn't it? The end of his career."

She takes my arm. "I'm telling you, it *can't* be him."

Surprised, I turn to her. "Tish?"

"Jacob Andrews," she says, not letting go of my arm. "I know he didn't hurt Sabine."

The hair rises on the back of my neck. "And you know this because?"

"Because I was with him today. I'm telling you right now, he would never do this."

CHAPTER 6

I rock back on my heels. "You were with Jacob Andrews? Today?" I sound incredulous and don't mean to and a furious look flashes across her face.

"He was at my house."

"What would Jacob Andrews be doing at your house?"

"Remember I told you about my dishwasher. The leak—"

"*A leak?*" A nervous laugh escapes from my mouth. "You mean to tell me Jacob Andrews was fixing your dishwasher? Are we talking about the same guy here?" *The guy running for county commissioner?*

"He was at my house," she repeats.

I stare at Tish, my best friend who tells me everything—who I thought tells me everything—and wait for her to say something else. That she's confused. It's the wrong man. The wrong Jacob Andrews, entirely. It's another guy from across town and not the one running for county commissioner. Not the man with the controversial business deals. Not the one people are gossiping about and accusing of going after the Millers.

Not someone who would be fixing Tish's dishwasher.

"We're seeing each other," she says.

And my mouth drops open.

I choke back on another laugh but only because I don't know what else to do, my stunned nerves making my eyes bounce up and down and all over the place until I'm forcing myself to settle down and search her face. Her jaw is set and no longer grinding, her eyes locked on mine.

"I was going to tell you," she says.

"When? For how long? *Why?*"

"What do you mean *why*?"

"Tish! Isn't he still married?"

Her eyes shoot down. "They're getting a divorce. Once the election is over."

"So he's hiding this from his wife?"

"She knows."

"She knows about you?"

"Not me specifically, but she knows the marriage is over."

I stare at her, dumbfounded, when what I really want to do is grab hold of her shoulders and shake her. "But it's not final until the divorce goes through… *Tish!*"

She sucks in her cheeks, her eyes cutting left and right. No one else is outside, it's only the two of us at the end of my drive, but the warning look on her face tells me to lower my voice.

"Tish, you can't have an affair with a married man. Especially not someone who's running for office."

Her eyes drop again. "Believe me, I've been battling with this."

"So no one else knows?"

She lifts her gaze. "No one."

"And he's not filing for divorce until after the election is over?"

"It would be bad for his ratings."

I cut her a look. "Isn't getting caught having a girlfriend on the side bad too? Wouldn't that be enough to crush his election chances? My God, Tish."

I shake my hands, but once again fall short of grabbing her by the shoulders. Another part of me is so frightened—stunned—I fight the need to pull her into a hug and protect her.

"What about the other guy?" I ask. "The one you've been seeing?"

"We broke it off…" Her voice teeters. "I wanted to tell you. I've been wanting to tell you about Jacob for a long time."

Now it's my turn to look hurt. "A long time?"

"Since January."

January feels like eons ago. Seven months that she's been hiding this from me.

"The event at the Davidson Center. We started talking. Mostly about the election and then we ran into each other again. We started emailing. We met up. It just… it sort of happened, you know?" She looks at me. Her voice has risen; she's imploring. But she's also talking excitedly—excited to finally be telling me about her new boyfriend—my teeth setting on edge at the realization it's Jacob Andrews. I try easing the shock out of my face.

"He's nice, Erica. Really. You'd like him. I don't think people give him enough credit. There's so much he wants to do. So much he's already accomplished. I really think you'd enjoy getting to know him."

I don't buy it. I'm trying so hard, I love Tish so much, but this is difficult.

"If he's so great, then why are people saying he'd go after the Millers?" I ask. "What does that say about the man?"

"They don't know him like I do."

"No one trusts him."

"They're wrong."

"He's *cheating* on his wife," I remind her. "He's already a scumbag."

She makes a face. Her anger flashes, but this time, it's combined with disgust. She spins on her heel and heads for the garage. "I thought you'd understand." Her words come out a muffled sob, the emotions rising in her throat as she marches toward the house.

"Wait," I say, calling after her, and run to hook her elbow with my hand. "I'm sorry. I didn't mean…"

Tish stood by me when I went through my divorce, just as I did for her. But she knows how much Derek hurt me—how his affair and repeated cheating blew my marriage up in my face. And now she's doing the one thing I absolutely despise.

She doesn't meet my eyes at first, her face ashamed and hurt.

But I also apologize. "I'm sorry," I say again. "You caught me by surprise… I wasn't expecting this."

Her chin trembles. She doesn't speak for the longest time. Finally, she looks up, thin blonde eyelashes disappearing against her pale skin. Tears forming, her eyes shining like wet glass.

"I'm scared, Erica. He has nothing to do with this. I know it."

I rub her gently on the arm and sigh. "Okay, tell me what happened. Tell me about today."

She steadies herself. "He came over. He was helping me in the kitchen. You called about the kids wanting to go to the pool and I'd already promised Charlie about the fireworks. Charlie thinks he's just a friend so Jacob stayed behind. He offered to finish up the dishwasher. It was so nice of him—"

"But that was hours before Sabine went missing."

"He stayed until past eight."

"How do you know?"

"He kept sending pictures. Progress of how he was doing."

I remember this now, sitting by the pool, the way Tish kept glancing at her phone, periodically typing responses. I thought she'd been catching up on work or checking Instagram. No clue she was checking in with her boyfriend.

"He sent me pictures so I could see how it was coming together. See?" She holds up her phone.

A series of text messages fill her screen. One picture after another. A man with dark hair. A blue baseball cap and white T-shirt. Dark brown eyes. The abbreviated smile.

The face of Jacob Andrews—but something's different.

"What's with the mustache?"

She cringes. "It's his way of disguising himself when he comes over."

I let out my breath. "Oh my God, Tish."

"I know, it's crazy. His idea," she adds, as if that makes it any better. "He uses a different car when he comes over too. It's a precaution," she assures me.

"This is so bad..."

But she continues scrolling through pictures.

There's Jacob Andrews, smiling and giving a thumbs-up while holding a wrench and some kind of rubber tubing. In another, he's pointing to a part number. In another, a close-up of where he's pulled the dishwasher out of the wall, pipes and wires and plastic molding showing in the cavernous space behind the counter.

I look closely. The checkered tile floor that is unmistakably Tish's kitchen. The blue dish towel with the rooster design I gave her last Christmas. The half-drunk bottle of wine we left beside the sink two nights ago—a bottle of pinot noir I brought over for her. The wine, one of her favorites.

Did she share a glass with him?

Tish's kitchen. The dish towel on the counter. Jacob Andrews *at her house.*

Evidence he was there and not somewhere else. Not breaking into the Millers' home. Not hurting Sabine. An alibi like Amanda said he would be needing.

But I can't get past the ridiculous mustache. The wave of anger that he would disguise himself and drive a different car so he can sneak over to another woman's house. His various ploys so he won't get caught.

The thoughts and fears and implications weigh heavily inside my head. Shock and outrage too. What has Tish gotten herself caught up in?

"You see," she says, swiping to another photo. "He was there for hours."

She points to the gray light that is falling outside her window, the dusk that is coming. In another selfie, Jacob is standing in front of the dishwasher, parts and pieces and wires finally put away, a satisfied look on his face as the project appears completed, the dishwasher repaired. The sky behind him turning dark.

Jacob Andrews was alone in her house while on the other side of the neighborhood, fireworks rocketed into the sky. And I sat, unknowingly, beside Tish and our kids.

Who knew the man could be so handy?

Who knew he'd been sleeping with my best friend?

"He was there past the time they said Sabine went home," Tish insists. "Past the time Mark called the police."

She points at the read receipts.

6:43 p.m.

7:15 p.m.

7:42 p.m.

If the Facebook post was right, he was texting Tish while the world was falling down around Sabine.

"He was texting when the fireworks started too."

8:15 p.m.

8:24 p.m.

By that time, Mark was calling the police.

"Don't you see, it can't be Jacob. He was there the entire time."

"Does he know what people are saying? About him? The accusations?"

"Yes. I hated it but I sent him screenshots of the Facebook group."

"What did he say?"

"He's upset. Outraged. Worried."

"Worried because his alibi is at your house?"

Tish shoots me another look. "Yes, of course. But also that people are saying those things. That they would even conceive he could do something like this. Those are potential voters."

"Doesn't sound like they're voting for him." As soon as the words come out, I bite my lip.

"Erica, please try to understand. Please try to be on my side."

"I *am* on your side. More than anything in the world. But this is freaking me out."

"I had to tell you. After what Amanda said. After what those people were saying online, I had to tell you. *Show* you." She shakes her phone.

I nod but my head is swimming. The message thread is blaring white hot in her hands.

"I'm so worried they're going to go after him," she says. "The wrong person. They won't know."

"Maybe the police won't ask."

"If people are posting things like this on Facebook, private group or not, the cops will find out. He'll be one of the people they consider anyway, don't you think? He's Mark's opponent."

"Will he tell them about you?" I ask. "The messages sent from your house. That's proof. Time stamps and all."

The look on her face sickens. "But it will get out about us."

"It's a hell of a lot better than being suspected of the disappearance of his opponent's wife, don't you think?"

Her eyes pinch again.

I glance at the house, the fact we've been standing out here long enough and should be going back inside. The kids will be wondering where we are.

But there's something else I need to ask Tish.

"Are you going to tell the police?"

"I don't..." She hesitates. "... I don't think that's my call right now. Jacob will have to do that."

"Have you heard from him again?"

Another long look at her phone, the screen fading black. "Not since before Amanda left." She blinks her eyes, tears springing at the corners. "He's not answering me. That can't be a good sign."

CHAPTER 7

We move back inside the house. From Taylor's bedroom, sounds of a movie playing and I'm thinking Lydia must have found something for the younger kids to watch.

Behind me, Tish takes a beer out of the fridge—the beer she didn't want earlier now a necessity. She pops it open and offers one to me, but I wave my hand to say no. After what she's told me, I can't stomach it.

Resuming her spot on the bar stool, she checks her phone for any messages from Jacob but by the way she places it face-down on the counter, he hasn't responded.

My phone buzzes. So does Tish's.

She instantly flips it over—her eyes bulge—thinking maybe it's him. I reach for my phone too—it's Amanda.

Mark Miller told the police it was Jacob Andrews. Erica, what you heard was right. They think Jacob Andrews tried something the night before.

Her messages ping one after another. Tish clamps a hand to her mouth and shakes her head with a cry.

Mark claims he saw Jacob driving in the neighborhood. The cops are talking to him now. This could be it.

"He's lying!" Tish slams her phone down so hard I'm afraid she's cracked it against the counter. But she doesn't check. A flush of red runs to her forehead.

My pulse races—erratic, shallow breathing as I watch my best friend respond.

"He didn't do anything!" she cries. "It's impossible! He was at my house, you saw it yourself. Each message places him in my kitchen. *Not* at the Millers'."

I hold her look, hating what I have to say next. The idea we must consider everything.

"Is there any chance he could have taken those pictures earlier?"

Tish blazes her eyes at me. "What do you mean?"

"Could he have taken those pictures and sent them to you later?"

"Like, made it up? Like, made it *seem* like he was at my house?"

I grimace.

"Don't say that!" she cries. "Don't you go thinking he did it too."

"I don't know… I'm not saying… I don't know anything about him."

"*I* know him. Doesn't that count?"

"Yes… yes it should—"

"It should?"

"Look, I'm just trying to figure this out. Same as you." It stings how much I'm hurting her feelings.

She sets her jaw. "So you think he left my house and sent me those pictures so I would think he was still in my kitchen? And *then* he went after the Millers?"

"I don't know…"

"Unbelievable." She picks up her phone. If the screen is cracked, she doesn't register it—she's too angry with me, too scared to think about what's happening to Jacob.

She pulls up her text messages and points at a picture, her fingernail tapping the screen until her dark nail polish chips. "Then how do you explain it becoming night outside? Huh? The light that's fading outside my window. See that?" She jabs at the screen again even though I've already seen the photo. Jacob Andrews still wearing the mustache I can barely tolerate looking at. "There's no way he was there," she tells me.

"He left and came back?"

"Oh my God, Erica! Stop!" she shrieks again.

I cut the air with my hand—a nervous glance toward the kids' bedrooms. It's my turn to remind her to keep her voice down.

But Tish doesn't quiet herself. "And that part about Mark knowing it was Jacob's car," she says. "Another mistake—or another lie. He drives a Tesla, cherry red. The car he drove tonight is a Buick LaCrosse. Black. One of those sedan-looking things."

Jacob's Tesla. I've seen that car before—everyone has. Flashy and bright red with Jacob being one of the few people in town who would drive one around in that color. He was parked outside the courthouse several weeks ago when I peeked through the driver's side window and spotted the matching red leather seats.

But Tish is telling me he drove something different tonight.

"So a Buick and not the Tesla?" I ask. "Has Mark seen him drive the Buick before? Is it a company car?"

"No, it's a rental. He rents a different one when he comes over."

I swallow down my dismay. The covering of his tracks is unbelievable.

Tish, this doesn't look good...

"Did he leave it somewhere else?" I ask.

"The other car?"

I tread carefully. "Yes, his other car. After leaving your place, did he switch vehicles? And there's a chance he took off in his Tesla and that's what Mark saw?"

She shakes her head. "No, that wouldn't make sense. He'd need somebody else to drive it over to him, and why? Why would he do that?" She lifts her phone again. "He was there the whole time.

Believe me. It's a big risk for him to be at my house without being spotted. Every time, he pulls right into my garage. He wouldn't want to take a chance of going out somewhere else and then back to my place. Definitely not to switch cars." She cuts me a look at what I've implied. "Certainly not to try and hurt the Millers."

Thoughts race through my head, a nauseous, sinking feeling, and I chew on my fingernails, something I haven't done in years. Not since the divorce. Not since—

"I'm scared for you," I tell her.

A whoosh of air comes from her lips, her mouth trembling. "I'm scared too."

"When this all gets out, the spotlight will be on you also."

"I know."

"The affair. Your involvement with him. I don't know what this is going to do…" I don't finish my sentence.

Tish sets down her beer and I reach my hand across the counter. I lift the same bottle to my lips, both our minds whirling.

"He's a good guy, Erica," she says after some time.

I don't respond.

"We're good together."

She presses the bottle back to her lips. "This isn't how it was supposed to come out. Not like this." She fights to control her tears. "We were going to do it properly. Wait until after the election. Go to dinner with you." She looks up. "Maybe a double date with you and that guy you've been talking to."

Terry. Well, that would be an interesting conversation. I think about the man I've started getting to know. *So… guess who we're going to dinner with…*

I look at her steadily. "Jacob's election chances are over, you know that, right, Tish?" She flinches. "There's no way he can come back from this. This is too…" I hate saying the word but say it anyway. "… scandalous. Even if he didn't do anything to the Millers."

"He didn't *do* anything," she insists.

"If the police are questioning him right now, then he's going to have no choice but to show those pictures too. The text thread with you. Everything you showed me. It will come out in the open about you two."

Her voice rises to a feverish pitch. "Then help me, Erica!" she says, pleading. "What am I going to do?"

CHAPTER 8

It's nearing midnight when Amanda calls.

"I think you're off the hook," she says. "With Mark notifying the police about Jacob Andrews, I'm pretty sure that's their guy. You don't need to worry about telling the cops too."

I make a sound, my breath exhaling in a loud rush of relief. But at the same time, my nerves skyrocket for Tish.

"They've had Jacob at the police station for the last two hours."

With my phone pressed to my ear, I turn away from the living room. Tish is on the couch, having switched from beer to a small glass of whiskey she cradles in her hands.

"Where are you?" I ask.

"The nature preserve. My search team was sent this way. Somewhere Sabine has been seen walking before."

"They think she'd run in that direction without flagging for help first?"

"They want us covering all ground. No chance in missing something."

"Any witnesses?"

"Not yet."

I think of the Ring doorbell app and security cameras Amanda mentioned before. "Any video?"

"Nothing that's been posted yet. I think the police are making the neighbors turn in their videos first."

I breathe out a sigh, calmed at the idea we won't have to watch a clip of Sabine running for her life on some Facebook post after all.

"You know," Amanda says, "it's harsh what people are saying about Jacob. But that guy is losing the election, which could make him have motive. There wasn't evidence before but after what Mark told police, it doesn't look good."

Evidence. I'm stuck on the word.

"Turns out it could be something after all," she adds.

I move further away from the couch, shielding my face from Tish. "What if it's not him?"

"Why would Mark Miller say he saw Jacob driving in the neighborhood? At about the same time he was going home to check on Sabine? The timing of it."

"Yes, but maybe he was visiting someone..." I squeeze my eyes shut with each word, not wanting to give myself, or Tish, away just yet.

"I suppose so. I mean, I guess he could have been. But the odds are slim. He lives out in Madison. His wife wasn't with him. What would he be doing in Green Cove?"

"Fireworks?"

On the other end of the line, Amanda snorts. "I seriously doubt it."

I cringe again and wonder how long it's going to be before Amanda hears about the text messages with Tish. How soon before that kind of information will get out about our best friend's affair. Proof of Jacob Andrews being at Tish's house while he's being questioned by the police. *He'll need an alibi,* she told us.

Amanda is bound to hear about it from someone in the sheriff's department or a city official and she'll hear about it soon. She's always had her finger on the pulse of everything, including tonight. Every update.

I cast a worried glance at Tish. She's still on the couch, staring into space with one hand wrapped around her phone waiting for an update from Jacob. Waiting for the moment he will tell her their secret has been kicked wide open.

Or worse—and what I can't get out of my head—that he's lied to her and knows something about Sabine.

*

It's past midnight when Tish asks to spend the night. She's stayed over numerous times before and with everything that's happened, especially with the numbing effects of whiskey and Charlie having fallen asleep next to Taylor, she doesn't want to leave. Her eyes, heavy and red-rimmed with fatigue, stare at her lap. Anxiety prickles her cheeks too.

She cries a few times as we sit together, silent tears that fall down her face. She wipes the tears away. All I can do is pull a blanket over our laps, the two of us sitting side by side on the couch, my hand clutching hers.

Through her tears, she asks, "What are people going to say about me? What are they going to think?"

All I can do is hush her. "Don't worry about that right now."

"How can I not? The talk. There will be so much of it." She grapples with her words, her breath raspy. "Our neighbors. Amanda. It's a secret I've kept from both of you, and now look." She searches my face frantically. "This is not how I wanted to tell you, Erica. Trust me."

"I know."

"I never liked that we were going behind everyone's backs."

"I know," I say again.

"The media. Won't they be all over this too?"

An idea comes to me suddenly. "Maybe he'll be able to keep your identity hidden. They won't have to release the name of who he was with."

She seizes on this. "You really think so?"

"Maybe." Although I don't have the faintest clue as to how this kind of thing works.

She presses a thumb and forefinger to the bridge of her nose and pushes hard. "God, I hope so… It will be awful for him but at least for me…" She can't finish her sentence.

"The affair, it's not good," I tell her, and she whimpers softly. "But If Jacob is innocent, then him being at your house will be his saving grace. If he didn't leave and come back like you said, if those pictures are confirmed as being sent from your kitchen while Sabine went missing, then everything will be fine."

She nods and closes her eyes, her fingers rubbing her forehead.

But soon, the tears return and trickle down her cheek, a wet streak coursing its way to her chin.

"But it won't be fine," she says. "Something like this will cost him the election, you said so yourself. People were so quick to judge him about Sabine and now this"— she throws her head back on the sofa — "having an affair. His career will be ruined."

My heart breaks for Tish. I squeeze her hand again, grasping her fingers between mine.

In her lap, her phone lights up. Mine too. But it's not Jacob, and another shattered look stretches across her face. It's a group text from the search.

Eric Nichols: *New team forming on Tammerack.*

Carolyn Castillo: *Golf course front nine is cleared.*

Scott Wooley: *Boats and divers seen on Mallard's Pond.*

Paul Tomlinson: *Group 4, turn back. Honors Row is shut down. Police door-to-door.*

We fall silent, scrolling as one message comes in after another. And as we should have anticipated, more gossip. The conjecture we knew that was coming even as members of the search team poke and prod in the grass, possibly even more irritated and wanting to throw out their theories since they're the ones stumbling around in the middle of the night in the dark.

Scott Wooley: *He did it. I'm sure he did.*

Lamar Jackson: *Did anyone else see Jacob Andrews' car?*

Alice Chin: *Mark Miller said he did and that's all the police need to hear.*

Carolyn Castillo: *Did he have Sabine with him?*

Scott Wooley: *I bet she's inside Jacob's trunk.*

Anthony Castillo: *Hope so. Then we can get this over with and go home.*

Carolyn Castillo: *I'm knee-high in mud and there's a chance she's inside his trunk?!*

Anthony Castillo: *Word is Monica and Carol think Jacob is behind this too.*

Eric Nichols: *Keep looking. Don't give up. We don't know where she is.*

Scott Wooley: *Pop open Jacob's trunk already.*

Tish lets out a sharp cry.

Dropping her phone, she lets it slide from her lap to the cushion.

CHAPTER 9

Tish and I fell asleep. I have no idea what time it was but with our bodies curled on the couch, we must have stopped speaking, our thoughts drifting, the pair of us exhausted as Tish gave up on any chance she'd hear from Jacob that night.

We wake up in the morning to Taylor and Charlie begging us for pancakes.

It's Sunday and I'm reminded of how we usually cook a big breakfast on Sunday mornings, a special treat so the girls can throw chocolate chips into the batter while I sizzle bacon in the pan. It's something my granddad did for me every weekend, coming over to the house early in the morning while my parents left for work. He's the one who taught me to cook, even if it was the most basic of recipes. And once we added chocolate chips, we felt as if we were eating like kings.

Tish presses a hand to her head. Managing a smile to her son, he leaps with excitement at finding his mom on the couch and jumps toward her in a wide-open hug that nearly knocks the air from her chest. With his legs kicked out, he nearly tips over the whiskey glass too and it teeters on the coffee table before rattling into place.

"Pancakes!" Taylor squeals.

I sit up cautiously, a crick in my neck that I rub gently with my fingers. The blanket Tish and I shared has fallen to the floor.

One look at my friend's face and her eyelids are puffy from both crying and battered sleep. The bun that was hiked on top of her head has come loose, her blonde hair hanging in several long strands down her back.

I run my hands across my face too, knowing I can't look much better. My hair, not as blonde as Tish's but honey-gold when I remember to keep up my highlights, is still tied in a knot, but it's come loose too. Tugging at the hairband, I re-tie the knot and then pat at my eyelids, feeling the creases of the sofa cushion embedded against my cheek.

Tish gives Charlie a squeeze and he cries, "Mommy!" while she clings to him, landing big kisses on his forehead as they hug and rock together. She grins too, trying her hardest to blink away the fear—the memory of what's happening shooting back to her, of what we're going through. She's doing her best to assure herself that all will be right in this world. She has her son. She has me. We will get through this together.

I smile at her and she raises her eyes to smile back.

I stand from the sofa. "Did someone say pancakes?"

"Hurray!" Taylor cheers as she and Charlie rush to the kitchen. Taylor has always liked mixing the batter and with Charlie's help, they'll count out the chocolate chips, each one organized into separate piles before sprinkling them into the mixture.

Tish checks her phone but frowns. She looks around for something until I realize she's searching for a charger. Her phone has gone dead.

"By the window," I tell her and nudge in the direction of the kitchen table.

She hurries to plug in her phone while I put on a pot of coffee, thinking we're going to need about a gallon, and set about grabbing the flour and baking soda, the salt and sugar and a carton of eggs.

The kids climb on the bar stools and watch as I pour out each ingredient and crack an egg, mixing in the milk and butter. Taylor begins counting out each chocolate chip.

As I mix, Tish impatiently drums her fingers on the table, waiting for her phone to power back on and return to life. Soon, the screen flashes and she's gripping with both hands to see what other messages have arrived.

She clicks on something, then something else, her eyebrows furrowing until a sharp crease lines her forehead.

She scrolls but then stops. Her thumbs hover.

"Anything?" I ask.

She doesn't respond. But her hand covers her mouth—she's reading something, her eyes skating back and forth. I can't take it anymore and hurry to sit at the table.

"Did they find her?"

She shakes her head.

My heart rises, then falls. They haven't found Sabine—that's great news. They haven't found her body. But that also means she's still out there. She's still missing. She wasn't in Jacob's trunk like people have been speculating. They can't find her anywhere.

"Have you heard from him?"

Another shake of the head.

I peer at the screen. She's looking at a news report, an update from WAFF 48 News, and angles the screen toward me so I can read it too.

The search was called off at 3 a.m. but police have announced they will resume again at noon.

A torn piece of clothing was found in the woods behind Honors Row. White cotton the police believe belongs to Sabine Miller. She was last seen leaving the pool wearing a white cotton coverup. The cloth was drenched in blood.

The blood, just like the trail found leading out the back door, has been confirmed as belonging to Mrs. Miller.

I put my hand to my mouth and Tish muffles a cry.

One of the search teams found a bracelet on the golf course. A silver bangle that had been snapped in two and flung to the ground.

My eyes shoot up—*another bracelet?* But this was one broken and ripped from her arm.

Not far from the bracelet the police found more blood on the ground near a road that leads away from the golf course. Police are investigating if, after running through the woods, Sabine Miller suffered multiple lacerations, fell at this location, and was then taken by the assailant who drove their car around to this very spot before taking off with her inside. Her condition is unknown but it is believed Mrs. Miller requires immediate medical attention.

Mark Miller is cleared as a suspect. He was not home at the time with dozens of witnesses placing him at the neighborhood pool. He's organizing today's press conference.

We reach the end of the article and Tish clicks on a different link, an update from AlabamaNews.com.

Security cameras are not installed on the golf course. The Millers have a Ring doorbell camera at their front and side doors but none of the footage reveals what happened inside the house or when Mrs. Miller is thought to have run through the backyard.

I raise my eyebrows at this: the Millers' cameras didn't catch anyone coming to the house. Not before Sabine or Mark returned home. No one lying in wait. No one driving up to the home and causing a confrontation.

Certainly not a red Tesla, or what Tish said Jacob had been driving last night: a black Buick LaCrosse.

But it doesn't make sense. Mark Miller claims to have seen Jacob driving in the neighborhood. So where was he? He didn't park in front of their house—that would have been too risky. Did Jacob park his car somewhere else and travel to the Millers' on foot? But how would someone not see his car on the side of the road or capture him on a security camera walking up to the house?

Unless whoever did this *left* their car near the golf course. They didn't drive around when Sabine fell—they purposely chased her in that direction so she would end up at that spot. They wanted her there. They chased her before shoving her inside the awaiting car.

Just like I questioned Tish earlier, Jacob could have left a second vehicle. He could have kept it by the golf course and driven off with Sabine.

I shudder. To think Tish was spending time with this man the day before.

Tish clicks on another article and we read.

At this time, there is no indication Sabine Miller has traveled outside of the city. Bus stations have been checked and police are reviewing security video at each train station too. Alerts have also been sent to all major airports including the privately-owned Moontown Airport but no one reports seeing a woman being smuggled onboard a private plane. There is no sign yet to indicate she boarded a flight at Huntsville Airport or the airports in Birmingham, Nashville, or Atlanta. She has not used her passport to leave the country.

There is no indication she or someone else has accessed her credit cards as her purse was left at the house. No money has been withdrawn from her accounts. No ransom calls have been made to Mark Miller yet. Her cell phone was left on the kitchen table.

A news alert announces a press conference that's about to go live. Tish quickly clicks on the link.

We see Mark Miller standing on the front porch of his home with two members of his team and the county sheriff by his side. Since he was seen sitting at the pool, the man appears as if he's aged overnight, understandably distraught with the once-sparkling eyes replaced with something haggard and bloodshot and spiked with fear. He chews on a cheek to keep from crying, a hand rising to his chest as he takes a moment to collect himself. And then another moment. He's ready to burst into tears.

The steady sound of cameras click in the background. A flash highlights his face.

"As you know," Mark begins, "it pains me to tell you my beloved wife Sabine Miller is missing. She has not been seen since just before seven p.m. last night when she went home to pick up something but never returned to the neighborhood pool." A hiccup of breath, a pause as he studies the sheet of paper clutched in his hands. The words could be written in gibberish, the letters swimming on the page, his voice cracking, for he's struggling to read them.

In all his years serving as county commissioner, I've rarely seen Mark read from a script, only when the event was huge or an announcement had to be carefully worded. But right now, in his despair, the man is barely able to stand in front of the cameras, let alone talk about his worst nightmare coming true—that someone would harm his wife and chase her through the woods. The reality that she's still missing.

A member of his team touches his elbow lightly and encourages him to continue.

Mark tries his best to look steadily at the cameras. "The police have several leads including information I've provided them. We're looking at everything—and everyone." For this, he pauses again, clearing his throat, the word *everyone* hanging in the air although he doesn't specifically identify Jacob or implicate his opponent to the press. But everyone hears him. "We assure you no one has been ruled out yet," he adds. Then, a shake in his voice. "Please, if anyone knows what happened to my wife or where she is now, you're urged to contact the police. I beg you," he says, those last few words ending in a sob. He looks down again, folding the paper in half and swallowing hard. He bites his lip before stepping to the side.

The cameras shift to the county sheriff, who announces a lengthier press conference will take place this afternoon. The live stream ends and Tish sets down her phone.

She sits back and rubs her temples. If she feels anything like me, her head is throbbing. Her heart aching for the Miller family.

The coffee pot hisses, the last of the steam bubbling at the top before it stops percolating, the intense, bold scent of dark roast filling the kitchen. I move as fast as I can to the counter, the strong need to pour Tish and I full cups, black for her, sugar and milk for me, and set the mugs on the table. Tish grips her mug tightly while the kids take over mixing the batter.

We don't say anything for the longest time, but instead blow across the surface, the smell of the coffee doing its part to wake us up, when the truth is, the adrenaline is already spiking. Everything we just read. What we heard Mark say. What we're picturing in our heads after reading those reports.

Images of Sabine running from her home and bleeding. A piece of her coverup ripped from her body.

Did the person grab her? Or did the material snag on a branch and tear as she hurtled by?

The bracelet that was left broken on the ground. Did they lunge at her again? Is this the moment she wrenched away to be free and the bracelet snapped in two? How long did she lie bleeding on the grass before they scooped her into a car and drove away with her inside?

I think of Jacob. Jacob Andrews at Tish's house. Photos of him at 6:43 p.m.

Sabine Miller arriving at her house at 6:52. Mark Miller arriving at his home at 7:40 p.m.

Jacob sending Tish another picture of himself two minutes later.

Mark indicating *no one* has been ruled out yet.

So how did Jacob swing it? How did he leave Tish's kitchen and show up at the Millers' home without being seen *and* have enough time to confront her before chasing her out through the woods?

Did he really switch cars? And if he did, how on earth did he manage to do all of that in the space of an hour?

Tish takes a sip of her coffee but it burns her tongue.

And a frightening thought occurs to me—*unless he had help*. He teamed up with someone else.

CHAPTER 10

Lydia joins the younger kids and helps them pour enormous amounts of syrup on their pancakes, butter slathered across each one too. The children devour their breakfast as I pour Tish and I more coffee.

Lydia stands up ready to clear her plate when Tish sucks in her breath. "*It's him.*" She clutches her phone to her face.

Lydia whirls her eyes. I do too.

I glance at my daughter and cautiously wave my hand, begging her to take the younger kids to their room. Quickly, Lydia ushers Taylor and Charlie down the hall.

My attention returns to Tish, her hands shaking. "It's him," she repeats, her thumbs typing frantically.

"What's going on? What's happening?"

She doesn't respond; she's too busy sending a message. But then she stops. "What?" Her eyes startle and it takes a moment to let whatever she's read sink in. "But I… I don't want to…"

She reads his message out loud. "*Don't worry. Everything will be all right. But you need to delete all my messages from before. Only keep the ones from last night.*"

Another buzz.

"*Please do this,*" she continues reading. Her mouth drops open; she's struggling to breathe. "*We can't talk anymore.*" Her eyes rip toward me. "Anymore? Why would he say that? But I—I don't understand." She finishes typing her response, the letters popping up on her screen:

Talk to me, Jacob. Tell me what's happened. Are you okay?

No response.

Tish types: *???*

Still nothing.

The battering of her thumbs. *Talk to me!!!*

This time, a message pops up. *Goodbye, Tish.*

*

People used to joke that Sabine and Mark Miller look like twins. It was almost uncanny how similar they appeared—golden blonde hair, hazel eyes, the soft downturn of their noses and high cheekbones to accentuate their gorgeous profiles. They met shortly after college, completing degrees at Samford University here in Alabama with Sabine majoring in French and Mark earning a degree in political science. Someone's parents introduced them at a dinner party and the joke goes that as soon as Mark saw her, he said, *That's the one. She mirrors me. That's who I want to appear on my campaign posters.*

It was either that or Mark Miller picked her out of a catalog, *Beautiful Wives for Politicians*, some people teased behind his back. It was terribly tacky and sexist—plenty of women are politicians too and not everyone running for office purposely marries for the arm candy—but then again, some of them do, and that was the running joke about Mark. The jokes turned endearing though once he proved to be an effective politician. A playful ribbing on the arm and pat on the back at event banquets and after Mark's speeches, everyone realizing he was becoming a true asset to the community and single-handedly turning our region into an economic powerhouse. It was just bonus he had a beautiful wife.

But there was still something corny and sweet and nearly too perfect about the Millers: Mark's grand political aspirations and Sabine's glamorous ways. It was hard to ignore they looked cut from the same cloth. Mark and Sabine were eerily perfect. Sickeningly perfect. The same looks. Same private university. So kind and giving. So genuinely altruistic. It was hard *not* to joke about them even as Mark continued to land one deal after another. A new auto manufacturing plant. A new data center. Sabine excelling at everything she laid her hands on too.

We loved them—and we were secretly jealous of them. Me included.

Sabine's work for the pediatric oncology center earned high praise. She trained as a nurse so she could entrench herself at the hospital and then fundraise for the nurses' higher pay. She led a benefit last summer that raised enough money to build a second computer lab at my kids' school.

Sabine stepped off stage last December when I saw first-hand how much of an effect she has on students. The principal presented her with a certificate of appreciation before introducing her to the new cyber team, the students eagerly lined up on one side of the gym. Sabine greeted each child as if they were her own, and the kids beamed with absolute honor and delight. It was as if she was royalty, her and Mark. Revered by the people. Another reminder of how much the couple helps so many families even when they've never had children of their own.

I watched Sabine leaving the school gym, her best friends Monica and Carol by her side and looking proud. Like ladies in waiting. Mark greeting his wife in the hall with a kiss.

The Millers. The beautiful, sunny, blonde couple with big hearts, even bigger wallets, and matching bleached-white smiles ready for their close-ups. The couple, photo perfect. Gracing Christmas cards and dozens of magazine covers. Their image perfect for campaign banners and billboards too.

Vote for Mark Miller. A man for the people.

This is who we want representing us.

And on the billboards, Sabine standing beside Mark, elegantly dressed. The two of them appearing on TV ads and interviews where Sabine wears head-to-toe designer suits and clutches his hand lovingly. And Mark, always with his American flag pin on his chest, smiling confidently and looking like someone you can trust. Someone who will take care of us. Someone who will take care of everything.

And someone who desperately needs to bring Sabine home. His heart will break if he doesn't find her soon.

CHAPTER 11

Amanda returns to my house. No knock on the door as she never does, appearing once again in my kitchen.

I peer at the time on the microwave: it's 9 a.m. How much sleep has she gotten?

She looks spun up again, hyper movements in her hands, cheeks twitching as she tosses her purse on the counter, her car keys skittering across the surface.

Not much sleep, if I had to guess.

Her eyes are puffy but not from crying—Amanda doesn't cry often—but what I can assume is the result of sleep deprivation after trekking around the nature preserve until three in the morning. Her movements are still jittery from being a part of a search-and-rescue operation like this—and possibly from already having downed three cups of coffee. Despite everything, I'm amazed she's here this early.

Amanda has showered and is no longer wearing the T-shirt she was in last night. No sign of the boots she retrieved after leaving my house either. Today, she's wearing track pants and a long-sleeved shirt, her curly brown hair held back with a clip.

She sees me eyeing her clothes. "I'll be hot but it's better than getting scratches. I got pretty torn up last night." She brushes a hand along her forearm and raises one of her sleeves to reveal a crisscross of red marks above her wrist, the kind you get from pushing through heavy brush. "The search is picking up again this afternoon."

Tish lifts her eyes. "You're going back out?"

"Of course." But then she stops and looks at us strangely. "Are you both still wearing your bathing suits?"

I look down. Tish does too. Neither of us has showered yet. We're in our swimsuits with sundresses on top, mine blue and wrinkled across my lap from having curled over and slept on the sofa. One of Tish's straps remains fallen at her shoulder. She doesn't move to fix it.

I wipe at my face and mash the back of my hand against inflamed eyelids that I'm sure could rival Amanda's, although, I admit, are not as swollen as Tish's. Another glance at my best friend and the skin below her eyes is puffy too.

"We sat up pretty late," I tell her.

"Crazy, huh?" she says, as if us waiting up half the night to hear about Sabine's recovery is enough of a reason for Tish and me to be in this state the next day. If only she knew…

Amanda spies the coffee pot and pulls a mug from the cabinet. "Did you hear the news?"

I shift in my seat. "Which part?"

"About Jacob Andrews?"

Tish flinches, her shoulders rising an undeniable inch, and I hold my breath. I'm almost positive Amanda will notice Tish's reaction but she doesn't. She's stirring two heaps of sugar into her coffee, the spoon clanging noisily against the ceramic.

"Jacob Andrews has an alibi."

Another jerked reaction from Tish, a sharp intake of breath.

Without Amanda seeing, I place a hand on Tish's arm and will her to be steady.

Amanda says, "Mark Miller swears he saw Jacob turning ahead of him. He was leaving the pool heading home when he saw the man's Tesla—it's hard to mistake that thing. The red one with the American flag sticker on the back. He remembers the guy having his blinker on and turning left—" Amanda makes a sound, almost a laugh. "Isn't that such an interesting detail to remember? Remembering the blinker? On top of everything, the guy racing away with Mark's wife but remembering to use his turn signal?" She takes a sip of her coffee and muses something in her head. At this point, I can no longer tell if she thinks Jacob Andrews is guilty or not.

But the build-up to revealing Jacob's alibi is practically killing Tish. Amanda is either loving drawing this out, or she's that armed with information we'll need to sit another minute longer before she lands the bombshell.

Tish shifts in her chair next to mine, her breath slowing to a crawl.

"No one else reports seeing Jacob Andrews driving," Amanda continues. "And no one remembers seeing his sports car since so many people were up at the pool watching fireworks. So it's Mark Miller's word against him right now… *but*… Mark claims Jacob threatened him in the past. He says he has proof." She raises her eyebrows. "That part I'm still working on as I'm sure we'd love to know what *that* was all about." She blows across her coffee and takes another sip.

"But after questioning Jacob for hours, they released him—for now." She arches an eyebrow, an incredulous look. "He has an alibi. And you're never going to believe it, where he says he was. What he was getting up to…" Her voice ramps up—here we go. I'm not breathing anymore. This is the moment we'll find out they know about Tish and Amanda has been biding her time, maybe even reveling in it for whatever insane reason, talking to us about scratches and turn signals while stirring sugar in her coffee, all so she can create this build-up in suspense before getting to the point. And I want to shout, *Come on, Amanda. If you know about Tish, you're torturing her. Don't do this. We're best friends here.*

But Amanda says, "He was at some woman's house. Someone he's been seeing. Someone in Green Cove he was visiting last night."

Tish lets out a peep that only I can hear, a wheezing breath stuck inside her throat.

Some woman's house.

Someone he's been seeing.

She doesn't say a name. And I realize, *Amanda doesn't know. She wouldn't draw this out for Tish.*

She laughs. "Can you believe it? An affair." Amanda's eyes bulge wide, the kind of energized look someone gets when they're the one who can deliver the exciting climax. She's amused and amazed. Horrified and disgusted, all at the same time. The gossip, deliciously fantastic. "He says he has pictures to prove he was somewhere else when Sabine went missing. That it's impossible for him to have been at the Millers'. The timing is uncanny. He's either smart as hell or got super lucky. Or, his mistress is covering up for him." She gives another amused laugh. "But either way, his election chances are toast—they were toast to start with."

I stare at her for the longest time. Tish does too. We're still waiting for her to drop a name. The identity of the woman—the fact that it's Tish Abbott sitting with us. The revelation that everyone will soon know she's the woman who received the photos and text messages, the woman with whom he's been having an affair. The proof Jacob Andrews showed to the police last night. His alibi sitting right here in my kitchen.

But Amanda doesn't say such a thing. She doesn't look pointedly at Tish. Nothing about her lets us know she thinks it's our best friend; she only turns to add more sugar to her coffee. The news delivered.

Tish's shoulders lower an inch, a rush of air from her mouth. Her relief, undeniable.

I'm lowering my shoulders too, not realizing I'd been sitting coiled in my chair. The crick in my neck lessens too, but my mind is racing.

When is *Tish* going to tell Amanda it's her?

Amanda prattles on. "Some girlfriend. Some mistress." She lets out a low whistle. "But why should we be surprised? A lot of them get up to that kind of thing. It's terrible, but you hear about it. The district attorney's office is notorious for having affairs. Rumors run rampant about the mayor's office too. So why wouldn't I think Jacob would have someone on the side also? We could have suspected something like this in the past, but now? What an idiot. I mean, seriously? During an election year when he's running for county commissioner? How could he be that flippant?"

She is tutting and stirring, the spoon clanging around in her mug. "And what a way for everyone to find out too. The man claiming to have"—Amanda lifts her fingers in air quotes—" '*traditional family values*'. But he's off messing around behind his wife's back. Lying to his kids. It's only coming out now because he had to be questioned about the disappearance of Mark's wife. Blood in the woods. His car spotted turning away from the Millers'. The possibility he might be making his girlfriend lie for him." Another choked laugh. "I mean, wow. You can't make this kind of stuff up—the thing of books and true crime exposés. A political murder-mystery podcast waiting to happen." She takes an excited breath. "Crazy."

I calm my heart. A pause from Amanda after a litany of details. But she is staring and waiting for us to respond, and now it's gone quiet, the minute hand on the kitchen clock ticking forward until it's the only sound in the kitchen. Our silence, deafening.

She looks at us curiously. Tish doesn't make a sound.

"It *is* crazy," I tell her to fill the space, but also because I don't know what else to say.

Anything I come up with, even the mildest of questions or statements, could give Tish away, or give me away, and let Amanda know we're keeping something from her. I don't want to be the one to tell her—that needs to be Tish's move. She came forward to me and now she needs to do the same with Amanda.

But Tish doesn't move a muscle. Her breathing is coming out in more even spurts, her fingers no longer tense, her face resuming an image of calm, although to me, a streak of terror still lingers in her features. But to Amanda, she has done a remarkable job keeping her panic hidden and our friend hasn't noticed a thing, which means, so have I. Both of us becoming great actors.

But I balk. Tish's silence also means she doesn't plan on telling Amanda right now. She won't be confessing, which means I have to continue keeping my mouth shut too. *But that can't be a wise move, Tish,* I want to shout. Amanda will soon find out and she'll be furious. She'll be upset for Tish too, of course, and worried, but she'll also feel betrayed. Blindsided. Like I did. I know Amanda. She'll want to get out ahead of the information and not be surprised with it later.

Tish should say something. She should fess up.

And my lips part, my eyes darting to her, waiting for her to speak or at least to comment on everything Amanda has just said, but she remains quiet. Only raises her mug to her lips and knocks back the rest of her coffee.

For the moment, Tish is thinking her identity is safe. She is relieved with Jacob. Either he has made sure to protect her identity, or his attorneys swooped into action last night and insisted the police not release the name of the girlfriend just yet. The news, for now, the particulars involving Tish, are under wraps. Not even to Amanda, who always seems to have the pulse on everything.

But it's not going to last. The truth, as we know, always finds a way of getting out.

FACEBOOK GROUP POST

Praying for Sabine Miller (Private Facebook Group)

Sunday morning

Eric Nichols

July 5 at 10:22 a.m.

The search is picking back up. Meet again at the corner of Chandler and Smoke Rise 12 p.m.

> **Tamyra Meeks** We'll be there.
>
> **Alexis Redfield** Count us in too. Bob has metal detectors.
>
> **Lamar Jackson** Great idea.

Jennifer Krel

July 5 at 10:30 a.m.

My heart is breaking for Mark and Sabine.

> **Christine Blanchard** Here's a picture of Sabine kicking off my daughter's summer camp with a party.
>
> **Jennifer Krel** I remember that! The girls had so much fun.
>
> **Christine Blanchard** She's a beautiful person. This shouldn't be happening to her.
>
> **Alice Chin** Mark must be terrified right now. Has anyone spoken to him?

Heather Stephenson The police have been at his house all morning. Word is he hasn't slept. He hasn't stopped crying.

Paul Tomlinson Everyone, please pray for them. We have to keep searching.

Alexis Redfield A volunteer team is preparing food and bringing it to Mark's house. Monica and Carol are sharing it with everyone joining the search. Let me know if you want to pitch in.

Lamar Jackson We will find whoever has done this!

CHAPTER 12

"Our flight times got updated. Did you see that?" Amanda holds out her phone.

"What are you talking about?"

It's jarring—my mind is on a single track about Sabine and Tish and yet Amanda is able to bounce from one task to the other, checking emails and responding to text messages about work while also catching up on Facebook posts about the search.

"Our flight," Amanda repeats. "To the BVI. The airline sent an update."

That's right, our trip to the British Virgin Islands. But that's not until next month. An all-expenses-paid trip that Amanda earned as an ambassador for the local Chamber of Commerce. Each year, if ambassadors sell a certain level of sponsorships, which Amanda did, they achieve a vacation for themselves and one other person. We pooled our money together so that Tish and I could both go, and also at a serious discount since we were able to pull some strings with a travel agent friend of ours too. It's the only way we could afford the tickets. We've been excited and talking about the trip for months, especially with this year's location: the gorgeous island of Tortola.

Amanda peers at her screen. "An email came in with new departure times."

"Earlier or later?" Tish asks.

"Earlier. Check your email, you should have something too."

Tish picks up her phone. To my amazement, the color in her face is restoring, the lines around her eyes still haggard, but beginning to lessen.

She searches her inbox. "We leave at eight a.m. Well, at least this gets us to the island earlier. We'll be sipping rum punches by sunset at this rate."

"Sounds good to me," Amanda says.

"*Meee* too," Tish agrees, sitting back in her chair.

I watch her carefully. On one hand, I'm relieved she's acting more normal, the tension lessening, but my irritation still sparks as to why she won't tell Amanda. Confusion too.

"By the way," Amanda asks. "Did you get those suitcases you ordered?"

I stand up and move to the fridge, putting away the milk and eggs. "I got the one."

"But I thought you ordered two?" Amanda asks.

"What happened to the other one?" Tish asks. "The one for me?"

I bring our coffee mugs to the sink and rinse them with soapy water. It seems odd to be talking about anything other than Sabine right now, but my friends' attentions are moving at rapid speeds. Tish's intent, I'm sure, is to change the subject whereas Amanda's brain is constantly able to multi-task.

I shut the water off.

"Something got screwed up," I tell them. "In the shipment details. I've been meaning to check with the store because only one suitcase showed up."

I know this is something I should have done last week. I've been meaning to call the main number to find out why only one box arrived on my front porch.

"They charged us for both so we should get both," Tish says.

"We will," I assure her. "I'm sure it's just an oversight. I'll call them this week."

Amanda frowns. "I bet it's the new mail service. It's been messed up for a while."

"You noticed that too?" Tish asks. "I thought it was just me."

"No, it's all over the neighborhood. Mail ending up in the wrong mailboxes. Packages going to the wrong doorstep. I heard the Montgomerys received Hector Suarez's meds. And Bethany ended up with the Carters' mortgage statement. What a pain."

"You think that's what happened to the suitcase?" I ask.

She shrugs. "Could be."

"But wouldn't somebody have called to say they received an enormous box with your name on it?" Tish says. "I was with you when you placed the order and I remember them putting your name on the delivery slip. Wouldn't somebody have told you if a package accidentally ended up at their house?"

"You would hope," Amanda says. "Unless someone is looking to keep your luggage." She grins. "What kind are they?"

"Nothing fancy," I tell her. "Samsonite carry-ons."

"Good enough," Amanda says, still grinning.

I wipe my hands on a dish towel. "That would be pretty crappy of them to keep it."

"Maybe they don't know who you are or can't find your contact info," Tish suggests.

Amanda rolls her eyes. "It's not that hard to look up Erica's phone number in the neighborhood directory. Or find a way to reach out to her on Facebook. Ask a neighbor."

"True enough," Tish says.

"Speaking of mail," Amanda says, "have you guys gotten your passports yet? I received mine."

"You know mine doesn't expire for another year so I'm good." Tish glances at me. "What about yours?"

"Not yet." And I sit back on my hip. "That's weird..."

"But we sent off for those months ago," Amanda says. "Getting them renewed shouldn't take that long. I was going to ask you about it but I figured yours arrived around the same time as mine."

"When was yours?"

"About two weeks ago."

I scratch my head. "Well, that sucks. I'm going to need to track that one down, and stat."

"If someone mistakenly got your passport and didn't hand it over, that's awful," Tish says.

"And a lot more complicated." Amanda looks at us. "A suitcase is one thing. You can claim you never received it and they can express ship it to you overnight. But a passport? Just trying to get someone at the processing center is a nightmare, almost impossible. It's all snail mail and a clunky website. It will take a couple of weeks for them to issue you a new one."

"Do you have a tracking number?" Tish asks me.

"I should." I think about the forms I saved when I submitted the application. "I should have it on my drive."

"Good," Amanda says. "At least you've still got time. We don't leave until next month."

"Maybe you could post something?" Tish says. "Ask if any of the neighbors received a package with your name on it."

"Not a bad idea," Amanda agrees.

I nod, thinking this is something I can do, but not for a few more days. Not now, when everyone is concerned about finding Sabine with group posts focused on the search. My request on Facebook about a missing passport would appear ill-timed, insensitive, or would be lost in the shuffle among everything else involving the Millers.

"And maybe post about that suitcase too," Tish says. "It'd be really great to find it. I need one."

Amanda brings her coffee mug to the sink. "Right," she says, gathering her car keys and purse. "I should get going."

"But I thought the search starts at noon."

"It does. But I want to stop by Eric's before we meet up." Eric Nichols, the man leading the neighborhood search, who's been posting updates on Facebook. "There's some stuff I need to talk to him about first." Amanda jostles her car keys, but then stops, looks at us, eyebrows raised. "But shower, okay, guys? I love you both, but you look like hell."

*

My attention returns to the coffee pot that needs rinsing and the sugar bowl I'm putting away when Tish crashes. The distraction of talking about suitcases and the nuisance of messed-up mail was temporary.

Something on her phone seizes her attention.

"Oh my God…" she says, her face sinking. "This is…" With every message, her eyes are widening. "I can't believe they would…"

"What's going on?"

She keeps her eyes glued to the screen. "Who the hell is Trevor Blankenship?"

Amanda would know but she's gone. "I have no idea."

"Why would he say something like this? Why are people responding?"

A clank inside my chest. "Responding about what?"

"Someone made a poll. On Facebook." The color drains from her cheeks and she turns the phone to me as I slide into a chair. "It's a poll wondering if Sabine Miller is alive or not."

"Oh my God." I cover my mouth with my hand.

Tish's fingers tremble. "People are actually voting." She reads a few more lines before her thumb hovers over the Facebook icon. She appears ready to delete the app.

"Wait," I tell her. "Let me see first."

And I look at the group, the group that started off so nicely, labeled *Praying for Sabine Miller* with calls for support and hashtags for #SaveSabine.

The hashtags are still there, but so is something else. Something twisted. The search for Sabine Miller is taking a dark turn.

FACEBOOK GROUP POST

Praying for Sabine Miller (Private Facebook Group)

Trevor Blankenship

July 5 at 10:40 a.m.

Group Poll

Is Sabine Miller alive or dead?

Alive, but only for a few more days. The clock is ticking—15 responses

Alive, and they should be expecting a ransom request any time now—18 responses

Dead, she was killed Saturday night—38 responses

Dead, she was killed this morning—24 responses

Heather Stephenson Take this poll down right now!

Lamar Jackson Who is Trevor Blankenship? Somebody report him. We need to flag his account.

Tamyra Meeks Who's the admin for this group? Block him and delete this, please.

Scott Wooley This is just for fun, guys.

Eric Nichols There's nothing funny about this.

Christine Blanchard Scott Wooley, is this you? Are you posing as Trevor Blankenship?

Scott Wooley I promise this isn't me.

Heather Stephenson We don't have anyone named Blankenship in our neighborhood. Someone has created a fake account and made this poll.

Amanda Kimbrough We can see where you voted, Scott.

Scott Wooley You did too, Amanda.

Amanda Kimbrough I voted her Alive.

Kerry LeBlanc The profile picture is a photo of a guy wearing a scuba mask. This is creepy as hell, you guys.

Hector Suarez How are 38 of you voting she was killed last night?? You're sick.

Scott Wooley Some of you are acting pretty high-and-mighty right now but we can see what you picked.

Anthony Castillo Let me know when they find her body in the back of Jacob's car and I can get back to the rest of my Sunday.

Jennifer Krel I heard he has an alibi.

Paul Tomlinson He was with someone. You guys can scratch him off the list.

Scott Wooley How are you so sure Jacob didn't have help? And he's got her dead in some basement?

Heather Stephenson She is ALIVE, people. You need to stop thinking otherwise.

Carolyn Castillo I heard he's got some BS story about visiting a girlfriend. They're releasing her name today or tomorrow. Maybe she has something to do with Sabine's disappearance too.

Alice Chin Like she helped him??

Scott Wooley Carolyn, let us know as soon as you hear something.

CHAPTER 13

I try not to drop the phone. Beside me, Tish looks ready to throw up.

In the time we've been sitting here, *Alive and expecting a ransom request* has moved up four more responses. *Dead, she was killed Saturday night* has ticked up to a total of forty-two.

What in the hell happened to *Praying for Sabine*?

Last night, so many people wanted her found alive and well. They couldn't think of anything but rescuing her and bringing her home, convinced every minute counted and they would find her huddled beside a tree or fallen in a ravine, ankle broken with cut-up hands and wrists, but making a full recovery. Most of the people who voted were out until three in the morning trekking through woods and mosquito-infested creeks, for goodness' sake. How could they turn around and vote in a poll like this? Something so heartless?

But one whisper of a culprit and a statement about a certain man's car from Mark Miller, and they're losing hope. They're pinning it on Jacob. Blood in the woods doesn't help either. The realization there has been no word from Sabine or her perpetrator. No demands for Mark to turn over everything he owns in return for his beloved wife, even as some people cling to hope for a ransom.

But wait—I spoke too soon. *Alive and expecting a ransom request* knocks down one less vote. To my horror, someone has changed their mind and they're assuming she's dead.

And the others? The ones who are already claiming her life has been taken, and so soon? My stomach churns as I watch a few more numbers roll in. *She was killed this morning* now exceeds thirty responses.

These people are either callous or numb or both. Maybe it's the desire to look plainly at the facts, at what we know, and they're reassessing the chances of finding her.

But showing their opinion in a grotesque Facebook poll for everyone to document and see is beyond me. It makes me sick. Many of our neighbors assuming the woman is dead and hidden away, already gone. Snuffed out. The continued search, a lost hope.

Except for the likes of Heather Stephenson, Paul Tomlinson, and Lamar Jackson. *Good for them,* I think. Those brave, positive souls. They will be the ones encouraging everyone to keep going. They'll continue rallying for the search team to meet, especially when Eric Nichols, former Eagle Scout leader and head of a biotech company, leads the call. Eric will want to keep organizing.

Outside, truck doors slam—that will be my neighbors, I'm sure, the Atkins family heading out for the day and returning to the corner of Chandler and Smoke Rise. Another car door slams with a shout from across the street, what sounds like Todd Hampton hollering from his truck window to my neighbors, the heavy diesel engine of his F-150 roaring to life next.

I glance at the time. Amanda will have arrived at Eric's house by now. They'll be discussing the poll and wondering who in the world Trevor Blankenship is. They might even be able to put in a call to some friends and ask about tracking the account.

Did Eric vote? I can't remember but probably not since he's busy organizing the neighborhood team and would never dream of taking part in something like this. But Amanda voted, and what did she pick—*Alive*? Looking through the responses, I see she has clicked on *Alive, but only for a few more days.*

Dear God, Amanda... Could you at least try to be a little more optimistic? Even when you're preparing to go back out in a hundred-degree heat, could you try to be the tiniest bit encouraging?

But out of the three of us, Amanda has always been the pragmatic one. She'll do her part as to what's neighborly and right. She'll head out with the search team every day until they find her, or until they tell everyone to stop. But like Amanda said, with every minute that passes, hope fades. For every hour she's gone, Sabine's chances of survival are becoming more critical.

And, yes, all of this bothers me—the poll, its very existence, Amanda's bleak vote, what so many are saying on Facebook—but what is troubling me the most—especially for Tish, who has resumed to a state of shortness of breath beside me—are the comments about Jacob Andrews and his girlfriend. Their belief that the mystery woman could be complicit. That her name could be released within a day. That as soon as the first person finds out, they will be expected to tell everyone they know. Including this dreaded Facebook group.

*

Tish heads for the shower, and I'm almost positive it's to hide and sob under running hot water. She barely looks at me as she slides out of her chair and pads toward my room.

With hands pushed against my face, I hold my fingers for several seconds, feeling the pressure in my eyes slowly receding to the back of my head. I welcome the relief. But then, white stars form and another sharp pang comes, this one at the base of my skull.

Like Tish, I need a long, hot shower and the caffeine from my two cups of coffee to kick in.

It's a few minutes longer before I hear the water shutting off and I walk to my bathroom.

Tish is standing in front of the sink wrapped in one of the towels she found in a cabinet. She's running her hands along the tubes and bottles I have spread out across the counter and picks one up, applying tinted moisturizer to her face. Wordlessly, she squeezes the lotion into her hands and rubs it along her forehead and cheeks, her motions robotic. If she's noticed I've walked into the bathroom she doesn't acknowledge me. She is staring into the mirror, her silence off-putting.

She didn't stay in the shower and cry long enough.

"Tish, you okay?"

She rubs the lotion down her neck in long, steady strokes.

"You can stay here all day if you need to. Taylor will keep Charlie out of your hair."

She doesn't respond but peers closely at the mirror, staring critically at the faintest lines forming around her eyes. She tugs at the skin.

After some time, she stares at my reflection in the mirror. "It's all going to come out now. I might as well get prepared."

"You didn't do anything wrong."

"They're already talking as if I did."

"But you didn't."

"In the court of public opinion..."

"But they don't know it's you yet. People love you. They know who you are, your character. You would never do anything—"

"I had an affair with a married man."

"You're not the one who's married, this isn't on you."

"But *he's* married. And now they're saying his girlfriend could be covering up for him. They're going to wonder," she says. "About me. If I knew something and didn't say a word. If he used my house as an alibi."

I try coming up with something—something that will ease her mind even though I have no idea if I'll believe it myself.

"They won't say that. And if they do, ignore them. It will die down as soon as the police clear everything up, you'll see. The cops' final call is what's most important." I move toward her. "But you really need to tell Amanda. About you and Jacob. She can help."

Tish's eyes widen. "How? How is she going to help?"

"I don't know… just having her on our side."

She presses her hands against the counter. "I thought she already *is* on our side."

"She is, but it would be good to tell her first. Before she hears about it from someone else. Or Scott or Carolyn telling the world on Facebook. You saw those posts yourself."

She takes on a faraway look before letting her gaze drop to an unidentifiable spot on the mirror. She thinks for a long, hard while. "I know I didn't do anything. *You* know I didn't do anything, and neither did Jacob."

"Of course you didn't. He was fixing something at your house. You drove over here. We went to the pool together and you've been with me ever since."

She makes a face. "But why would they think the girlfriend would automatically be an accomplice?"

"They're stupid. They want to jump to conclusions that he's the one, and while they're at it, assume he faked his alibi. That his girlfriend would be in on it."

"But I wouldn't let him send me text messages so he can cover up his tracks." Tish's lips set into a hard line. "And you saw those pictures. He was standing in my kitchen. He was there the whole time. The sky was getting dark outside. He never left. How would that explain—?" She doesn't finish her sentence. "I just hate how they're pointing fingers at him, talking trash about him, how they're going to be talking about me too, and it will all be for nothing. Someone else has her."

"Who?" I ask.

"How should I know? But definitely not Jacob."

I watch as she pulls her hands through her long, wet hair and runs her fingers to the end, combing out the tangles. She tugs at another strand before flicking her eyes to me. "I was so nervous in the beginning," she says quietly. "About those text messages and the cops. But now I'm glad we have those messages as evidence." She tucks her hair behind her ears. "I never thought I'd be so relieved to have my dishwasher go out like that, you know? What good timing." Her smile borders on nervousness. "If he was ever going to come over, last night was as good as any."

She drops her hands while I provide a nervous smile in return.

But then she shakes her head. "And now I've been dumped."

"You didn't get dumped—"

"Oh, yes, I did." She repeats his words: "*Erase our text messages. We can't talk anymore.*"

"He's backing away because there's a lot of heat on him right now."

"I know." She sighs, a deep painful breath. "But what about me? It's like he left me on my own. I'm terrified for him but scared for myself too."

"You're not on your own. I'm with you."

Her eyes lock on mine. "Thank you, Erica. You're the one I trust."

CHAPTER 14

It's my turn to shower and afterwards as I'm toweling off, Tish is returning to the bathroom and holding something for me to see.

Silver bracelet. Blue charm. A bangle held up with her index finger.

"Is this yours?"

I take a good look at the bracelet, then back at Tish.

"I think it's Sabine's."

"What are you doing with her bracelet?"

"I found it by the gate. Last night. I was going to give it back." I fold the towel tighter across my chest.

"Charlie was looking in your pool bag for a toy he thought was with your stuff." She peers at the jewelry closely. "You found it at the pool?"

"She must have dropped it before she left."

"The police found another bracelet of hers on the golf course."

"I know." I take the jewelry from her hand, feeling the need to wrap my fingers around it. But the band feels hard and cold against my fingers and I set it beside the sink. "I plan on giving it back to her when they find her."

"You think it's connected?"

I look up, confused. "What is?"

"That look she gave you, and then you find her bracelet. She goes missing." She shrugs, biting her lip, thinking this over. "For whatever reason she picked you to give some sort of warning. She knew something was going to happen, she was scared, and you're the one she looked to for help." She points at the bracelet. "Maybe she dropped it for you to find on purpose too."

I steady my gaze. "It's just a coincidence."

Tish goes to say something else but closes her mouth. Her eyes leave mine until she's only staring at the bracelet.

*

An onslaught of text messages from friends are filling my screen. It's many of the same people from last night.

Tamyra Meeks: *Someone posted a video.*

Lamar Jackson: *What is it??*

Tamyra Meeks: *A street view of Honors Row. They think it's whoever took Sabine.*

Alice Chin: *Is it that Jacob Andrews guy?*

I wrench my head. Tish is in the bathroom blow drying her hair while I throw mine in a loose knot. It will take her at least ten more minutes—her hair is that long—with a good chance she hasn't seen these messages yet or she'd be slamming the hair dryer down.

Another ding sounds from my phone. A neighbor is texting along with several others who have been posting—and, yes, voting—in the group poll too.

Jennifer Krel: *I just watched the video.*

Carolyn Castillo: *I need to see this! Where?*

Tamyra Meeks: *Check the Facebook group.*

Hector Suarez: *I just watched it. This doesn't make sense.*

My thumb jams against the Facebook icon in two seconds flat. My heart is racing as I search my notifications.

And then I see it. The video hasn't come from one person but instead the link is repeated several times in one post after another—everyone wanting to share the same info with dozens of comments stacking up. I click on the most recent link.

The caption reads: *Video recorded last night 7:38 p.m.*

The camera angle is from someone's front porch looking onto Honors Row, one of the Millers' neighbors with a grand sweeping yard and landscaping filled with rose bushes. Their sidewalk is swept clean. And across the street, the beginning of someone else's driveway.

It's not yet dark but the sky has settled into a gray, dusty haze. Sabine would have already returned home by this point. And based on Mark Miller's statements, he would be on his way home to check on her.

At 7:38 p.m., this video should capture the moment Mark insists he saw Jacob Andrews driving near his house.

With a heavy breath, I press play. The street for now is empty.

A car appears in the frame—coming in from the left. The driver is moving slowly, slow enough that I can make out the outlines of the vehicle but not the driver himself. The windows are darkened by the shadows of overhead tree branches and the fading light. The distance of the camera doesn't help either.

But something stops me abruptly—that's not a Tesla. Not a flashy red sports car with its sleek design and low curved body. Not a chance of it having matching red leather seats as I spotted in Jacob's.

This car is a sedan. A long body that rides low to the ground. Black in color.

I squint but there is still no way to make out the driver.

The car passes and comes to a halt at the stop sign. The driver pauses before turning left—the left blinker flashing. Turning, the driver heads down Quarter Lane toward the waterfall entrance before exiting the neighborhood. The car disappears off-screen.

The left blinker was on. What an interesting detail to remember, Amanda said.

Mark Miller was right about that detail.

But he's gotten everything else wrong. How could he mistake this car for a Tesla?

My pulse quickens in my throat as I watch the video again.

If this person has done anything to Sabine or is holding her captive in the trunk, they are in no hurry. If they're hiding something or have just attacked her inside her kitchen, they are in no way trying to get the hell out of there either. There is nothing about their driving to indicate panic.

And more importantly—and what I'm sure everyone who's watched this video is noticing—that car isn't Jacob's Tesla. It's a black Buick LaCrosse.

The cortisol spikes in my shoulders.

What Tish said: *The car he drove tonight. It's a rental. He rents a different one every time.*

A black Buick like the one Jacob used to visit Tish.

But what else is puzzling: why would Mark lie and say he saw him driving something else?

FACEBOOK GROUP POST

Praying for Sabine Miller (Private Facebook Group)

Alexis Redfield

July 5 at 11:55 a.m.

Did Jacob Andrews switch cars or something?

> **Jennifer Krel** Why would he switch cars?
>
> **Heather Stephenson** Maybe there's a chance it wasn't him after all.
>
> **Lamar Jackson** The man says he was at a woman's house. And that's not his Tesla. So…
>
> **Scott Wooley** I still have my money on him. He had someone help him. Sabine is in the trunk of that Buick.
>
> **Christine Blanchard** Scott, can you remove yourself from the group posts? I'm sick of seeing your accusations.
>
> **Scott Wooley** Whoa! We can write what we want in here.
>
> **Carolyn Castillo** Christine, if you don't like it, why don't you leave the group yourself?
>
> **Heather Stephenson** Everyone needs to calm down.
>
> **Eric Nichols** We're heading out in five minutes.

CHAPTER 15

Is Mark Miller lying? Is he making up the fact he saw Jacob Andrews, or did he see him in the Buick and left that detail out on purpose?

And how did he know Jacob was in a rental car in the first place?

I think of Sabine's best friends sitting by him at the pool. The way Monica said *they won't try it again*. If he and Monica are so sure they know who *they* are and they claim Jacob threatened them in the past, then why would Mark lie about seeing the Tesla? A cherry red sports car with an American flag bumper sticker is highly identifiable. The detail about him using his left turn signal is incredibly specific too. Why would Mark say those things but describe the wrong car?

And not to mention the most chilling part—what Tish is going to freak out about the most—the vehicle captured in the video looks like the one Jacob must have driven to her house.

I pace in the kitchen and agonize over when Tish will see this video herself. The moment she'll watch it with bated breath as I did, only to discover it's a car looking very much like the one her boyfriend was driving.

Did Jacob Andrews lie to Tish? He told her he was in her house until after 8 p.m. but he snuck out early. Either that, or someone else happened to be driving a black Buick at the same time Mark Miller was going home. What are the odds?

Which means Jacob returned to Tish's house only to take more photos of himself in the kitchen. He wanted to show that it was dark outside. He staged it all.

But I still don't understand how Jacob could have swung it. How he could leave Tish's kitchen, show up at the Millers' house, *and* have enough time to confront Sabine before chasing her through the woods. And even more time-consuming, take Sabine to where she still hasn't been found and *still* beat it back to Tish's house for a couple more photo ops? With him wearing that wretched mustache on his face and standing in front of a repaired dishwasher with nightfall outside her window? We're talking about an hour block of time. Maybe less. It almost seems impossible.

But as shrewd as Jacob Andrews is, wouldn't he also know that by driving down Honors Row, someone was bound to have a security camera? They would capture him traveling down their very street? That eventually the police will find out he'd rented a Buick earlier in the afternoon?

I steal a glance down the hall to my friend.

Does Tish have any idea who she's dealing with?

*

When Tish emerges from my bathroom, I don't want to tell her. I'm trying not to look jumpy, trying not to panic.

Has she seen the video yet?

But Tish isn't carrying her phone in her hands and instead says, "I'm going to check on the kids," before heading for Taylor's bedroom.

My phone dings with several news alerts. Every local station is parked outside the Millers' home with additional crews staked out on the golf course where her blood was found. A CNN crew has shown up too, the news of what has happened to Mark Miller's wife reaching national levels.

I scan through the alerts, viewing images of the Millers' back porch and a close-up of their back door, the one that shows glass smashed in—the door they believe she ran from and escaped to the woods. In another article, yellow caution tape stretches across a bank of trees, the golf course in the distance. Additional crime scene tape marks off the golf cart path, and beside it, several wooden stakes are shoved into the ground.

Is that where they found her broken bracelet? More of her blood?

I read the headlines:

Day Two: the search for Sabine Miller
Jacob Andrews released from police questioning for now

I lift my eyes:

Mark Miller to give another press conference at 2 p.m.

Is there new information?

And then another striking headline:

Jacob Andrews' Tesla Roadster remains at his property

Underneath the copy reads:

Wife Meredith Andrews cannot confirm her husband's whereabouts between the hours of 4 p.m. and 8 p.m. but does confirm his sports car was parked in their driveway. Mark Miller is to provide a statement about his sighting of this vehicle in the Green Cove subdivision which is located eighteen miles from the Andrews' home. Is Mark Miller mistaken?

I shake my head. Both men have a lot of explaining to do…

My phone lights up with an incoming call, and for a split second, I'm wondering if it's Terry—the man I've been dating.

He's finally checking in or he's heard the news while on his work trip and wants to make sure we're okay. But, no, it's Amanda.

"Hey," she says. She is once again breathless, reminding me of the last twenty-four hours where she's sounded nothing less than shocked, and my heart ratchets a few beats.

What else have they found? What has she learned? Does she know about Tish?

"It's Monica," she says. "They've brought her in for questioning."

I pause. "Monica? Wouldn't that be a formality? She was with Sabine last night."

"Yes, but they've already questioned her. Carol too. But something else happened. They found something else. Hate mail."

"Hate mail? You're kidding."

"Some horrible letter she wrote to Sabine. Something vicious."

"They got in a fight. What's the big deal?"

"Trust me. What she wrote is making everyone's head spin. It's stunning."

FACEBOOK GROUP POST

Praying for Sabine Miller (Private Facebook Group)

Anthony Castillo

July 5 at 1:05 p.m.

Unbelievable. Looks like Monica Claiborne is in the hot seat now.

> **Tamyra Meeks** What have you heard??
>
> **Alice Chin** She wrote some letter. The cops found it balled up in Sabine's house. It doesn't look good.
>
> **Kerry LeBlanc** Where are you guys hearing this?
>
> **Carolyn Castillo** We've got connections.
>
> **Tamyra Meeks** What did she say? Have you guys seen the letter?
>
> **Anthony Castillo** Not yet. But from what I understand, she threatened her.
>
> **Kerry LeBlanc** What in the hell? They're best friends. Why would she do that?
>
> **Christine Blanchard** Aren't you guys supposed to be out there searching?
>
> **Alice Chin** We are. Just stopping to check Facebook.
>
> **Hector Suarez** There were about 300 people at the pool who can say they saw Monica, Carol, and Sabine

together and they looked fine. There was no fighting. No animosity.

Alexis Redfield I saw them too. They looked happy.

Hector Suarez If there's a hate letter, they've gotten over it since then.

Hillary Danners Why would someone write something like that and then actually go after the person? Wouldn't that immediately give them away?

Carolyn Castillo People are stupid.

Scott Wooley She probably thought Sabine tore the letter up but she didn't.

Alice Chin You guys, this is crazy... but I just I heard Monica used to date Mark Miller back in the day.

Tamyra Meeks No way!!

Carolyn Castillo I heard that too. They dated in college before he met Sabine.

Scott Wooley So that's it then.

Alice Chin I think she's always been jealous. She wanted him back.

Anthony Castillo Could be motive...

Heather Stephenson Why don't we wait until we hear the next news report?

CHAPTER 16

At the last minute, Mark Miller cancels his appearance at the additional press conference. Instead, the spokesperson for the police department makes brief remarks—a total of one minute and four seconds, which sends the media into a frenzy asking questions and demanding to know why Mark is suddenly refusing to speak to the press when he appeared only hours earlier.

Tish finds me watching the event streaming on WAFF 48 News and sits beside me on the couch, tucking one knee under her chin as we listen to reporters call out with questions that go unanswered. The spokesperson is stepping away from the cluster of microphones and trying her best to smile when several more reporters throw in a few extra requests.

Is Mark Miller mistaken about what car he saw?

Why would he say it was Jacob Andrews?

Who is the woman Mr. Andrews was with last night?

By now, Tish has caught up with every message on her phone. She's finished watching the movie with the kids and collected her phone from the charger, her eyes widening the moment she checked the video post, the color in her face blanching.

The revelation the car is a black Buick LaCrosse isn't lost on her. Her mouth dropped open the moment she hit play—a sickening worry filling her eyes. But she hasn't said a word to me about it. Every fear and doubt and question about whether that's him or not—the same questions running through my head—are, I'm sure, filling her brain. This latest revelation hangs heavy in the air between us.

Mark Miller is lying. And Jacob lied to her too.

Another reporter calls out:

Can you discuss details about Monica Claiborne?

Is she now a suspect?

But the police spokesperson waves her hand; she's done. And no one else is moving to replace her at the microphone stand. They're shutting down the press conference.

Well, that won't go over very well. A lack of transparency from authorities will either mean they don't have the first clue or they're hiding something before coming clean with the public.

If I had to guess, with half the police department including the lead detectives and that very spokesperson already working with the county commissioner's office, they're supporters of Mark Miller. He's that popular and that loved. More than likely, they're good friends and voted for him in the last election, which means they plan on voting for him again in November.

But now this. They're in damage control mode. Turmoil not only for Mark Miller's family and the safety of his wife on the grandest of national scales, but for his political campaign too.

Behind closed doors I can only imagine a team is scrambling to help him make sense of his story. What he thinks he saw. What he thinks he knows about Jacob Andrews. Whatever threat he claims the man has made to them in the past. If he's going to have to backtrack on his original accusation.

And now Monica.

Did he make up the part about Jacob Andrews' car to protect her? When I heard her say at the pool, *they won't try it again*, did Mark automatically jump to accusing Jacob because he couldn't imagine it would be Monica—a close family friend and someone devoted to his wife? Someone who, coincidentally, also used to be his girlfriend.

*

Taylor and Lydia don't want to leave. We're finishing a thrown-together dinner of spaghetti when my ex-husband Derek rings the doorbell ready to take them back to his place.

This is what we do: the children transfer back and forth to our houses every week with Sunday evenings being the most convenient time to pick them up. But it's never easy. It hurts every time I see them go.

Lydia doesn't get up from the table; her hands remain tucked in her lap as she shoots me a look. She's worried and doesn't want to leave me alone. But Taylor scampers to the door and swings it wide open. "Daddy!" she squeals.

I slide my eyes to Lydia. "We'll be all right," I tell her. "I've got Aunt Tish." But even as I say this, Tish is mindlessly pushing noodles around with a fork, lost in her thoughts, ready to hide or scream or curl up into a ball.

Lydia says, "What about Aunt Amanda?"

"She's stopping by again tonight. She wants to talk to Tish and me about some things." And I glance at my friend wondering if she's seen the latest text—if this is any indication Amanda has learned Tish is Jacob Andrews' alibi.

Taylor pulls on her dad's hand until she's led him into the kitchen. He doesn't greet us, only smiles at Lydia, who eventually stands from the table and gives her father a hug, her head pressing against his chest before she steps away. "Hi, Dad," she says.

"Hey, sweetheart. Do you have anything you want to bring?"

She shakes her head.

"I've missed you," he says, scooping both girls in for a hug. "I've missed you both so much."

When he says this, he accidentally makes eye contact with me. But I know good and well his sentiment doesn't include me. It never has, not since he started running around on me behind my back.

As the girls say goodbye, he says, "I'll bring them back Sunday." When he stops on the porch, he adds, "Make sure you lock your doors." A worried glance toward the front yard. "Something in Green Cove isn't right."

CHAPTER 17

Amanda sends a heads-up she's five minutes away.

Tish immediately turns in my direction. She's finally speaking. "I'm telling her as soon as she gets here. You're right. I need to get this over with."

I finish rinsing the plates from dinner; the pots I leave in the sink to soak. Tish asks if she can borrow my iPad and brings Charlie to the couch so he can watch cartoons. He settles against the sofa cushions, his head tilted to one side as she presses play.

When she returns to the kitchen, she asks, "Do you want to tell the police about finding Sabine's bracelet?"

I silently place the sponge on the counter.

"Or tell Amanda you have it?"

I shut off the water. "I don't think it has that much significance."

"But what if it does?" Tish looks to the door that will soon open with Amanda's appearance. "You said it yourself, she can help. I'm telling her about Jacob and maybe when you tell her about the bracelet it might mean something. She's hearing so many details and something like this could click."

"But you saw her at the pool, the amount of jewelry Sabine was wearing." I shrug. "It fell off. It doesn't mean anything—"

The door yanks open.

It's Amanda, hot and sweaty with her curls mashed beneath a white baseball cap stained with sweat. Dirt and grass marks run from the hem of her track pants to her knees.

I turn from the sink. "I thought it was just the golf course?"

She brushes past me and reaches for a glass, filling it to the top with water. "It was. But there are a lot of hazards out there. Sand dunes. Tall grass." She chugs the water greedily before wiping her mouth with the back of her sleeve. "It's hot out there." She fills the glass for a second time. "Be glad you're inside."

Tish sits at the table. She opens her mouth, ready to tell her, her shoulders rising in preparation for what she has to say, but Amanda doesn't give her a chance.

"They think Sabine may have cut through the woods to another side of the trees before she got to the golf course. Like she ran in a zig-zag pattern or something as if she was being chased." She takes another big gulp of water and this time instead of her shirt sleeve, she tears off a piece of paper towel and runs it against her mouth. "Monica and Carol said she'd been wearing a couple of bracelets at the pool and since the cops found one of them snapped in two, they had us looking for anything else that could have been yanked from her body." Tish rips her eyes to me but I give the tiniest shake of my head to hold off for now. "There was also a charm someone found near the golf course," Amanda says. "But they're not sure if it's hers or not."

Tish clears her throat. "What did it look like?"

"Red, I think. Someone said it could have been a heart since Mark gave her an *I Love You* charm a few years back. The police are asking him to identify it." She balls up the paper towel and tosses it in the trash. "I'm hearing several other comments too."

"Like what?" I ask.

"How Sabine disappearing in the middle of Mark's re-election campaign is either hurting his election chances or helping him. Causing turmoil. Costing him valuable time where he could be out there campaigning."

I scoff. "People really care about that during a time like this?"

"His team does. I've heard them talking. But they're confident he's getting the sympathy vote since there's not a speck of evidence against him, with everything pointing to an outside job. Pinning it on Jacob Andrews, for example. Their marriage was on the up and up," Amanda continues. "Mark is the devastated husband who won't rest until his wife is found." She sets down her water glass, meeting our gaze. "And can you believe this craziness about Monica's letter too?"

Tish jumps forward at this—the chance this latest revelation could direct any heat away from Jacob. "What do you know about it? Do they think Monica could have done something to hurt Sabine?"

"I don't know what the letter says word for word, but it's bad enough that she's been at the police station for the last three hours."

"How long ago did she write the letter?" Tish asks. "If it was recent, that would be pretty telling, wouldn't it? She could have planned something. She could be behind this whole thing."

Amanda gives her a curious look. She notes the excitement in Tish's voice—or the desperation.

"Monica is a piece of work, don't get me wrong," Amanda says. "We would never be friends. I've never understood how Sabine or Carol can tolerate her either, she's a total snob. But the woman was at the pool the entire time, same as you. Waiting on the fireworks."

Tish doesn't give up. "But there's a chance she could have done something? Maybe she's working with someone else. They planned it."

Amanda nods. "The rumor mill is going rampant right now. Monica. Jacob Andrews."

Tish flinches. "Why do people keep thinking Jacob would do this? Risk doing something so brazen? Especially when a lot of eyes are on him during this election year. It makes no sense."

"You've seen it on Facebook," Amanda says. "A bunch of people have their theories."

"But *why?*" Tish asks, straining her voice. "There's a threatening letter from Monica saying God knows what. And now Sabine is missing. How much more proof could people want?" She smacks her hands on the table, a flush blooming across her cheeks.

Amanda gives her a worried look. "You okay?"

She presses her hands together to calm herself before throwing a worried glance at her son, who remains on the couch watching cartoons, blissfully unaware of his mother's reaction. She returns her eyes to Amanda. "I have to tell you something—"

But Amanda cuts her off. "I already know."

"What do you mean? What do you..." Her voice trails. "About me?"

Amanda walks to the table and pulls out a chair to face Tish directly. "There's a lot about this case I probably shouldn't know, things I haven't told you both. Stuff that I'm gleaning from my colleagues. But yes," she says to Tish, "I know about you and Jacob. About him being at your house. I found out just before I came here. In fact," she says, "that's a lot of the reason why I'm here."

Tish lets out a gasp.

"Wait." I hold up my hand. "How do you know about Tish? The cops haven't called her in yet."

"I'm friends with an assistant at the attorney's office. Jacob's attorney." She takes stock of our startled faces and says, "I know, it's bad—attorney-client confidentiality and all that. But she knows we're good friends and wanted to give me the heads-up. I'm giving you the heads-up too."

Tish is turning white as a ghost. "So the police are going to want to talk to me any minute? I thought maybe Jacob had bought me some time, that he'd found a way to protect me."

"He did. For a little while, at least. The police know it's a girlfriend and that's all they've been told, but Jacob's attorney is going to have to provide your name soon. They'll need to ask you a few questions just to verify that, yes, Jacob was at your house. That, yes, he sent you those pictures. That, as far as you know, he was at your house the entire time. Those text messages and time stamps have given him enough of an alibi for them to back off for now. You'll just need to verify."

"He has an alibi," Tish says. "So why do people still think he did it? Monica's letter sounds damning as all hell. A direct threat. Why would anyone think he could be the one?"

"The cops let him go, remember?" Amanda says. "Monica's the one being questioned right now but…" She looks away. "It doesn't explain some of his unusual behavior. A black Buick that's seen driving near the Millers' home last night. The same car Jacob rented yesterday afternoon before visiting your house. *With cash*," Amanda says, "so he could come over to your house without being detected. That doesn't look good either."

I wonder if Amanda also knows about the mustache he wore as a disguise—and she must. The assistant at the attorney's office may have divulged that information too. I squirm where I stand, hating the amount of information that is leaking from this case. It's unbelievable, not just to Amanda but even the people in that Facebook group. The ones that already knew about Monica's letter.

Amanda stares quizzically at Tish. "Do you know what he was doing? Do you know why Jacob was driving down their street?"

But Tish insists, "It doesn't have to be him."

"Did he say anything to you before you left to go to the pool? Did he say he was going anywhere else?"

She shakes her head. "No. With his text messages, I just assumed he was at my house the entire time. There's no reason why he would leave and come back."

"Was he checking on them or something?"

"Who? The Millers?"

"I don't know. I guess."

"Why would he do something like that? What reason would he have?" Tish chews the inside of her lip. "And it's killing me because he won't answer my calls. I want to ask him, but he told me to delete his messages. I haven't been able to talk to him about any of it."

"I'm sure his attorney is helping him develop a story—"

"It *won't* be a story," Tish snaps. "It's not him. Or maybe it *is* him, but he just went for a drive or something." But by the way her voice is trailing I know she's struggling. "Will the assistant at the attorney's office tell you more? When she hears of anything, will she call you?"

"I don't know. It's pretty dicey that she told me your name in the first place."

"She could get fired." I speak up, and Amanda glares at us both.

"That's why we're not going to say anything about her, okay?" she says firmly. "She told me to help you. I'm here to help you, you got it?"

Tish nods slowly.

"If Jacob is innocent, Monica's letter is what will get him off the hook for good. She may have hurt the woman," Amanda adds.

Tish nods again but she doesn't say anything more. She picks at spaghetti sauce that has spilled from one of the kids' plates, a blob of red that is hardening on the table, her finger picking up speed until she scrapes at it violently.

And the guilt is rising in me too. What I heard Mark and Monica talk about at the pool. The bracelet that's tucked away in my bathroom. There is so much information coming out, and yet, I'm keeping a lot of things quiet. Several details I'm holding close to my chest.

But I know I need to talk to the police. I'll need to talk to them very soon.

*

A statement is released from Mark Miller's camp this evening.

"Due to a phone conversation between Mark Miller and Jacob Andrews which Mr. Miller considered to be hostile in nature, Mr.

Miller, in an emotional and panicked state once he discovered his wife was missing, believed the car he saw on his way home was a Tesla belonging to Jacob Andrews. The threatening phone call in question occurred the night before Sabine Miller went missing.

"Mark Miller has now retracted his statement about the vehicle. However, police are investigating a black Buick LaCrosse that was spotted. Police are also following additional leads at this time. Anyone with information is strongly encouraged to contact the missing persons tip line set up with the Huntsville Police Department."

I drop my phone, my blood running cold.

CHAPTER 18

Amanda says she's leaving to go home and shower. She won't be joining the search tomorrow since she'll be at work.

"What about you two?" she asks.

"I'll call in sick. With the kids at Derek's, I can help with the search in the morning."

She turns to Tish. "Are you thinking about lying low for a few days?"

"I can't imagine being at the office." She glances at me. "I'll send a note and call in sick too. Charlie can take a break from summer camp. We need to get through the next few days somehow." She places her hands on the table and pushes to a standing position. "But we're going home, Erica. Thank you for having us for so long but we should go."

"You don't have to leave. Stay here as long as you need to."

She casts me an appreciative look. "I should get Charlie back to his room and his things… that will be best." She sighs at the sight of Charlie with his head sunk lower, his legs scooped beneath him as he watches cartoons.

"If the police contact you, call me," I tell her. "I'll come over and watch Charlie. Or I can bring him here if I need to."

"Thanks." Tears form in her eyes and she blinks them away.

Amanda stands too. "If I hear anything else, I'll let you know." She puts a hand on Tish's back and pulls her in for a hug. I do the same.

"We're here for you," Amanda tells her.

"We've got you," I whisper too.

Tish falters a little in my arms. Her body trembles and I'm starting to reconsider, thinking maybe it's not the best thing for her to be going home alone after all. But she eventually pulls away and insists on putting on a brave face—and with a start, I realize, I've seen that look before. The same resolve Sabine Miller had when she turned away from the pool. These brave women who are trying to power through everything.

I stand at the garage door and watch them go, their cars pulling out of the drive as Charlie waves goodbye from the backseat. Tish waves goodbye too when my phone dings. I look down and my heart does a double beat. It's Terry—he must finally be home from his work trip.

You doing okay?

I'm relieved to hear from him. An entire weekend isn't going to pass without us talking to one another.

I'm okay, I respond. *How about you?*

I just heard the news. Any sign of her yet?

No, not yet.

It's so close to your home.

There is so much to say in response to this, but I don't know where to start. I don't know how much I can say either, the last twenty-four hours being unlike anything I've ever experienced. The disappearance of Sabine Miller and surrounding circumstances—hell, one of the suspects—hitting way too close to my circle of friends.

It's very close, I tell him.

Are the kids scared? I hope they're all right.

They're worried, especially Lydia. But they've gone back to Derek's.

I add: *Do you want to get together this week? It would be nice to see you.*

A pause. He doesn't respond right away and an irritated pang hits the back of my throat. Why is he taking so long to answer? Does he have to think it over?

Relax, I tell myself. He's probably checking his calendar and wants to make sure he's not booked. He's been traveling a lot these last few months, he told me, his job taking him to countless sales meetings and conferences.

Waiting for him to agree feels like an eternity when in reality it's more like twenty seconds. But in a new relationship where nothing is locked in, firm or steady, any hesitation can shake my insecurity about dating. It makes me wonder if we'll see each other again, if he's really that interested. If I should have asked him out in the first place.

A message appears.

Sorry about that. A package delivery at my door.

Another text and the pang in my throat subsides.

Sure, he says. *How about tomorrow? Lunch. I'm pretty slammed this week.*

Lunch? Okay, so I was hoping for dinner, but lunch will work too. Maybe his calendar will free up more this weekend.

Sounds good.

Terry writes:

I've got a meeting on Hwy 72. Can you drive that way to meet?

I'm about to ask him where when I already know what's on his mind.

How about 11:30 at that bar & grill on West Elm? he asks.

West Elm, the same place we met the last time, except it was a Thursday night and I beat him in darts. The grill is about a thirty-minute drive from here.

You sure have a lot of meetings in Scottsboro, I tell him.

Sorry about that.

Next time, some place closer, okay? And I get to pick the place.

He sends me a smiley face emoji. *Sure thing. Have a good night, Erica.*

He adds: *I sure hope they find that woman.*

*

On Monday morning, a text from Amanda tells me the search in Green Cove is halted for now and I don't need to meet up. She's on her way to city hall and was told the sheriff's department is no longer organizing neighborhood groups but are expanding their search with additional police precincts and FBI agents. It's been nearly thirty-six hours and with no sign of her body or her safe recovery in Green Cove, they have reason to believe she's been taken elsewhere.

Overnight, it's also been confirmed that Jacob Andrews was driving a black Buick LaCrosse when he was initially called in by the police, that he did in fact leave his Tesla at home as his wife confirmed, but the car he was driving on Saturday may not be the same vehicle that was seen traveling down Honors Row. The license plates for the vehicles don't match up. Police are now trying to track down the owner of the other Buick.

But, Amanda reminds me, anyone can switch license plates. It could take a person five minutes, which means Jacob isn't in the clear yet.

I know we shouldn't be saying that about Tish's boyfriend but… and she doesn't finish the rest of her message.

Amanda adds:

Also, Monica needs to be sweating right now. I found out what she wrote in her letter.

I bolt straight up.

You've seen it?

No way. That's police evidence.

I raise my eyebrows. *Well, to be fair, Amanda, you've gotten ahold of a lot of other information you shouldn't have been privy to…*

They got in a huge fight, Amanda texts. *Some dinner party at the Miller house Friday night. Everybody got way too drunk and Sabine accused Monica of having an affair.*

With Mark?!

Monica says someone else.

Does anyone believe that?

Not sure yet. Didn't know they used to date before.

I think about the revelation made in that Facebook group.

Me either.

According to the cops Monica said they were yelling at each other and it got super-heated. She was emotional and said things she shouldn't have. Sabine too. Monica's husband got upset. Carol was yelling. Sounds like a complete shitshow.

So what about the letter? I ask.

It happened Friday night. The same night they got spooked. Before Sabine went missing.

I think about the statement Mark's camp released about Jacob making a threatening phone call the night before.

Monica admits she wrote it in a drunken rage. Scribbled it on a piece of paper and threw it on the floor. It wasn't supposed to mean anything. She regrets it. Doesn't want anything bad to happen to Sabine.

Her letter said: I hate you. I wish you would die.

I hope your life ends the way you said it would. And we'll never see you anymore.

Dear God.

Reading this, it takes me a moment to catch my breath. The anger from Monica, so visceral. Her threat, so cut-throat.

Amanda is sending this to me by line-by-line as a text, but I can only imagine the dramatic ink-to-paper fashion in which Monica wrote it. Drunk. Wailing. Tears streaming down her face—or maybe no tears—only pure rage, her eyes turning as dark as her black hair. Leaning across the table, she must have clutched a pen and written these words in hard cutting lines across the page, the ink blotting, the jab of the *i*'s and slash of the *t*'s as she told Sabine exactly how she was feeling. Writing to her such horrible things I'm assuming she would wake in a few hours to regret—*if* she regretted them.

What's crazy is the letter was written Friday night, but by Saturday afternoon, Monica, Carol, and Sabine were at the pool together, laughing and talking and watching their children swim. Even if Sabine had never found the letter—say, after the last dinner guest left, Sabine went to sleep and never saw it on the floor, Mark never picked it up either, the letter swept into a corner of the room or drifting beneath a table—there had still had been a vicious fight between those two. An accusation made by Sabine. Monica either lying through her teeth or defending herself in front of her husband.

Carol would have been present, her husband, Monica's husband, and Mark too. They would have witnessed the argument. Mark would have already been on edge after the phone call he said he had with Jacob. He would have seen how upset his wife was after fighting with her friend.

How did Monica and Sabine go from screaming at each other to sitting poolside and sharing wine spritzers twelve hours later? How in the world does something like that happen?

But a new message flashes across my phone and I can't answer Amanda anymore. I'm sprinting from my bed.

It's Tish.

I need you. The cops were here.

CHAPTER 19

It takes me less than a minute before I'm leaping into my car and racing to Tish's house. She doesn't live far, and the only stop sign between my house and hers, I blow right through. It's still early; most people are either asleep or at work so I don't have to slow down behind anyone else. There's one jogger and he steps out of the way as my car careens around the corner.

Tish's street is laid out just like mine: cookie-cutter-style houses with arched windows and bleached-white sidewalks. But something I haven't paid much attention to before: the location of Tish's house. She lives at the far end of the street. The very last house. No cul-de-sac but a dead end.

No one passes Tish's place unless they're needing to turn around—or they're pulling directly into her garage and out of sight, just like Jacob would have done. Visiting her is made simpler this way.

I swerve into the drive where police cars would have just been.

Swinging open the door I find Tish waiting for me inside her living room. I run to her. "Are you okay?"

By the way she's pacing, her hands flexing as she pulls at her fingers, mindlessly popping her knuckles and wrangling her wrists, I can tell she is anything but okay. Her long blonde hair is down and stringy—she didn't have a chance to brush it—and she's wearing a thin bathrobe I'm guessing she quickly pulled over her pajamas when she heard the police knocking on the door.

"They came so early. It scared me half to death. Charlie was asleep but now..." She glances at her child, who lies on the floor coloring a book.

Tish keeps pacing. "But it's done. I provided my statement. I showed them my phone, which corroborated the messages I received from Jacob. I told them how I left and went to the pool with you." She gives me a warning look. "There are plenty of people who saw me swimming with the kids but they'll want to talk and confirm times with you too."

"Absolutely, Tish. Yes, I'll confirm everything."

She points to the kitchen. "They even took photos. The dishwasher. The counter. They dusted it for fingerprints to confirm Jacob was really here." She grits her teeth. "I haven't cleaned it yet."

"I'm so sorry, Tish."

She keeps talking. She's so rattled, the nervous chatter rolls right off her tongue. "They asked me about the Buick and I told them, yes, that's what I saw him driving. *Did he say anything about leaving, about going anywhere else?* they asked. I told them he was heading home when he finished here. There's no reason to think he would go to the Millers', that he would do anything like that."

She spins to me. "It has to be another car. Someone else was driving, it just *has* to." She grips my arms. "Someone is trying to frame him. They knew about me—they knew about us. And somehow, they found out that's the car he rented Saturday. They rented the same model on purpose. That's what they drove past the Miller house. Not Jacob. *Never* Jacob."

"Who would know about you two seeing each other?"

She chews on her nails, her eyes returning to the floor, the wall and back to the floor, thinking. "I have no idea. We were so careful..."

"And who would want to frame Jacob?"

She gives a strangled laugh. "I don't know, pick a number."

*

Monica Claiborne is telling the police she did not hurt her friend, that she did not hire anyone to hurt her friend, nor did she collaborate with anyone, including her former boyfriend, Mark Miller, to kidnap Sabine.

She and Mark were an item in college more than twenty years ago. They've moved on since then with their lives and careers and families and there is nothing between them, Monica insists. It's only happy coincidence she would become best friends with Mark's wife after they moved to Green Cove and pure luck they would end up living side-by-side on Honors Row. She swears she and Mark are now friends and nothing more. Her allegiance is to Sabine.

Monica also tells the police the letter was not written with any intent to hurt her friend. She was merely drunk and angry and doesn't understand why Sabine would announce at the dinner party—and in front of her husband, no less—that she thinks Monica is having an affair.

Monica insists she is *not* having an affair and that her argument with Sabine was a big misunderstanding. She is now heartbroken over the disappearance of her best friend and wants Sabine found immediately. As of last evening, she and her husband have contributed to the financial reward with the amount now sitting at a quarter of a million dollars.

All of this we glean from Amanda, who continues to dig up information while she's at work. City hall, she says, is abuzz with nothing but talk about the ongoing case.

"It's all anyone can focus on. That big of a reward is nothing to sneeze about. And there are missing person posters everywhere. Heather Stephenson and her PTA crew have been hanging them up since yesterday. A whole stack of them showed up in my office a few minutes ago."

Amanda is on speaker phone while I'm at Tish's house. My legs are scooped under me on the couch while Tish's knees continue to shake at a frantic speed.

Tish has told her about the police visit this morning and Amanda doesn't sound surprised when she says, "Well, at least that's out of the way."

And it's not that Amanda is being dismissive, it's just that her main motivation behind this phone call is Monica. The hate letter that is the gossip spewing from everyone's lips right now. The idea that if anyone had issues with Sabine, many are saying her letter spells it out clearly.

But Monica's defense as of this morning? "A new bombshell," Amanda announces.

Monica is claiming that Sabine Miller was planning on leaving the country. She says she's been talking about going somewhere and Monica thinks she took off.

"Wait," I interrupt. "If Sabine wanted to go traveling, this is *not* the way to do it."

"Agreed," Amanda says. "I can think of a thousand different ways to take a vacation without someone chasing me from my house while I'm bleeding from my arms and legs."

Tish waves her hands. "This doesn't make any sense. Monica gets caught with a letter telling Sabine she wishes she would die and her explanation is to say, no, Sabine up and left the country?" Her eyes grow wide. "How does she explain the blood? And the broken glass? And what people found in the woods?"

"It's insane," Amanda says. "Could be a desperate way to deflect the heat off her."

"And how come no one's heard from Sabine?" I ask. "If she left the country, why hasn't she called?"

"Because maybe she was trying to leave Mark?" Amanda suggests.

"No way," Tish says. "She wouldn't leave him. I think they love each other too much. They renewed their wedding vows back in January."

I look at her. "Where'd you hear that?"

She shrugs. "Facebook. They posted pictures of the ceremony. It was beautiful, actually."

"Maybe stuff has soured since then," Amanda pitches in.

"I don't know," I say. "He was joining her at the pool and made it seem like they had plans to meet up with each other."

"I don't buy it either," Tish insists. "Sabine wouldn't want to leave Mark and not in this way. Not so drastic and heinous. Monica must be feeling really desperate if this is the theory she's coming up with."

"Well, whatever's happening," Amanda says, "it's the crazy story Monica is sticking to right now—that Sabine wanted to leave the country. But she didn't take her passport and there is no indication she purchased a plane ticket or traveled anywhere. Trust me—the cops have bulletins all over the place. The FBI is on this too. Someone would recognize her and flag her ID in an instant."

"And it still doesn't explain the blood," Tish reminds us. "Or her leaving without a trace."

"Or…" Amanda says but she lets the sentence hang.

"Or what?" I ask.

"Unless she used a fake name."

"Wait—what?" Tish leans closer to the phone. "What are you talking about?"

Amanda's voice quickens. "Unless she used a fake identity." A muffled sound comes through on the speaker and I imagine her tucking the phone under her chin and pressing it close to her neck. The sound of fast typing comes next.

"I'm emailing someone," she says. "Going to ask around and see if that's been looked into."

"Wouldn't the cops have already considered this?" Tish asks. "Looking to see if she staged it. If she flew out of the country using someone else's ID?"

"Yes, I'm sure. They would look at everything." The sound of Amanda's clacking against the keys comes to an abrupt stop. "Erica," she says. "Your passport."

My legs sweep out from under me. I lean forward, same as Tish. "What about it?"

"You never received it, right?"

"No." I think about the sticky note I left beside my purse last night, the one reminding me to check with the passport processing center later this week.

"Do you think there's a chance?"

"A chance of what?" Tish asks.

But I'm the one who answers her. "That Sabine received my passport instead of me."

CHAPTER 20

Tish nearly trips on the rug, and within seconds, she's returning to the living room with her laptop in her arms. She places it on the coffee table in front of me.

"Do you really think..." she starts to say.

But I don't answer; I'm too busy logging into Gmail and accessing my Google Drive. I search for a folder titled Miscellaneous where I'm almost positive I saved the receipt and passport tracking file. The document opens and at the top of the page, the tracking number.

I search for the US Department of State website next. Under the *Passports* tab, I click on *Application Status* and enter my information.

Status: Delivered by mail.

June 23.

Two weeks ago—about the same time as Amanda's.

"Does it say which address?" Amanda says through the speaker phone.

I search the page. "It confirms what I entered. My address. Everything is correct." I scratch my head. "But my passport never arrived."

Tish peers over my shoulder and confirms the search results. "112 Holly Pond Road. That's you."

Amanda is typing. "What's Sabine's address?"

With a click, I navigate to the Green Cove website, although I'm almost certain that's where Amanda is searching too. The private directory requires a password and it takes a second for me to remember mine. I haven't used the directory in ages.

I enter my last name—Holloway—plus my alarm code: 14-27, my kids' birth dates, and presto, I'm in. I search for the Millers.

There's the sound of keystrokes on the other end of the line before Amanda says, "Found it."

The page I'm looking for pops up too. Tish and I stare at the screen:

Mark and Sabine Miller

112 Honors Row

I sit back on the couch and the number glares back at me: 112.

The Millers and I share the same house number. It's not something I would have noticed before. Our street names sound a bit similar too.

And with the mail service being as messed up as it is, if the Montgomerys did in fact receive Hector's meds and Bethany ended up with the Carters' mortgage statement like Amanda said they did, who's to say a brown manila envelope with my passport didn't end up in the wrong mailbox by mistake also? Who's to say Sabine Miller didn't open the package before realizing what it was and who it was for?

So why didn't she call me?

Our contact info is listed right there in the directory. A simple email would have done the trick. Why didn't she let me know? She had to know I'd be waiting for it, that I'd want this important document as soon as possible.

Except... and I look at Tish....

"No way," Tish says. "There's no way this is related—"

But Amanda cuts her off. "It's a huge coincidence, don't you think?"

"We have no idea if that's where Erica's passport ended up," Tish cautions.

"It says her passport was delivered."

"But that doesn't mean it ended up on Sabine's front porch."

112 Holly Pond.

112 Honors Row.

A simple mistake… right?

Tish is pacing in front of the couch again. "So Sabine got your passport and used it to leave the country? *She staged her whole disappearance?* The blood and everything? No way," she repeats.

Quickly, Amanda tells me, "Erica, check your bank. Credit card statements. You've got LifeLock, don't you?"

"Yes." LifeLock is an identity theft protection service I signed up for last summer.

"Check to see if there's been any suspicious activity. If someone ended up with your passport. That someone hasn't taken your info and compromised it. Like bought an airline ticket or used your money to book a hotel or something."

My head is spinning at every one of her orders. I begin typing but it's difficult at first. A nervous bubble rises through my chest causing my fingers to shake.

I check my email for any LifeLock notifications but nothing turns up except for an alert from four months ago when I opened a department store credit card to buy clothes for Lydia. LifeLock sent an email to verify the activity was in fact me and I clicked confirm.

But there are no other warnings in my inbox. No big purchases or international transactions that would have flagged the identity theft service. No dings to my credit either.

A huge part of me sighs with relief.

"Anything?" Amanda says.

"No."

I search my bank next and choose a thirty-day history just to be safe. Scrolling through my checking account, I review my regular activity: weekly fill-ups at the gas station, occasional lunch deliveries at work, Rosie's Mexican Cantina for dinner with the kids last week. There's also a debit at the West Elm Bar & Grill when I bought a beer waiting on Terry. He joined five minutes later and purchased the rest of our drinks.

A check cleared for my July mortgage. There's a monthly transfer to savings. The bakery where I bought donuts for Taylor after she helped me tidy up the house. From what I can tell, everything appears to be in good shape.

"Check your credit card too," Amanda prompts me.

The last two months of credit card statements take longer to inspect. It takes a moment for the PDFs to download and as soon as they open, I'm leaning forward to check each one. Amanda and Tish wait patiently—well, as patiently as they can. Tish is hanging so close over my shoulder I can feel her breath hot in my ear. Amanda is furiously typing something on her end while telling someone—an office aide, I imagine—to hold her calls and not come in. She barks at someone else and the door subsequently bangs closed.

I read out loud: "Phone bill. Utility bill. The suitcases I ordered on June eighteenth." I keep scrolling. "A hundred and twenty dollars at the grocery store." Switching over to July's transaction doesn't show much either as we're less than a week into the new month and I haven't made as many charges yet. "A trip to McDonald's for Taylor's kid's meal. Sparklers we bought at the fireworks place." I reach the end of July's history. "The only thing related to travel are the airline tickets we bought for our trip but that was months ago." I log out of the website. "I don't think anyone has stolen my identity. No one has used my passport to go anywhere internationally. They certainly didn't take any of my money to buy a ticket."

"So not Sabine?" Tish asks.

"We don't know that yet," Amanda pipes up. "She could have used her own funds. She could be traveling under Erica's name."

"Is there a way to check?" I ask, thinking I could look at a travel website next.

"Any emails about a flight confirmation?" Amanda asks.

I return to Gmail and search. But the only flight details are the ones involving our trip to Tortola—the same email Tish and Amanda received about an earlier flight time.

"Nothing," I say again.

But Amanda keeps typing. She must have set her phone on the desk and placed us on speaker because there's a clatter, the clicking of her mouse set up right against her phone.

"You can fly nationally with a passport too. Sabine didn't have to go out of the country. She could still be in the US."

Tish steps closer to the phone. "But wouldn't she need an ID to back up that she's Erica Holloway? She can't just show up with Erica's passport." She turns to me. "Is your driver's license missing too?"

I shake my head. "No." I don't move to check my wallet, my purse I flung to the floor as soon as I entered Tish's house. But I know my driver's license is intact. I showed it at that hole-in-the-wall place where Terry and I met for beers during our first date. The bartender joked and asked if I was of age, and we shared a laugh since I'm very much of age and forty-three.

"I still have my ID," I tell them.

"Then how would Sabine get away with this?" Tish asks.

"She could get a fake one, I suppose," Amanda says. "That's not unheard of. Let me check into it..."

I sit straight up, an alarm ringing through my chest. "Are you going to tell the cops?"

"No, let me ask a friend of mine. I don't want this getting out of control if it turns out to be nothing."

"It *is* nothing," Tish insists. "Erica's passport is circulating in God knows which mailroom at some post office. Or it's stuck inside someone's mailbox and they've been out of town and haven't checked—"

"They've been out of town for two weeks and didn't have someone check their mail?" I picture Amanda rolling her eyes on the other end of the phone.

"Or it's sitting in someone's house in a big pile and they haven't gone through everything yet," Tish continues. "They haven't seen Erica's name on the front of the package. They haven't had time to—"

"Or, it ended up at Sabine's house and it got Sabine's wheels turning," Amanda says.

"You're only saying that because Monica has this B.S. story about Sabine cutting and running," Tish tells her. "And Monica is only saying this crap to get out of the hot mess she finds herself in. *She's* the one who hurt Sabine—*not* Jacob, I just know it. *She's* the one who the police should be looking at. Sabine did not leave on her own."

But I keep thinking about Amanda's theory: Sabine taking my passport on purpose. Her idea to leave Huntsville while pretending to be me.

Could it be possible?

The mailman leaving my package at 112 Honors Row. Sabine not bothering to notify me about what was contained inside the brown envelope because that was the green light she needed to escape.

Did Mark find out? Did Monica confront her about these plans also? Was Sabine wanting to cut and run part of the epic blow-up fight that happened at the Millers' home Friday evening?

I wonder if Monica told Mark she thought Sabine was planning to run away. They tried stopping her. They told her not to go—that she would ruin everything. Mark's re-election campaign would be at risk if Sabine left their marriage.

But wouldn't attacking her and kidnapping her be even worse?

And why in the world would Sabine leave? She has the perfect life. The perfect marriage. The most gorgeous home.

... Doesn't she?

But she fought with her best friend. Who knows what else Monica has said to her in the past if she's capable of writing such hateful words in a letter?

And what else do we not know about Mark? He's already lied about Jacob's car. After everything we're learning, what else is he capable of lying about?

CHAPTER 21

From the floor, Charlie drops his crayon and stares at his mom.

"Mom, I'm thirsty." She ignores him. "*Mooom*," he repeats.

She shushes him. "Not right now, Charlie." She's pacing again.

"But *Mooom*," he insists.

"I'll help him." I look at Charlie. "Give Aunt Erica one minute, okay? I need to do something first." He gives a dramatic sigh.

Navigating back to the US Department of State site, I click on *Passport Status* and submit a trouble ticket regarding my missing passport. Wherever it is, whoever's got it, doesn't change the fact I still need a new one. A claim will need to be filed since there's no way I'm jeopardizing my vacation to the BVI next month.

A couple of clicks later, I close Tish's laptop and say to Charlie, "Okay, let's go."

But he takes my hand as soon as we enter the kitchen.

"You okay, buddy?"

He points.

A fine layer of dust covers the length of Tish's counter, a thin veil of it swept across the marble and along the top of the dishwasher with more of it brushed on the floor. It's the fingerprint dust the police officers used earlier.

A trail of it leads messily toward the door that opens to the garage. That's where Jacob would have parked and walked in, and I peer around the corner. On the doorknob, another smattering of dust. The doorknob is something he would have touched, the dishwasher too, but in the police officers' hurry, or just plain carelessness, they have let the fingerprint dust fall wherever they swept it from the container, making a mess, and not bothering to clean it up after.

"They put yucky stuff everywhere," Charlie says, rooting his feet right where he stands. He points at the fridge. "My juice is in there."

I tiptoe across the floor and move around another clump of dust left on the kitchen tile. In the fridge, I find a juice box.

Turning back around, there's the bottle of wine next to the sink, the one Tish and I shared a few nights ago that is now pushed out of the way. The dish cloth with the rooster design I gave her is tossed to the side also. And across the dishwasher buttons, a fine coat of fingerprint dust settles between the creases.

I picture Jacob Andrews standing at that spot. The pictures of him pulling out pieces and parts while he posed with that horrible mustache smiling for Tish. It's enough to make me tighten my jaw.

Again, who knew he could be that handy…

Charlie rips the juice straw from its plastic wrapping. "Mom said they were painting but I don't think that's what they were doing."

I stare at the fingerprint dust.

"It's a special kind of paint," I tell him, playing along.

"There were so many people working in our house. Painting and asking Mommy questions. And that man who fixed our dishwasher? He said he wants our dishes *nice and sparkly*." Charlie takes a sip of his juice, his cheeks sucking in until his eyes grow big and he stops to take a breath.

"That man? Are you talking about Mr. Jacob?"

"Yup. Mr. Jacob fixes things for us all the time."

"Like what things?"

"The dishwasher, silly." Charlie laughs. "I told you that."

But something registers inside my belly, a strange wriggling feeling.

Kneeling down before Charlie, I ask, "You said he fixes things all the time. What other things?"

He looks at me funny. "The dishwasher, I said."

"Only the dishwasher?"

"*Every* time," Charlie says. "Always the same thing. Over and over." And he laughs again. "He must really want us to have *sparkly* dishes."

*

Tish runs into the kitchen. She stops short at the entry, nearly slamming into us.

"There's a van outside my house."

"What kind of van?"

She gestures to her son, not wanting him to fully understand, and says between clenched teeth, "The kind with reporters."

I scoop my hand behind his back. "Okay, let's go to your room. Mom has a visitor and we need to stay quiet."

He kicks out a foot. "I'm so tired of being quiet."

I jostle against his back. "I mean it, Charlie." And with a gentle push, he moves.

"What should I do?" Tish's voice drops to a whisper.

"Tell them, *no comment.* Isn't that what you're supposed to do?"

She pulls frantically at her hair. "I don't know." Yanking at her bathrobe next: "I look like hell. I can't go to the door like this."

"You talked to the cops that way."

She screeches, "This is different! They were banging on my door and—"

The sound of voices outside. Tish's eyes bulge open.

Another look at Tish and she's right. I don't appear much better but at least I'm not still in my pajamas. I'm not ready to leap out of my skin.

"Okay, I'll handle this." Stepping toward the window, I look over my shoulder at Tish high-tailing it down the hall with her son.

I peek out from behind the curtains. Not only do I see one TV news van but also a marked SUV with the call letters WAFF

48 wrapped on one side. The videographer is setting up a wide shot of Tish's front yard while a reporter walks steadily down the sidewalk toward the front door.

I brace myself. Here we go.

Opening the door, I don't give the reporter a chance to knock even though she has her hand lifted, a smile on her face that broadens the moment she thinks there's a chance we're not leaving her out here empty-handed.

But she's wrong.

"No comment," I tell her without so much as stepping foot on the porch. "We have no comment at this time." And I shut the door with a loud, and I admit, exaggerated, slam.

The reporter calls out, "Can we speak to Tish Abbott, please? Can you ask her to come to the door? We only have a few questions."

The adrenaline runs through my body, my protectiveness of Tish.

I stand still on the other side and will the reporter to turn around and leave, the crew from the other news station too.

She knocks, followed by the ring of the doorbell. "Can you please ask Tish Abbott to speak to me?"

I shout through the door, "This is private property. Please step back!"

The reporter mumbles something unintelligible under her breath and gives up, the soft click of her heels against concrete as she returns to the van. To the videographer, she asks, "Did you get B-roll of the house at least?"

Another peek out the window and the crew is packing up their cameras and returning to the van. The door to the SUV also slams closed and both cars take off.

I breathe a huge sigh of relief.

But I know this is just the beginning. The reporters will try again this afternoon. They'll want to call too.

When I turn around, I see the whites of someone's eyes staring back at me from the hall. It must be Charlie not wanting to listen to his mom. But then I realize, it's Tish. She's standing frighteningly still, one of her hands clenched in a fist. Another look of terror.

FACEBOOK GROUP POST

Praying for Sabine Miller (Private Facebook Group)

Trevor Blankenship

July 6 at 9:08 a.m.

Updated Group Poll: We have a winner.

Is Sabine Miller alive or dead?

Alive, but only for a few more days. The clock is ticking—32 responses

Alive, and they should be expecting a ransom request any time now—25 responses

Dead, she was killed Saturday night—92 responses

Dead, she was killed this morning—78 responses

Eric Nichols Whoever this is, you're sick.

CHAPTER 22

A text message from Terry reminds me about our lunch.

I don't respond immediately, thinking, *I can't leave Tish—not anymore*. I can't leave her alone while she's hiding in her hall waiting for the next group of reporters to come calling. She needs me here.

I'm about to respond, *no*, when Tish returns to the living room. She steps gingerly, peeking around the corner when she spots the look on my face. "What's wrong?"

I try playing it off and hike a thumb over my shoulder. "The reporters."

"No." She gestures at my phone. "You got a message. Is it Amanda?"

I look down, then at her slowly. "It's Terry. He wants to go to lunch."

"He's back in town?"

"Yes." But I hold out a hand. "I'm not going. I'm staying right here with you."

She turns her head to the front door, a glance at the living room curtains I've pulled shut. "I'll be fine," she says.

"You didn't seem fine five minutes ago."

"I don't need to answer the door, do I? And neither do you. I thought of that while I was hiding. I don't have to answer the door, or my phone either. That's as good as *no comment*, if not better. I shouldn't be scared."

"But what about Charlie?"

"I'll keep him inside. We won't go to the playground. We won't go anywhere."

"I shouldn't leave you, Tish." I begin typing *I'm sorry* to Terry.

"It's just lunch," she says. "You should go, it's fine. But will you check on me later? That would be good." She stares again at the front door. "It would help to know you're coming back."

A conflicted feeling spreads across my chest. Guilt for leaving Tish, but also the desire to see Terry.

"Are you sure you'll be okay?"

"Absolutely," she says. "It's not like you're going to be gone that long."

"I can tell him, *no*. We can go another time—this weekend, in fact. Right now is too crazy."

"Actually, this will work out. You can bring us food. I don't have much here and it's not like Charlie and I are going anywhere." She reaches for her purse. "Will you order us cheeseburgers or something? I probably won't eat but Charlie…" She tries handing me a twenty-dollar bill.

"Not necessary. I've got you."

She returns the money to her purse and I hit backspace on my message, telling Terry: *See you at 11:30.*

*

I head home knowing I've got less than an hour to throw on some makeup and make the thirty-minute drive to Scottsboro.

It's my first time leaving the neighborhood since before Sabine went missing, since before this horrible weekend, and I don't dare take the route leading me closer to the Millers' home, wanting to avoid Honors Row and the waterfall entrance at all costs. Police and news crews will be camped on that street, I'm sure.

Instead, I take a side road where the exit out of the neighborhood will shoot me closer to the bypass, and then ultimately, Highway 72 leading to Scottsboro.

But at the edge of the neighborhood, the sight of something large and white rocking gently in the wind causes me to slow down—a Missing Persons poster taped to the bottom of a Stop sign, the edges of the poster shifting slightly with the breeze. To my right, a long row of posters is staked along the grass with several more wrapped around the lamp posts. Along the fence, an even larger poster with Sabine's smiling face staring back at me in full color. The word *MISSING* in bold black letters at the top, and beneath her picture, *$250,000 Reward.*

They've picked a photograph of her sitting outside, her shoulder-length blonde hair backlit by the sun with a beaming smile that brings a shine to her eyes. The photo has been taken mid-laugh, her mouth slightly parted with eyebrows arched, her hazel eyes crinkling at the corners with long lashes that have been touched up with the slightest dash of mascara. Another happy, relaxed day in the world of Sabine Miller.

I idle my car for several more seconds as I let my eyes wander to the additional posters lining the fence. Just like Amanda said, Heather Stephenson and her PTA crew have been busy. I can only imagine the waterfall entrance is covered with these things, the length of Honors Row too. The perfect backdrop for a TV reporter's live shot.

I stare again at Sabine's picture, her face that is tilted to one side as she laughs. She had no idea what was coming for her, only a feeling, and I say a silent prayer before shifting my car into drive and pulling onto the bypass.

Terry isn't at the restaurant when I arrive. I timed the drive perfectly, pulling into the parking lot just before 11:30 and taking a seat at the back of the restaurant, not wanting to be late. Technically, he isn't late either, not yet, but as I tap my watch, in another two minutes, he will be.

I'm not sure why he insists on meeting in this place. I get that his work takes him to Scottsboro sometimes, but why this bar and grill is beyond me. It's classic hole-in-the-wall with its gravel parking lot, a door that creaks on hinges when it opens, and a concrete floor that echoes my footsteps along with the classic rock music playing in the background, the occasional *thwack* of a pool stick hitting against the cue ball.

The place is dark too, lights dimmed except for the glow of neon signs hanging above the bar. Besides me, there is one bartender, a waitress with an apron tied over her jean shorts and three men solemnly perched on bar stools. An older couple are the ones playing pool.

But Terry insists they have the best barbeque sandwich and it's served in a bun he swears is homemade by the owner. I tried the sandwich the last time we were here; I'd beaten him in darts and he ordered us dinner. After one bite, I admitted to him he was right. It was one of the best things I'd ever eaten.

"*See?*" he said, proudly, as if he'd made the sandwich himself.

Another thwack of the pool stick as I glance at my watch again. 11:35 a.m. He's late, and I settle against the vinyl booth.

The door opens, sunlight pouring in and blinding me as the person enters and is caught in a dark shadow. But I can already tell it's Terry—the tall stance with his shoulders held back, the way he turns his head to stare directly at the corner where I sit, the exact same spot we met last time. He said he liked having a booth that's out of the way. We can have a private conversation and not be disturbed.

I give a small wave and he walks forward, the bar light catching the side of his face so I can see him more clearly now: the thin mustache above his mouth, golden with flecks of brown, and a black baseball cap that he's pulled tightly over his head, his blonde hair covered, although I catch a few strands above his ears. He's wearing a white polo shirt and jeans, which seems casual for a day at work, but then I remember how he works in software sales and many in that industry, especially software developers and their managers, work in hoodies and T-shirts most days.

Terry cracks a smile and his eyes brighten. "How are you?" he asks, sliding into the seat across from me. "Did you order those sandwiches yet?" He throws me a wink which matches the cute Southern twang in his voice.

"I'm good," I tell him, smiling too. "I figured we'd look at the menu first."

"But that's what we got last time." He laughs and pushes the menu away. "You can't tell me you're gonna try anything else. Not here."

"I might." Teasing him, I scan the menu but it's sparse. Besides offering a deli club and a platter of chicken fingers, the pork sandwich is what is highlighted at the top. Next to it, the words *World Famous*, although another look at this place and West Elm is far from spotlighting the world map. I pretend to agonize over my choices as the waitress appears, notepad at the ready, and I relent, asking for two barbeque sandwiches and glasses of water.

When the waitress leaves, Terry says, "Thank you again for meeting me here."

I glance out the window but it's spotty and covered with grime. The parking lot and shopping center across the street are barely visible through the glass. "Do you have more work to do this afternoon?"

"Two more appointments," he says, his eyes settling on my face. "But I'm so glad we could meet up."

"I called in sick," I tell him. "I wanted to help with the search but it's been called off in the neighborhood for now."

"I heard about that." His eyes turn down. "The poor Millers. I can't believe they're going through something like this."

"Me either."

"Did you know Sabine?"

And I flinch—his use of past tense. Surely he's not like the people in that Facebook group who are counting her out.

"I saw her at the pool..." I start to say but don't finish. I'm not sure if I want to monopolize our lunch telling him about what has transpired the last few days. Sabine's look that continues to haunt me, and certainly not about Tish and Jacob Andrews.

"Do you think they'll find her?" he asks.

"I sure hope so."

He settles against the booth and takes another long look at me. "It's good to see you."

My chest warms over. The heat rises in my cheeks and I glance away, not wanting him to see me blush. "It's good to see you too."

The waitress returns with our waters and says the sandwiches will be another five minutes. But Terry's phone rings loudly and he fumbles in his pockets. He pulls out a phone but its screen is black; there's no sound. "Shoot," he says, and digs in another pocket, bringing out a different phone. He studies the screen as it shrills a second time. "Work call," he says, apologetically.

Terry places the phone to his ear. Whoever it is says as little as five or six words before Terry is making a face, his mouth twisting with frustration. He holds out an arm to catch the waitress's attention, who is just starting to walk away. He tells her, "Can I take that to go?" His eyes dart to me. *I'm so sorry*, he mouths.

Seriously? He has to leave so soon? But we haven't had lunch yet.

Terry listens to the person on the other end of the line. His other hand reaches up to his face as he absently pulls at his chin before rubbing his index finger along his mustache. I've seen him do that before. The last time we were together, I asked him a question about his family and where he'd grown up. He asked me the same and I told him about Louisiana, the small town of Pearl River where my granddad took care of me most days, the front yard covered with magnolia blooms, and he listened, running his hand along his mustache and patting it down smoothly. I remember thinking how we hadn't kissed on the lips yet.

Terry's eyes dart to mine and once more, he mouths, *I'm sorry*. And then to the person on the phone, "I'll be there as soon as I can."

Disappointment blooms in my chest and I wave the waitress back over, adding two cheeseburgers and fries to the to-go order. I can't leave without bringing home what I promised Tish.

Terry ends the call. "I'll make this up to you," he says. "How about this weekend? We'll try again. I promise—" But his phone rings again and he's already moving out the door.

CHAPTER 23

My lunch date having been reduced to a dismal fifteen-minute event, I'm back on the highway when I call Tish and tell her I'm bringing lunch sooner than expected.

She doesn't ask why, only says, "No. Meet me at your place. More reporters were here. Sitting around and waiting for another group is driving me crazy." She tells Charlie to put on his shoes. "We're going to Aunt Erica's," she says. And then to me, "How far away are you?"

I've only just left the outskirts of Scottsboro. "Another twenty minutes."

"I'll let myself in."

"Don't forget to punch in the code."

She tells Charlie, "Your shoe. It's under the bed," followed by a sigh and the door slamming, the jangling of car keys. "See you soon."

*

Cheeseburgers are eaten—well, only Charlie, since Tish can't seem to sit still long enough to open her to-go box—and I've also had my sandwich. The barbeque is good, Terry is right about that, the bread having a soft baked taste in my mouth. I wipe at the sauce on my chin, squeezing the napkin absentmindedly and trying not to be too irritated as to why Terry left so suddenly.

But another look at Tish and I'm also wishing she would sit down and relax.

She's turned her phone on silent as several reporters have tracked down her number and she's tired of answering with, "No comment." She leaves the phone face-down on the sofa and walks circles in the living room.

"I thought you said you were okay. I wouldn't have left..."

"I thought I was okay." She breaks from her path to look out the front window. Since coming home, I've closed the blinds just in case anyone followed her, or the news stations take a guess and assume she's hiding out at my place. A couple of calls is all it would take to find out I'm her best friend living two streets over.

Tish retreats from the window. No one's out there—I could have told her that. But her anxiety is increasing every minute.

"I refuse to look at the news," she says. "I don't want to check Facebook. I'm sure it's already out there."

I'm not looking either—I'm tempted, but I don't peek. The revelation Tish Abbott is Jacob's alibi and the woman he's been seeing is, no doubt, spreading across the internet like wildfire. We don't have to see it to know it's happening. Any minute now my phone will start ringing with colleagues and nosy neighbors asking for the scoop. *As if I would tell them.*

Tish returns to pacing holes in my carpet.

"I need something to do," she says. "Something to distract me. Something to get my mind off... I can't sit and wait ..."

"We could do a puzzle? A board game?" Although under normal circumstances, Tish can't stand playing board games. A time like this would be worse.

But Charlie's ears prick up. "Yeah! A board game!"

Tish shakes her head and his shoulders droop.

"I'll play with you." And his eyes light up. "Run to Taylor's room and find something." He scurries away as if I've just promised him a hundred bucks.

"I need to do something with my hands," Tish repeats. "Like cleaning. Organizing. Scrubbing."

I glance at my kitchen. "Want to tackle my oven?"

"What about your shed? You've been dying to get that thing straightened out."

I frown; that's a mess I don't want to tackle right now. "The air conditioning unit went out a few weeks back and I haven't had anyone fix it yet. You'll be sweltering in the heat." I motion at the kitchen. "Seriously. The oven. If you want to take out your frustrations, that'll help." I try to joke. "One less thing I have to do."

But Tish is heading to my bedroom. "Your closet then. I'll sort through your stuff. Your clothes are a wreck in there." She marches down the hall, mind made up, on a mission. I don't say anything, thinking at least that will keep her from peering out the windows every five seconds and giving herself a panic attack.

Charlie holds out a Connect 4 board game. "How about this, Aunt Erica?" He tugs on my arm so I can return to the sofa.

Tish is in my bedroom for what feels like ages, when really, it's only been about half an hour. But long enough that Charlie and I have played twenty rounds and he's slowly tiring of the game. He tells me sweetly, "I don't want to beat you *this* many times, Aunt Erica," and I ruffle his hair, crowning him the official Connect 4 champion.

While we play, my phone buzzes but I don't respond to anyone, only looking out for messages from Amanda. She's gone quiet since this morning. I'm sure she's seen the news alerts and assumes we're still hunkered down together.

But just like I expected, that doesn't stop neighbors or work colleagues from sending text messages asking if Tish is okay. Tish's boss sends me a note too. A call from Carolyn Castillo goes unanswered. They're not concerned, only looking for gossip to share.

Charlie sees me put away my phone. The look on my face must say I'm done with playing because he asks, "Can I go to Taylor's room now?"

"Sure thing." When he leaves, I no longer hear Tish rummaging around in my bedroom.

Has she finished tossing the empty hangers? Or is she done sorting through my shoe rack and the absolute mess it was in, the shoes never lining up properly on the shelf? Maybe she's found a pair of her sandals she tossed in the corner last month or her dress left from St. Patrick's Day and wants to bring it home later.

I push off the couch, telling myself I should check on her. Make sure that reorganizing my walk-in closet hasn't let her thoughts drift and she's turned into a crying heap against the wall. But what I find is neither. Tish is sitting in the middle of the floor with a box of photo albums she's pulled from the shelf. Photos from my college years are scattered at her feet, an old party cup from a sorority mixer and some keepsake matchbooks from a graduation party. In her hand, a postcard my parents sent from their one and only vacation to the Smoky Mountains when they'd saved enough money. I remember when they left for that trip and I stayed with Granddad.

Well, this isn't the frenetic cleaning I thought I'd find from Tish, but I'll take it over her storming around the living room and sobbing into her hands.

I lean against the door and Tish doesn't look at me. She's placed the postcard aside and is now flipping through a small photo album, one of those old plastic ones they used to hand out at the supermarket when we collected our pictures from processing. The album holds twenty photos max, and from the looks of the party shots, I'm guessing they're from my days in college, good ole Louisiana State University.

She points at one. "You look so young here."

I sit beside her, my legs folded Indian style, to stare at the picture. My hair was longer back then, a dirty blonde that went past my shoulders, my face smooth and clear with the youthful shine and optimism of a teenager. Those were the days...

"I was." I nudge her playfully on the arm. "We both used to be so young."

"It was so simple back then, wasn't it?"

I can't remember exactly where this picture was taken but it's a house party. A black beaded choker is around my neck and I'm wearing a red tank top.

I point at the beaded necklace. "Geeze, do you remember those?"

She makes a face. "Very nineties."

Tish hands the album to me and rummages through the rest of the box, something I haven't gone through in ages—not even after we moved into the house and unpacked—when she pulls a soft jewelry bag out from the bottom.

She teases, "Something fancy? You kept that necklace all these years later?"

I reach out my hand but she's sliding the jewelry out until it's nestling against her palm. Silver bracelet. Blue charm.

She gives me a funny look. "Wait, did you put Sabine's bracelet in here? I thought you said you were giving it back."

A jilt to my voice. "I am."

"Well, what's this doing in here?"

She jumps up and heads for the bathroom counter. Next to the sink, she finds the bangle I left earlier, the one from my pool bag. She holds it up in her other hand, both bracelets dangling from her fingertips.

Her eyes bounce between the pieces of jewelry until focusing on me. "Why do you have two of Sabine's bracelets?"

I don't answer.

She narrows her eyes. "What's going on?"

I stand up. "One of those is mine."

"I don't understand."

I take the bracelets from Tish and clutch them in my hands. She holds my look, waiting for an explanation.

Finally, I say the words out loud I haven't said in a long time. "We used to know each other in high school."

Tish's mouth parts—disbelief, confusion, her eyes pinching as if she misunderstood. "You knew each other before? But you never said. You don't even talk to each other."

A knot forms at the back of my throat. This will be hard for her to understand. Even harder for me to discuss.

Leading her back to the box of mementos, I realize the only way may be to show her instead.

Pulling out a yearbook—the memories going back to 1995 when I was a senior at St. Mary's High School—I flip through some of the pages, the mostly black-and-white images from my alma mater and the Jaguar mascot that someone from the yearbook staff has stenciled in the corners. Without a word, Tish kneels slowly by my side.

I find a picture of me at the head of a table, the caption reading: *Erica Holloway, Student Council President.*

I show her several more pictures in the yearbook: Baccalaureate Mass. Students assembled in the cafeteria, group photos of the track and baseball teams... until I find women's soccer. With my finger, I trace along the second row until I come to a stop. There I am, my hair in a ponytail with a blue scrunchie to match my uniform.

And down in front, a girl with blonde hair kept shorter than mine, not in a ponytail, but tucked behind her ears with gold dangling earrings that would never be allowed on a soccer field.

The caption below it reads, *S. Taylor.*

Tish sucks in her breath. "*Is that her?*"

I find a snapshot of a group of kids sitting at lunch. At the table is the same girl from the soccer team, and below the picture, featuring the girl with blonde hair and hazel eyes and the same parted mouth that makes her appear as if the picture has been captured mid-laugh, is the name *Sabine Taylor.*

Tish points at me—the fact that I'm sitting right next to Sabine.

Her eyebrows crinkle. “But I thought you didn’t know her before? I thought Sabine grew up somewhere else.”

I’ve gone quiet.

“You never mentioned her from *high school.*”

And I look at my best friend—the things I haven’t told her yet. What happened so long ago. Why Sabine and I stopped being friends. Why our past is a big reason for what went down between us last year, that heated argument in front of our neighbors. Emotions sky-high and reminding us of another vicious argument from so many years ago.

It’s time I finally come clean. Almost.

PART TWO:
TWENTY-FIVE YEARS AGO

CHAPTER 24

1995, Louisiana

"Hand me that, will you?" My backpack drops to the linoleum floor with a thud—four textbooks and three binders filled with notes—reminding me of the weekend ahead of studying. First quarter exams getting in the way of our seventeen-year-old fun.

Sabine slides me a lunch tray. On it, chicken nuggets and mashed potatoes, a fruit cup and oatmeal raisin cookie. "Can I have your milk?" she asks, reaching for the carton.

"Go for it."

She pinches the top of the cardboard and peels it open.

The cafeteria at St. Mary's Catholic in Slidell, Louisiana, is nothing but a beige concrete block. Rows of laminate tables and plastic chairs that squeak against the floor, although the nuns at St. Mary's do their best to mop after us. I have no idea how they put up with us day after day, the sounds of two hundred kids talking one on top of the other, cackling and howling, slamming books and scraping table legs, especially as a group of football players are busy rearranging where they sit for no other reason than to be obnoxious. One of the teachers waves his arm, warning them not to knock the table against the wall.

St. Mary's, unlike so many of the schools in the Roman Catholic Archdiocese in Louisiana, is co-ed. Boys and girls walk the halls and attend class together. We kneel together in the gym for Mass. The girls wear crisp white blouses and blue plaid uniform skirts while the boys dress smartly in white collared shirts tucked into gray pants, the St. Mary's insignia embroidered on our front pockets.

Zach Howes, one of the football players, drags a set of chairs toward his table. He happens to also be Sabine's boyfriend and I catch her flashing a smile before he sits down. They've been together six months, which is a super-long time to be going steady with someone. Sometimes I catch her adding his last name to hers as she scribbles in her notebook: *Sabine & Zach Howes*, with a red heart bubbled around the letters. From across the cafeteria he smiles back at her.

We're a small high school, just two hundred students in all four grades. But sitting in the cafeteria at the same time, all of us crammed in for the same lunch period—the nuns believing it's imperative we squeeze religious studies class in after lunch—the high-pitched chatter is enough to drive me mad. After taking my time reaching the cafeteria, I've asked one of the girls to grab my lunch first.

Sabine nudges my arm. "After next week, our exams will be finished and we're off to Lake Tahoe."

Her reminder makes me smile as the two of us say, "*Fall break…*" in unison. A week-long holiday from school.

Sasha pouts. "I wish *we* could go."

Our other friend Heidi says, "Me too," and pushes a spoon through her food. "How come your parents didn't invite us?"

Sabine's smile weakens—she feels badly, I know she does. But her parents only said one friend.

"I wish you could. But it's a long road trip. You really think my mom and dad could put up with all four of us for that long?"

The girls mumble something and Sabine shoots me a wary glance, hoping they'll be okay.

In our pack of four, Sabine and I are the closest. We've been this way since freshman year, since the day we were assigned the same homeroom and found ourselves across from one another at lunch. We've been joining each other in the cafeteria ever since, inseparable on the weekends, sharing the same clothes, swapping makeup, confiding in each other about our boyfriends, the assholes and good guys among them, the ones we've broken up with even though Sabine is still holding strong with Zach. Sharing the same packs of cigarettes.

The first time I got drunk was sophomore year sneaking booze into Sabine's parents' garage. That night, I realized how much I hated malt liquor. Sabine laughed at me, even though she was cradling her head the next day too and saying, "I think we should stick to beer."

On Saturdays, shopping trips to the mall. Sasha and Heidi tagging along, but always with Sabine and I making plans for the next sleepover. After soccer practice, raiding each other's fridges before pushing through our homework, several hours of studying needed as our grades are becoming a bigger deal. It's our senior year and we have college applications to complete.

Lately, I wish we could take a night off and blow off some steam.

Sabine says we need to keep studying. She's been sharing her note cards and helping me with practice tests, but the truth is, I'm overwhelmed. My hands are full organizing the Homecoming committee. The dance is in three weeks and I'm tired of planning and wish I hadn't agreed. "But it's good for your résumé," my parents tell me. "Colleges will want to see how much you're involved."

My parents never made it to college. They work long hours to make sure they can afford my private school tuition and hope one day I'll graduate with a bachelor's degree. It's why I don't see them as often as I'd like. My parents work extra shifts at the manufacturing facility while my granddad greets me at home and takes care of me.

Something else, besides planning Homecoming, is the fact I don't officially have a date to the dance. But not to worry, Sabine tells me. Zach's best friend is going to ask—they're arranging every detail and Sabine is thrilled since we can double-date and pose for pictures together. Nick and I dated off and on before deciding to become friends again. "Maybe Homecoming will get you back together," Sabine hints.

Heidi releases another sigh, her mashed potatoes falling from her spoon with a *plop*. "We're going to be *so bored*."

I shove a nugget into my mouth and chew quickly. "We're not leaving yet."

"What about this weekend?" Sasha asks.

"We could go to the movies," I suggest.

"No, we should hang out and study," Sabine tells us.

"Great," Heidi mumbles. "Consolation prize before you ditch us for vacation."

"It will probably be a boring trip anyway," I pipe up.

"Seriously?" Sasha stares. "Lake Tahoe? You can ride jet skis across the lake. The water is so clear you can see right to the bottom. Kylie went with her family last year and said the lifeguards are gorgeous."

Sabine shares my look. "But three days driving by car?" She rolls her eyes and shudders. "With *my* parents? Symphony on cassette tape and Catholic hymns on the radio?"

Heidi says, "You'll have your Walkman."

Sabine tucks her hair behind her ears, revealing the gold earrings the group of us recently pitched in and bought for her eighteenth birthday. She loves those things—shiny brass with just enough swing. The flashier the jewelry the better when it comes to Sabine. And as I watch her and consider our upcoming trip, I'm almost positive she'll swim in the lake wearing those things too.

She nudges my arm and glances at our friends who are still sulking.

"I'll probably sleep," I say, making it up again. But this time, it's not a complete exaggeration. "After exams, I'll want nothing more than to sleep."

"See?" Sabine laughs, turning to our friends. "You're not going to miss a thing."

*

Just like I thought, studying for exams is brutal, but surprisingly, I complete the tests feeling more confident than I expected. There's a chance I might be able to keep my straight As after all. Sabine worries about getting a low grade on her physics test but the grade comes back with full marks, and she sighs with relief. The pressure we place on ourselves, unrelenting.

It's Saturday morning, the start to fall break, and Sabine's parents call for us to load up the car. A grueling 32-hour drive lies ahead with Mr. and Mrs. Taylor talking non-stop about how amazing it will be to cross five state lines.

"Think of how much we're going to see before we reach California," Mrs. Taylor says excitedly. "So much of the country." She's breathless, her eyes twinkling, the same hazel eyes she's gifted Sabine, the pair of them looking so much alike with their blonde hair and perfectly shaped noses with rose-bud lips that seem to permanently smile no matter what they're thinking.

Mrs. Taylor sets a thermos of coffee in the center console for her husband and he reaches for her hand, placing a kiss across her fingertips in thanks. He glances over his shoulder to make sure Sabine and I are buckling our seatbelts. His hair is blonde but darker at the temples with gray streaks appearing through the strands, and he smiles, tapping his hands across his chest to show off the goofy T-shirt he insists on wearing on road trips. The one that says, *Drive or Bust.*

They're giddy, and I'm not. I wasn't totally making it up when I said the trip is going to be boring. But I meant the drive. Sabine and I know once we get there it will be amazing.

Flying would have been simpler but I don't have the funds to pay for a ticket and I don't expect the Taylors to cough up that kind of money either. They're cash-strapped too since they're saving up for whatever college tuition Sabine doesn't receive in a scholarship. We're going on this trip because Mr. Taylor's boss announced it as his yearly bonus. The only catch? The location is two thousand miles away, a long haul, but not unachievable by car. After much consideration, the Taylors decide we'll make the trek because, well, why not? None of us have been to Lake Tahoe before and we heard it's incredible. But also because, as Mrs. Taylor put it, this is one of our last family vacations together. "Soon you girls will be heading for college," she says emotionally, "and we'll hardly see you anymore."

When I hear this, my heart warms over—how they include me as family. Sabine and I are only children and we cling to each other as sisters, another reason we bonded so quickly our freshman year. Our parents treat us as if we're each other's long-lost twin. If I'm not at her house on weekends, she's at mine.

Mr. Taylor backs out the drive and away we go. Three full days of driving with, as Sabine said, religious talk radio on the AM dial. But occasionally, the Taylors flip to a local station and we'll listen to Hootie & the Blowfish or Bon Jovi, Mrs. Taylor bopping to TLC's "Waterfalls". An hour later, Mr. Taylor will switch back to a news station or highlights from a football game. At one point we listen to an hourlong sermon since we're missing Sunday Mass.

And I sleep. I knew I would be exhausted from exam week, but there's not much else to do in the back of the van. Sabine's Walkman runs out of batteries, and soon, she's sleeping too—in fact, she's sleeping so much that at one point it's hard to rouse her and on day two of the trip, her mom is placing the back of a hand to her forehead, worried she might be sick.

"I feel fine," she says drowsily. But her head tilts to one side and she hikes her knee against her chest and falls asleep again, the swaying of the car and the endless stretch of interstate enough to make anyone drowsy. I close my eyes too.

But Sabine isn't eating much either, even when the Taylors make stops along the way and force us out of the van to take a break inside one of the many roadside diners. Sabine says she's carsick or has a little bug. She pushes aside her food, and for her mom's sake, swallows down a few crackers.

Back in the car, I stare out the window. Sabine isn't talking as much as I'd hoped and my backside aches from so many hours in the car. It would be nice to have someone to pass the time with but Sabine is dozing every chance she gets.

Along the way, the Taylors point out sites that might be of interest. The busy labyrinth of interstate overpasses in Dallas with the city's towering skyline. The flat open spaces of west Texas as we cross into Amarillo and Canyon State Park. The rising elevation and backdrop of the Sandia Mountains as we approach Albuquerque, New Mexico. Only at the outskirts of Las Vegas does Sabine perk up—she presses her hands against the glass and marvels at the bright city lights glowing in the desert night in the distance. Mr. Taylor keeps driving. We veer onto the interstate again.

Turning away from the window, I ask, "You feeling any better?"

"Yes." She adds quietly, "I'm just ready to get out of this car."

"You and me both." I reach over and squeeze her hand. One more night in a travel motel to go.

On day three, signs for Lake Tahoe. Dropping off Interstate 580, a smaller road winds us through the national park, our drive taking us along the eastern shore of the lake. But the sugar pines are too thick to spot any water through the trees, the white firs towering above us and on either side of us, the snow-capped mountains of Diamond Peak straight ahead. It's only as we're passing through Sand Harbor and coming around the curve of Crystal Bay that Sabine seems to come alive.

It's the sight of the lake that wakes her up—me too. The shimmering magnificent blue water with its indigo waves lapping against the docks. Miles and miles of lake stretches beyond and across the

Nevada state line to the opposite shoreline where commuters cross to California. We spot sailboats cruising with sails at full mast. Powerboats and jet skis with vacationers revving their engines. A row of college-aged lifeguards on the beach, just like Sasha said. Rosy-cheeked children splashing in the water.

Sabine's smile spreads to her cheeks. "I've never seen a place more beautiful."

And her mom turns from the front seat. "Totally worth the drive, don't you think?"

*

The rental house we're staying in is in the King's Beach area of Lake Tahoe, a chalet retreat with mustard-painted walls and an alpine roof. The home is quaint with its red door and brown shuttered windows, and in the back, a patio and pitch of grass that extends to our own private beach. But the best part? The spectacular view of Lake Tahoe. Navy water stretches before us. The rise of the Sierra Nevada and Carson mountain ranges dramatically rise into the sky on either side. Our own boat dock.

The four of us race from the car to stand and gape, mouths open, not wanting to unload our bags just yet and allowing the sun to shine against our faces instead, enjoying the break from ninety-degree temperatures in Louisiana and the cooler weather of the west coast.

I stretch my arms overhead. My God, it feels good to be stepping out of that van. It feels fantastic to be a part of this bright sun-filled day with puffy white clouds soaring above us.

Sabine runs for the lake and the wind whips at her hair, blowing it back from her face with a sudden gust that barrels off the water. She lets out a laugh I'm relieved to hear. It's good to see her smiling and moving around again. Whatever ailed her the last few days on the road is made better now that she's taking in fresh air.

I run to catch up, then kick off my shoes and dip my feet at the edge of the water—it's freezing—and I shriek, causing Sabine to laugh. She slips off her shoes and steps into the water too. Another shriek.

"That's mountain water for you," Mr. Taylor calls.

I catch a sight of him wrapping his arms around his wife. He's holding Sabine's mother close, the two of them swaying together and watching us fling water between our toes. A few minutes later, Mrs. Taylor announces we'll be enjoying our first night's dinner outside on the patio.

*

Sabine finds the bracelets at a gift shop the following day. Matching bracelets made from sterling silver with charms dangling in the shape of Lake Tahoe, the charms set in a blue-fire opal inlay.

"Let's get them," she says.

"They're beautiful." I clutch the bracelet to my wrist.

She fastens one around hers too. "This way, we'll remember our trip forever."

We're having such a wonderful time. A morning bicycle ride to the King's Beach rec area, a long walk along the beach, lollipops in our back pockets from the corner drug store followed by discovering this little shop tucked behind an ice cream parlor.

I rub the charm between my fingers.

She cracks a beaming smile, taking in the view through the window. "Don't you love this place? Don't you want to come back one day?"

We've been here less than twenty-four hours and I know I already love it as much as she does.

"Maybe when we're older," Sabine says. "A college road trip. Or we'll bring our kids back." Her eyes light up. "Wouldn't that be fun?"

I laugh. "Kids? You're thinking that far ahead?"

"Absolutely. We're best friends forever, aren't we? So of course we'll bring our kids. We'll pack them in the car like my mom and dad did." Excitedly, she sucks in her breath. "We can stay at the same house! The exact same chalet. Wouldn't that be amazing?"

I *do* love this idea. And I smile, thoughts of our forever friendship and future children that we'll lead on bicycle rides around Lake Tahoe.

At the front of the store, Sabine whips out cash to pay for our bracelets while blocking my hand from reaching for any money. "My treat," she tells me. "I've got this." Glancing to her right, she spots a rack filled with Lake Tahoe postcards and pulls one out featuring picturesque King's Beach. "Let's send the girls one."

I eye the postcard. "But we'll get home before it makes it through the mail."

"It would still be fun. Let them know we're thinking about them."

Laying the postcard flat on the counter, she borrows a pen from the shopkeeper and scribbles a note:

Missing you. See you when we get home!
Love, S and E

She signs our initials in giant looped letters.

Adding Heidi's address, she says Sasha can share the card and buys a stamp and drops the postcard in the shopkeeper's mailbox. We step toward the ice cream shop, Sabine reaching for my hand and swinging it as we admire our bracelets, the blue opal charms sparkling in the sun. "Lake Tahoe forever," she tells me.

CHAPTER 25

It's one of those trips I don't want to end. But it does, and as Mr. Taylor puts it, "That's the thing about good times. They come to an end. But that way, we can look forward to more great times."

Mrs. Taylor grins before turning to check on Sabine. "You feeling okay?"

She's doing much better on the return ride home, not as carsick as she once was, even though we sleep away the hours to help pass the time.

At one of the rest stops, her mom orders a coffee and is chatting with home only a few hours away. She's snapping back to business, thinking about school and asking Sabine about college. "We should work on your college applications soon, all right? When we get home, over the next few weeks, start putting those essays together. It's so important you get into Samford."

Samford University—Sabine's parents' dream she follow in their footsteps and attend the private Christian school in Alabama, their alma mater where they worked hard and earned scholarships to attend. Sabine will have to do the same for the Taylors to afford her tuition.

"I know, Mom," Sabine says. "It's at the top of my list."

She gives her a worried smile. "Don't let Homecoming distract you. I know it's coming up."

"It will be fine, Mom. I've got this."

But Sabine doesn't *have this.*

Something changes within days of us returning. She's quiet. A paleness to her cheeks, and I worry she might be sick again. Whatever ailed her on the road trip is coming back.

But it's not that. She says there's something on her mind she doesn't want to talk about. She even turns down a day of shopping for Homecoming dresses.

Blowing me off, she says she's busy. She claims she doesn't have time for Zach either. When pressed, she tells us she's worried. The scholarship process for Samford is more difficult than she anticipated and she's terrified she won't be able to pull it off. Her parents' disappointment will be excruciating.

But there's something else—I know it. I know Sabine like I know my own mind. A college application for a girl as bright and accomplished and studious as her would not have her acting this way. She's withdrawing. She's keeping a secret.

My best friend I've known for years—the determination during exam week, the laughter and pure happiness from our time spent in Lake Tahoe—is gone. A switch turned off in a matter of days.

"Tell me," I beg. We're sitting on her bedroom floor. She's asked me not to come over, that she doesn't want to talk, she's busy, but I came over anyway. Sitting beside her, I ask, "What's happening? Tell me. I can help. But I need to know how."

She looks away and it cuts right through my heart, a frustration also welling inside my belly. She's tired of me badgering her. She wants me to stop. I'm not going to get an answer so I'll leave still not knowing what's wrong and—

"I'm pregnant."

At first, I don't think I've heard her correctly. She repeats the words again, "I'm pregnant," and squeezes her eyes shut. "I know what I have to do."

The breath goes out of me, my ribcage deflating as I stare at my best friend.

"There's a clinic in Mississippi. I'll take care of everything." She says these statements so resolutely, so robotically. My brain hasn't even caught up yet. *A baby?*

And I realize what she's saying. My heart seizes. "Wait? You can't... slow down... Let's figure this out." My thoughts are scrambling too much inside my brain as I take this all in, desperately trying to keep up and wanting to understand. But Sabine's plan is already cranking into place. She's had time to think about this, but I haven't.

Sabine. And Zach. *Pregnant.*

I flash back to last week. The car ride where she slept so much. Not wanting to eat and pushing away her food.

We thought she had a small bug or was carsick. At the lake, she seemed so much better.

My eyes search hers. She pulled herself together for our sakes. But now...

"Sabine..." I whisper.

She blinks back the tears. "Mom and Dad *can't* know. They would never forgive me. What I'm going to do is..." Her eyes stretch wide with panic. "It's against everything they believe in. The church. An absolute abomination. They'll never forgive me." She searches my eyes desperately. "Zach can't know either."

"Oh my God. But we need their help. Your parents, they'll understand."

"*No!*" And she leaps to her feet. "None of them can know—only you. You're the only one." Her tears can't hold back any longer and they fall heavily down her face. "I have to do this. Get this done and move on. Finish my essays. Get into Samford. Make my parents proud. It's the only thing." She's panicking, convincing herself while also forcing herself into action mode even when every part of her is stunned.

"But Sabine—"

She won't listen to me. "I need your help. Please, Erica. You'll drive me. The appointment is in two days. I'll need to stay with you after so we'll tell my parents we're busy. We're working on college essays together. They'll never know."

My head is spinning. All of this—it's too much—too fast. An appointment in two days? A baby. Something *this* catastrophic and important.

And I'm driving her. I'll need to care for her.

I turn my eyes to Sabine. Of course I will. "Yes, I'll help you."

She collapses to her knees, the tears pouring more freely, her face twisting with pain until it breaks my heart in two. The anguish that's cracking open. Pressing her head against my chest, her body trembles, the full sobs wracking her body until she wails, "I'm so sorry. I didn't mean… I didn't know. Please forgive me…"

And I'm not sure who she's asking an apology from: me or her parents or Zach, because with me, she doesn't need to apologize. I'll be here to support her no matter what. But then I know. The baby. Her heart is breaking and she will never be the same again. She's pleading for forgiveness from the baby she will never meet.

*

When Sabine limps toward the car I know something is wrong. She leans her body against mine, her feet shuffling, body bent at the waist, and I'm gripping the discharge papers from the clinic, guiding her across the parking lot. She winces, followed by a cry as she lowers herself into the front passenger seat.

The front of the building sent goosebumps across my body when we first arrived. The dingy waiting room and interminable wait after they led Sabine behind closed doors. And now this, Sabine hurting, and far more than I thought would happen after a procedure like this. Something's not right.

"Sabine…" I say, nerves flying through my belly. "This isn't good… Are you okay? Tell me what to do."

She rests her head against the headrest and grimaces, her upper lip curling with pain. "Take me to your house," she whispers.

As we drive, my heart is hammering a sickening thousand miles a minute. I keep darting my eyes to her face, the tightening of her jaw every time we hit a bump, the bracing of her arm against her stomach as she bites her lip and whimpers with every turn, even though I'm driving as carefully as I can. But inside, I'm freaking out—racing at break-neck speed and wishing we could be home, get this day over with. Her head lolls to one side.

"Sabine." I reach out my hand to check her. Her skin is clammy. "We should find another doctor. Something's wrong." The fear edges up the back of my throat.

She rattles the bag clutched in her hand, holding onto the prescription bottles they've given her like a lifeline. "I have meds. This is normal..." But her voice is hoarse.

"This is *not* normal!" I cry.

At the off-ramp, I veer into a merging lane and someone stops ahead of me suddenly—a red light—and I have no choice but to slam on the brakes. Sabine lets out a howl and my heart explodes inside my chest.

"I'm so sorry! Sabine!" And she's crying, scrunching her body against the seat, her face drenched in sweat.

I can't do this—I can't do this on my own. Sabine needs help. She's in trouble. Something's gone terribly wrong and they screwed up the procedure. I can't hide her in my bedroom while my parents are out of town. We need adults. We need—

I drive her straight to her parents' house.

"What are you doing?" She lifts her head but is too weak to protest.

"Sabine, I'm so..." I don't finish what I'm saying because I pull into the Taylors' drive and run for her parents' door.

Pulling on their arms, I don't tell them much, only that they must come quick. *Come now.* Sabine is in my car and she needs help.

The Taylors clutch their daughter. Her dad carefully scoops her out of the front seat and carries her into the house while, hysterical,

Mrs. Taylor tosses pillows from the couch and clears a space for Sabine to lie down. Mrs. Taylor's eyes are wide as saucers, the panic ripping through her face as Sabine's dad asks repeatedly, "Are you all right? What happened?" Their eyes are on me, a pointed look in my direction. "What's happened to our daughter?"

*

Sabine misses school for two weeks. She doesn't go to Homecoming and doesn't answer my calls. She also breaks up with Zach, but I'm sure it's because her parents convince her to never see him again.

The Taylors keep her home while she recovers. They enlist a family friend, a retired doctor, who ensures Sabine's infection will subside and her fever will dissipate as long as she keeps taking her antibiotics. I only know this because after repeated attempts of knocking on the Taylors' front door, her mom finally lets me in. She says Sabine is recovering but that I'm not allowed to see her.

"But Mrs. Taylor. It's me. Please—"

"I love you girls," she says. "I love you so much." She turns away, barely able to meet my eyes. "But what you've done… what Sabine has done. It goes against everything we stand for. This family. Our religious beliefs. I'm sorry she had to bring you into all this."

I'm sobbing. "She didn't think she had a choice. She was terrified. I was only trying to help—"

"You should have never taken her."

I stop short, my breath stuck in my throat. My voice wobbles. "I'm so sorry!" I whisper again, and I want to rush to her, hug her, feel her wrap her arms around me too. This woman I've known for years, almost a second mother. Our happy times together during our trip.

But Sabine's mom wants nothing more to do with me.

She bristles. "She could have been seriously hurt. That place…" Her eyes fill with tears. "She was seriously injured."

I tear my eyes toward the stairs. "Please let me see her."

But she's nudging me out the door. Swallowing a sob, she says, "I think it's best if the two of you stay away from each other."

Stunned, I step back from the porch. "Mrs. Taylor?"

"We need Sabine to get back on her feet. Recover from this ordeal. She has college applications to focus on."

"But Mrs. Taylor—"

"I'm praying for you, Erica. I love you so much…" She reaches out an arm and shuts the door.

CHAPTER 26

I don't know what to do. I'm a shell of a person without Sabine. I stay at home and wait endlessly to hear from her, but nothing. I'm chewing my nails, a horrible habit, and sitting in a corner with nothing else to do but wait.

My parents work so much and are hardly home, and even when they are, I don't bother them with what's happening. I try to hide it as best I can. Granddad notices, though. He stops by and helps me with laundry. The two of us stand at the sink and rinse dishes that have piled up on the counter. He asks me why I'm being so quiet, why he hasn't seen Sabine come around for a while, but I don't say a word. My family would be horrified by what we've done too.

At school, it's only worse. Heidi and Sasha ask me what's going on and I don't know what to say. I keep lying to them, and to everyone, and the girls badger me daily asking if I've heard from Sabine. After their own phone calls to the Taylors go unanswered, the girls visit their home.

"She has the flu," Heidi says at lunch. "Her mom wouldn't let us upstairs but that's the deal."

I raise my eyes, wondering if they really believe that.

Sasha adds, "Poor Sabine. I heard the flu is pretty bad this year."

They believe them.

I want to throw up where I sit, my hands shaking. Clamping my fingers beneath the table, I will myself to be calm, hoping they don't see the torn ends of my nails. Heidi asks me repeatedly why

I haven't tried to visit and of course I tell her I've tried. I leave out the part about the door slamming in my face.

Zach, Sabine's boyfriend until a couple of weeks ago, is beside himself with worry too. He still sits with his friends at lunch but his head droops. He's barely eating. Occasionally, he lets his eyes drift across the cafeteria and I quickly turn away. Other times, I stand up and dump my food in the trash.

One day after school, Zach runs toward my car and holds his arm against the door not letting me get in and drive off. I've been avoiding him for days and he's sick of it, but I know he's worried sick about Sabine. The green of his eyes flashes. A tuft of brown hair he rakes across his head.

"What's going on?" he asks. "She won't see me. She canceled Homecoming." His brows squeeze tight. "She said we're breaking up and I don't understand. *Why?* What did I do? What's happening?"

I push my backpack beneath his arm and hurl it across the seat. "I don't know, Zach. She won't talk—"

"Bullshit!" His face is inches from mine but it's not threatening. At any second, he's about to cry. And my heart hurts, it really does. Not seeing Sabine. Lying to everyone. Watching Zach be in so much pain.

Sabine, I was only trying to help.

It's what you asked. I was so scared you were hurt...

"She talks to you about everything," Zach says. "You know every little thing when it comes to her. *What's going on?*"

I can't tell him—I mustn't. And I want to push past him, close the door and crank the engine, shutting him out. But he won't let me. His arm blocks my path.

"Erica! Please. She says she doesn't want to be with me anymore but I don't believe her. Her parents told me she has the flu but that's made up too. You know something, I know you do. You have to tell me."

But my words sound hollow. "I can't, I'm sorry."

He tightens his grip against the door frame, his eyes narrowing. "She doesn't have the flu, does she?"

I fumble with my keys and look away.

"She said something to me a few weeks ago. Something I couldn't figure out. It came out of left field." His eyes soften. They turn heavy. "She asked about kids. I told her I didn't want any, not yet at least. I mean, we're only in high school. I've got my football scholarship and years of ball ahead of me. And she looked so sad. So heartbroken. It didn't make any sense. A few days later she said she felt sick." His eyes stare into mine, the seconds excruciating. And a shocked realization hits his brain, his face tilting up, pained with the question: "Was she pregnant?"

I don't make a sound but my face gives it away. Zach knows me too well. My silence is the only answer he needs.

"Oh my God." He stumbles back, his arm dropping limply from my car. "That's what it is, isn't it? That's what happened..."

My heart squeezes—*Fix this, Erica!* Convince him otherwise. *Do something!* But Zach is sprinting across the parking lot and jumping into his truck.

*

Sabine calls me from her parents' house phone—I can't believe it, she's actually called me back—but my stomach twists. I know why. I've been pacing my bedroom floor, a sickening dread, knowing Zach has gone straight to her place.

But Sabine tells me her parents didn't let him in. They barred him at the door like they've done with everyone else.

But Zach found a way upstairs anyhow. He sprinted past Mrs. Taylor and ignored everything she said. And now Sabine has asked him to leave and her voice is screaming at me through the phone.

"You told my parents! And you told Zach! *How could you?* How could you do this? What were you thinking?" She's talking so much and so fast, I don't have a chance to say anything in return. I only want to pound the floor with my fists and beg for her to listen. Beg for her to understand where I'm coming from.

I was trying to save you.

If you'd stayed with me, you could have gotten worse. You could have died.

I didn't tell Zach. He figured it out on his own.

She's crying so hard she's hiccupping. "I trusted you. I asked you to help. You knew how much I didn't want to do this but I had to and no one was supposed to know. Only you." Another sob. "Only you, Erica."

"Please listen—"

"No!" she says. "Don't! My parents—*they're devastated.* Do you know what this is like for them? How they've always wanted the world for me. All their prayers. My first Communion. They thought I was perfect, and now this. They can barely look in my direction. Can barely sit in the same room. And now they're talking about sending me away."

What?

"Boarding school. In a few months. They're sending me away to some boarding school!" she wails. "And it's because of you! Everything's ruined. How can I get into college now? A transfer in the middle of the year looks bad. But my parents think it's the only way for me to focus, to not get in trouble again. Because of—"

"You can't leave."

"I don't have a choice!"

"I'll help you. We'll work on those applications. We'll get you into Samford."

"Don't you understand?" Sabine cries. "My parents don't want me to have anything to do with you anymore!"

*

When Sabine returns to school, she doesn't want to sit together at lunch. She places her backpack in my chair and turns her head.

For whatever reason, Sasha and Heidi come up with an outrageous idea I have a thing for Zach and that's why we're no longer friends. Sabine doesn't deny it, she's too wrapped up in her own grief to respond, and the girls stay by her side, leaving me alone. An anger and a hurt that cuts deep inside.

A month later, she's sent to the boarding school she warned me about. No goodbyes. No hugs but a letter she places in my mailbox.

My heart is broken. I know yours is too. But you broke my trust and I'm not sure if I can forgive you. After what happened, I'm not sure if I can forgive myself.

Throw away that bracelet. It's meaningless now. Lake Tahoe is one of the last times I remember being happy, my parents too. But no one has joy anymore.

Take care of yourself, Erica.

She signs the letter, *S*.

And at the bottom of the page, a blemish where something has dried. A spot on the paper the size of a teardrop. Evidence I know Sabine cried, that she still cares.

Four months later comes the devastating news her parents have died in a car accident and my heart shatters into a million pieces—a horrific nightmare to process since they'd been driving to visit Sabine at her school. In my agony, I picture Mrs. Taylor with her thermos of coffee and Mr. Taylor wearing his *Drive or Bust* T-shirt. How they only wanted the best for Sabine. How they didn't understand the agonizing choice she'd made in the end.

And my soul tears open, the pain I know my friend must be going through, how I want to run to her and help. But she barely speaks to me at the funeral, which is agony in itself as I'm grieving for the Taylors as if I've lost a member of my own family, something that would kill me inside. At the service, my parents and Granddad sit beside me. My mom, tired and overworked, reaches for my hand. She cries into a handkerchief my granddad gives her and prays quietly for Sabine's parents. I lean my head against her shoulder and close my eyes.

I'm hurting for my friend, who I know is going through so much. And by the end of summer when we leave for separate colleges, I'm starting to come to terms with the fact we may never speak again.

I try reaching out to her once by phone, and then stop. I'm hurting too—the way she's cut me off, how she ended our friendship. And years later when I move to Green Cove, I can't believe it when I see her. What are the chances of us living in the same town? I mean *seriously*. The same neighborhood? But utterly worlds apart. We're hardly recognizable to one another.

But seeing her reminds me of what happened. The abrupt ending. Her anger raged at me when I was only trying to help. Her going away without even a proper goodbye.

Sometimes when I see her out and about—Sabine along the walking trail or leaving the kids' school—I bite my tongue. I squeeze my wrist where my bracelet used to be, the one she told me to put away, and the memories light like a torch, tearing me up inside, an anger and a hole that's been left in my life. And I struggle daily with what I'm going to do about it.

PART THREE: PRESENT

CHAPTER 27

Monday afternoon

Tish asks, "Why didn't you tell me?"

She's staring at the photo, at Sabine having lunch, holding a soda can and smiling for the camera with her hair down, gold earrings dangling above the collar of her school uniform. Three other girls sit alongside her lifting their soda cans to make a toast too, including me.

Tish takes the yearbook from my hands and flips through the pages. Another photo captures Sabine once again in the cafeteria but things are different now. The light and laughter in her eyes have vanished, her cheeks sunken, the forced closed-lip smile for the photographer as Zach and I are the only ones who know what she's going through.

I'm no longer sitting with Sabine. Only Sasha and Heidi remain at the table posing with big smiles, oblivious to the fact our friend is going through so much pain—and it's not their fault; they didn't know. All they're aware of is I've been relegated outside the group.

For Sabine's change in appearance and mood, the girls must have assumed she was worried about exams. Her breakup with Zach. Completing her college application essays in time. The pressure of earning that scholarship. On other days, she must have faked it with enough of a smile to assure them she was all right.

But this snapshot has caught it. Without realizing it, this photo documented what happened to Sabine in her senior year—what happened *to us*. The searing divide.

Tish says, "You guys didn't just go to school together, you were *really good friends*. But why..." She looks at me strangely. "I don't get it. Why didn't you say something before?"

I shut the yearbook. It's hard for me to look at the pictures right now, memories of Sabine rushing back full force. The years that have gone by since then.

"It was a long time ago. We went our separate ways. We had a fight. It was rough but those things happen."

"But years later you end up in the same neighborhood and you don't even acknowledge each other? I've seen you walk right past her. We'll be at the grocery store and she'll move right past us too. You don't act like you're upset, or she's upset, or there's anything wrong. You act like strangers. Except for..." And her eyes widen. "What happened that night at the event. The school auction. That's the only time..." Her eyes search mine. "Is *that* what went down? A fight from high school and neither of you are over it and *that's* why you got in each other's faces?"

I don't answer.

"The way you screamed at each other," Tish remembers. "It was so out of left field. I didn't understand before... but now..."

I look away and lean forward, pressing my fingers to the bridge of my nose and pushing tight. A headache looms, my heart pounding with the memory.

That charity event. The neighborhood clubhouse decorated with flickering golden lights and a jazz band that played in the corner. A fundraiser for the school where Tish talked excitedly about the silent auction. "They always have those fantastic gift baskets," Tish said. "Maybe we can find something for the kids' birthdays."

And she was right. The auction paired gift certificates for roller-skating parties and ice-cream cake. A party pack for kids' bounce houses that also included pizza. Entire birthday packages ready to go with convenience and fun tucked inside cellophane-wrapped gift baskets. You just needed to be the winning bid to bring the prize home.

And with Taylor's birthday in less than two weeks, winning one of these would be a special treat. It would also ease my wallet.

The night should have been simple. It shouldn't have gone the way it did.

Within minutes, I'd found the perfect party package: a children's paint class complete with cupcakes where children could paint their own canvases. As a budding first-grade artist, Taylor would be over the moon.

Adding my name to the bid sheet, I marked my first entry at $60.

Tish called me over for another glass of wine, telling me about a petting zoo party for Charlie that she was almost positive she would win, joking that no one else seemed interested in the animals and wanted laser tag parties instead. I hoped the same for the painting class.

But when I returned to the table, someone had outbid me at $100. They didn't bother with the suggested increment of ten dollars but shot straight to a higher bid. This was a school fundraiser, but still. Who would do that?

I stared hard at the name written on the page in cursive, looped letters: *Sabine Miller.*

Why on earth would she be needing a child's painting party?

I glanced around and found her standing near the event organizer, laughing and sipping champagne. But when she burst out with raucous giggles a second later, it sounded odd. Reckless. Loud. She was half-drunk and didn't seem to notice I was staring at her.

Picking up the pen, I increased my entry by another twenty bucks.

Amanda swooped by, asking me to check out a pair of earrings on the other side of the room. If she didn't win, she had bid sheets marked for a spa day and shopping spree too. We reviewed the number of boutiques together, each shop boasting their latest fashions, when the bell rang marking the last five minutes of the auction.

A scurry of activity ensued as people checked on their bids. Some were laughing and poking fun at one another, increasing their amounts and telling their neighbors to back off—friendly competition.

But I was livid. In the time I'd stood with Amanda, it appeared Sabine had walked back to the table and entered $300, more than twice the original value of the painting party.

Tossing back the rest of my wine, I glared at the numbers. It shouldn't have bothered me. I know I shouldn't have let her get under my skin... but she did.

I was picking up the pen when the sound of her voice came up behind me—a voice that hadn't been issued in my direction in years. "I really want to win that," she said, her voice slurred. Husky. An intense orange scent wafting from her expensive Dior perfume.

I halted—it was the first time we'd spoken since high school. And now here she was outbidding me for a kid's birthday package.

"I said, I really want to win that," she repeated.

I wrapped my fingers around the pen. How much could I put down? This was mad—it would be cheaper for me to book the party on my own, but then the money wouldn't be a fundraiser for the school. *But $300?* How would I top that? Something told me Sabine would be marking over my next bid anyway. No restrictions to her unlimited credit card.

After I found out she moved here, her address on Honors Row gave away her newfound life of luxury. It's a far cry from how we grew up and now she could do whatever she wanted, including bidding on auction items as high as she fancied.

I dropped the pen and faced her. Hazel eyes. Blonde hair pulled into an elegant twist. For the first time in years our eyes connected.

But my anger subsided. Seeing her. Being this close.

A memory hit me of the two of us side by side at the lake. Her hair whipping loose while I spun around in the sunshine and laughed. A time when we'd been so carefree carrying lollipops in our back pockets. The gift of matching bracelets.

How had we let that year come between us?

My face must have crumbled, my mouth softening to a tremble, because she flinched. Something registered in her eyes too—the emotion of seeing me again, the pair of us standing together after all this time. But she blinked, another sip of her champagne, then one more, until her glass was empty. Something hardened in her eyes. The moment, disappearing.

"I want that gift basket," she said coolly.

"What for?" It was the first thing I'd said to her in twenty-five years, the first words to come out of my mouth and it was the wrong question to ask apparently because she snapped.

"*What for?* What, just because I don't have children, I wouldn't want to buy something? I wouldn't want to gift that to somebody? Carol's daughter perhaps?"

Stunned, my shoulders rolled back.

Heads turned as I spotted guests at nearby tables sneaking glances in our direction. The curious stares as to why Sabine Miller would be raising her voice at me over an auction item, for goodness' sake, and me standing guard in front of a child's gift basket as if it was a stack of gold bars. Heat rose to my cheeks. Embarrassment and anger that Sabine would be talking to me this way.

One table over, Tish and Amanda threw confused looks, ready to step in if needed.

"I want this for Taylor's birthday," I said defiantly.

Sabine's eyes glowered. "Then put down another bid."

"Why? You're just going to put a higher number on top."

A strange little smile. "That's how it works."

"Why are you being like this?"

Her eyes swirled. She wobbled in her step. "It must be so nice planning your daughter's little birthday party," she said. "So wonderful to be able to do that for your child."

"What are you talking about, Sabine?"

And then I saw the look in her eyes—the flash of pain. How this was about much more than winning an auction for Sabine. It was a child's gift and Sabine didn't have any children. Seeing me wanting this for my daughter must have reminded her of what she'd missed.

But I thought they chose not to have kids so Mark could focus on his career? So that Sabine could support him every step of the way. That's what I'd heard.

The bell rang for a second time. "Less than one minute," someone called.

My eyes veered back to her face. "It doesn't have to be like this."

"Like what?"

"Like this."

She scoffed. "You have no idea what I've been going through—all of it. Not a damn clue. Now, get out of my way so I can win this thing." A startled gasp from someone as several more heads turned our way.

Monica appeared, of course she did. The two of them rarely not seen together. She gently pulled on Sabine's arm while simultaneously throwing me a strange look—not so much an apology for her friend but something more akin to shock. This was so unlike Sabine and everyone knew it. As far as Monica knew, the two of us didn't have any history. We weren't friends. But she could tell Sabine was drunk—by now everyone noticed. She needed to drag Sabine away before a bigger scene turned this party upside down.

But I couldn't help it; I'd had too much to drink too. Hurt and anger rose through my stomach.

"Nothing in your life is perfect, is it?" I shouted. "You're struggling just like me. I see that now."

Sabine wrenched free from Monica's grasp and closed the gap between us. Inches from my face, her perfume was suffocating. "You don't know me. You don't know anything!" And then she stopped, ready to cry. "If only you knew..." But Monica yanked on her arm and escorted her away.

The bell rang a final time. "Auction is over!"

And I looked down at the bid sheet. Sabine had won.

*

Sitting with Tish now, I let the yearbook slide to the floor, telling her, "We can't handle being around each other at a school fundraiser so it's better if we go back to ignoring each other, don't you think?"

"Neither of you have wanted to try?"

"Clearly she's still upset and so am I. We're different people now. We have nothing in common. She's got her own circle of fancy friends. An important husband. A lifestyle I'll never match."

"But you have *history*."

"Yes, but I guess sometimes that's not enough."

Tish rests back on her hands, thinking. "Wow. That must have been some fight in high school for both of you to still react that way. What happened?"

I look at her warily.

She sees the apprehension on my face. "Erica, tell me. You can trust me."

And I muse over the word *trust*. The 800-pound gorilla sitting on my chest. But Tish and I aren't teenagers.

I tell her about high school. Starting off slowly, I speed up, glossing over some of the Lake Tahoe details because it's just too painful. I describe those final months and a horrible argument that came between us. How much it hurt when I found out her parents had died and we didn't speak at the funeral.

But I don't tell her about the clinic or the reaction from her parents. I will never betray Sabine about that again.

"And you had no idea she'd moved to Huntsville? The two of you had no clue you were in the same neighborhood?"

"I moved for a job, you know that. Same as you. It wasn't until the divorce when I bought this house that I ran into her for the first time."

"That must have been intense."

I take a breath. "It was like time stopped. Literally, physically stopped. She was standing in the produce aisle of the grocery store—can you imagine? The grocery store of all places. And I came around the corner and froze. She froze. We were both shocked and turned away."

"And that was it? Neither of you tried making contact?"

"What for?" I splutter. "The odds were so insane. I never imagined we'd end up living in the same town. We both left college and I lost track of her after that."

"But didn't one of you want to reach out to the other?" Tish asks. "Weren't you even tempted?"

"*No.*" And I say this so firmly that Tish jumps. "We were done."

Tish shakes her head. "I keep thinking about that look she gave you at the pool, and then you finding one of her bracelets. I said before it seemed like maybe she was sending you a message. She was reaching out to you—someone she used to be really close with. Something bad was happening in her life and she saw you. Maybe she thought you'd understand." Tish's voice is gentle. "Do you want to tell the police now?"

My body stiffens. "You also said before I should stay out of their mess." I flick my eyes to her. "Aren't we involved enough as it is?"

Tish winces and I instantly regret what I said.

"It's just a bracelet," I say, softening the edge to my voice and I touch her arm. "Anyone could have found it. She didn't leave it for me at the pool."

"You don't think she was asking for help?"

I draw up my legs and wrap my hands around my knees, feeling a looming dread inside my bones. "Of all people, I don't think she'd pick me to help."

CHAPTER 28

It's approaching 3:30 in the afternoon when I hear Amanda saying, "Don't be mad," which is never how I want to hear someone begin their sentence, "but I talked to someone at work about your missing passport. Sabine's address is too similar."

I grip the phone, squeezing my eyes shut. "Amanda…" I warn.

"If Sabine got your passport in the mail, she could have used it."

"But we—"

"You look enough alike. Blonde hair. She could say she got recent highlights. Her hazel eyes can look brown like yours depending on what she's wearing." Amanda pauses. "She could have done this. She could have—"

I'm still waiting on the bombshell. "Amanda, what's happening? Who else did you tell?"

"They pushed it up the chain."

"*The chain?*"

"I didn't think they would."

"But you said you were going to ask a friend. That you didn't want this to get out if it turns out to be nothing."

"Turns out it might not be nothing. And it also turns out who my friend told is super tight with Monica's husband. They shared this information with the cops. I think it's their way of getting Monica off the hook."

I slap my hand to my head. "They can say, yes, she wrote the letter, but she didn't do anything to hurt Sabine? This can support their theory of Sabine leaving on her own?"

"Exactly."

"Amanda—"

"Look, I'm sorry. I didn't want to get you involved but what if it's true? What if there's something to this?"

I rub at my temples. "So what happens now?"

"Well, for starters, don't travel anywhere. The cops are searching for flights where she could have used your name. Anywhere that Erica Holloway has booked a ticket or shown up on a plane manifest."

"Anything yet?"

"They're still searching. But if this is happening—if this is really what she's done—who's to say she's not waiting before she travels?"

"But then she'll get caught. They'll flag my name and they'll find her."

"True," Amanda says, and pauses. "Or she left Saturday night before all hell broke loose."

*

Tish is still reeling from the discovery that Sabine and I were friends in high school and now I'm telling her our passport theory has moved from Amanda's lips to someone who has notified the police.

"Why would Amanda do that?" she asks.

We've moved out of the closet—the yearbook and bracelets I insisted be stored in the box and shoved on the shelf—and back in the living room where I've finished Amanda's phone call.

"She's just trying to be helpful," I tell her.

"But now Monica will grasp onto this. She'll want the cops to think this too."

"She's already got the cops thinking this."

"But now they know about your passport."

"Yes, they do."

"This is ludicrous," Tish says. "Where do they think she would go? Where would she hide? *Why?*"

"I have no idea."

"She wouldn't be trying to get away from Mark. This is Monica's doing, I know it is," she says. "She's jealous of Mark and Sabine. This is all part of her set-up and now she's going to use your passport mishap to throw everyone off her."

A pounding at the door.

Tish sits straight up, and so do I.

My first thought: the police.

Tish's first thought: the reporters found me.

She whirls off the couch and retreats to the kitchen. "Tell them, *no comment*."

But it's not a news crew because a voice on the other side of the door says, "Erica Holloway? Detective Matthews with Huntsville PD." Another loud bang. "Open up, please."

My stomach squeezes. A panicked tremor along my jaw until my teeth ache and my mouth runs dry.

"Answer it," Tish encourages me.

The man on my porch introduces himself as Detective Matthews. He's short, less than five foot eight, and wearing khaki pants and a button-down shirt. He's not smiling as I imagine his search for Sabine Miller has been twisting and turning with every hour with still no sign of her.

The detective looks over my shoulder at Tish. "Hello again, Ms. Abbott."

She croaks a *hello* in response.

He slides his eyes back to me. "Can I come in? I have a few questions."

I lead him to the dining-room table, thinking this is a more formal setting for having a police detective in my home. I certainly don't want him sitting on the couch where there are bound to be crumbs or colored ink from one of the kids—the same place where Tish and I fell asleep two nights ago, the cushions crumpled with one of them still tossed on the floor.

The detective's eyes are steel-gray in color, his nose sharp and bent like a hawk's beak with thinning hair combed across his scalp. Another study of his face and I spot dark rings below his eyes, shades of black and plum radiating below slowly blinking eyelashes. He looks like someone who hasn't slept for days.

Removing a notepad from his pocket, he asks, "Ms. Holloway, what is this about your missing passport? Can you explain it to me?" His last question is followed with a sigh.

But the way he asks—so bored and so without urgency—strikes something cold inside.

He unfolds the notepad but there's no pen in sight. The lack of keen discovery in his face, the fact, now that I come to think of it, he has arrived here with no partner—certainly there must be a team of police officers working this case—but he's arrived here on his own. His eyes, dead and lifeless. He's not just tired; he doesn't care about my passport. He doesn't think this is a worthy lead. He's only here as a formality. And I realize, Monica and her husband may have friends in high places, they want people to believe this latest information involving my passport, but Mark Miller has trumped her. He has friends in even higher circles, and they'll want to protect any notion Mark Miller's wife would ever leave him. The idea of that is preposterous especially when the couple renewed their wedding vows earlier this year. Mark's team is working every day to protect the couple's reputation, including this detective. Someone has taken Sabine Miller and any other theory is a distraction.

Amanda was so right about having the wool pulled away from her eyes. These city officials of ours really are something else.

Sending this one detective could merely be checking the box for the police department on behalf of Mark Miller and his camp. Questioning me will confirm that my passport has never shown up, but it doesn't prove Sabine has it or intended to use it to leave

Mark. She didn't fake her own disappearance or create some sort of elaborate ruse.

I answer a total of five questions before Detective Matthews excuses himself and says he has everything he needs. Just as I thought, he doesn't write down any of my answers.

But what comes next makes me jump from my seat. With the detective gone, someone else is banging steadily on my door—their ferocious knocking followed by an urgent cry.

CHAPTER 29

Monica and Carol don't wait for me to turn the doorknob before they're barreling inside my home. I step back, the women pushing past me to the living room.

Monica says, "He was here less than ten minutes." Her voice is shrill, her hands shaking. "They don't want to think it's true."

She moves closer to the couch, Carol following, the two of them panting as if they've run a half-marathon to be here despite Monica's monstrous black Escalade I see parked in the driveway. I slam my front door.

Monica's eyes are wild, pupils dilated as she blinks repeatedly. Her dark hair falls on either side of her face; she hasn't bothered to pin it up. Long gone is the signature green visor I'm used to seeing her wearing, Carol too, their coordinated ponytails and meticulous looks. But with everything that's happening—their world flipped upside down—the glamor is over for now.

Without a stitch of makeup, Carol's face is stark against her bright red hair. Thin blue veins ripple at her temples. But not those green eyes—eyes that are fierce and leveling me with a gaze that says she wants to get to the bottom of this. Monica too.

But get to the bottom *of what*?

These women have never been to my house before, and honestly, I didn't think they knew where I lived. I've never had a reason for them to visit, not that I've visited their homes on Honors Row either. But here they stand, the great Monica Claiborne and Carol Troy, looking very much like women who no longer have their acts together—or their lives together, for that matter. In the few seconds they're before me, they look seconds away from coming unhinged.

Tish joins me at the elbow. This isn't a confrontation per se, but a line has certainly been drawn in the sand and we can both sense it. Tish and I stand on one side as we wait to hear what is raging through Monica and Carol's minds.

"The passport!" Monica says. "When did you know it was missing? Did Sabine say anything to you? What do you know?"

I give her a startled look. "I only realized yesterday that it never turned up."

"When should you have received it?"

"A couple of weeks ago. Look, I just told the detective the same things. I don't have to tell you."

"But your passport," she insists. "This could help. They think I hurt Sabine but they're wrong. It was only a letter." She shoots Carol a look. "Tell them it was only my stupid drunken words. I didn't mean any of it."

"She didn't mean *any* of it," Carol repeats. "This is being blown completely out of proportion. Sabine should have torn it up and we wouldn't be dealing with this part right now."

"Is there a chance she took it?" Monica asks, flashing her eyes at me. "She took your passport and went somewhere? Did you get an alert about someone booking a flight? Have you checked?" She jabs a finger at me. "Tell us, Erica! What do you know?"

Tish's face blooms bright red. "Monica, stop it! You're only latching onto this because you wrote those threats to Sabine. You're only trying to get yourself off the hook."

"We said Monica didn't mean it." Carol says.

Monica spins away, looking both horrified and guilty. "Everything has gotten so screwed up. We had that fight Friday night before everything happened. It was awful. Sabine didn't mean what she said to me either, I know she didn't." She is rambling, her gaze darting from one corner of the room to the next. "Something was off—I knew it the moment we sat down for dinner. Sabine and Mark were already arguing about something. The mood was terrible. Sabine finished a bottle of wine, so did I, and we said those things to each other."

Dumbfounded, I say, "Why are you telling us all this?"

"Because we want you to know. We need someone to believe us."

"Aren't the police?" I question her. "You haven't been arrested."

Monica reels at the word *arrested*. "No. But your passport, as soon as we heard." Her eyes light up. "We thought it could be connected somehow."

I grit my teeth. "So what else happened?"

"I've never seen Sabine be so cold, and Mark in return was furious. After Jacob called, it sent everyone over the edge. Especially Mark." For this, she looks at Tish. "He claimed to know something about Mark misusing campaign funds, which is entirely wrong, by the way. We thought it was nonsense. It was just a way for his opponent to get a rise out of him—you know, dirty politics."

Tish doesn't say a word.

"But Sabine started freaking out. She got really scared. It was like she was doubting her husband. She was turning on him."

"So you went after her to silence her?" Tish says. "You wanted Mark for yourself? You couldn't believe she'd accuse him of anything?"

Monica swings her arms around. "*Are you crazy?* Why would I do something like that?"

I step forward, shielding Tish, but she doesn't back away.

"I would never hurt her. Never!" Monica screams. She cuts me a look next. "You've argued with Sabine before too. *In public*. And no one's ever said you wanted to hurt her."

My mouth drops open. "That's not even close to being the same thing."

"It's certainly not a hate letter," Tish reminds her, folding her arms. "And how do you know that's what Jacob told him anyway? I've never heard him talk about Mark misusing funds. He never said he was going to pull something like this over him to win the election. How do you know that's what he said to him on the phone?"

"Because Mark told us," Monica answers. "He came back to dinner and repeated everything. He said Jacob warned him about dangerous people who were watching. Some business deal that went terribly wrong and they're going after Mark. Planting cameras. Monitoring the house."

They won't try it again, the words repeat in my head. When Monica said this at the pool, had they been worrying about multiple culprits?

Monica says, "Everyone was pretty shaken up and we drank some more. Sabine kept asking Mark if there was something he was hiding—she wouldn't let up. It was like she knew something. Like she had found out something—"

"Like what?" My voice cracks. I find I'm getting caught up in their story until I'm breathless.

"I don't know, she wouldn't say. She was hysterical," Monica tells us. "At one point, I was trying to console Sabine. Tried convincing her that Jacob was only trying to get under our skin. I tried consoling Mark too and that's when she turned on me; it was crazy. She brought up all this stuff about me wanting to get back together with Mark—*which is ridiculous*—it was so long ago."

"We've never seen Sabine act like this before," Carol insists.

"She kept talking about my marriage. How I didn't love Frank anymore and wanted to leave him, but that's not true. Frank was so appalled he could barely look at me. But I knew Sabine had had too much to drink. Her emotions were all over the place. She'd accused her husband for no reason. She accused me, and I think this was her way of lashing out. She took it out on us instead of facing the truth about herself."

I narrow my eyes. "What truth?"

"That she wanted to leave her marriage. That getting a divorce from Mark wasn't the right option. He'd never allow it. She had to do something else."

Stunned, Tish asks, "Why would she want to leave him?"

"She hasn't been happy for a long time. People don't know this, but a lot of things have changed with Sabine."

"Why can't she leave him?" Tish asks. "Why is that not an option? *He'd never allow it.* What does that mean?"

She gives a tight smile. "A successful politician like him can't afford a messy divorce."

"So now you're saying he hurt her?" Tish scoffs. "He didn't want a divorce so he hurt her instead?"

Monica's eyes grow big. "No, Mark would never do something like that!"

"We told you, we think Sabine took off," Carol says. "She only made it seem like everything was okay the next day so she could run off and disappear."

"Mark is the one who suggested we go to the pool," Monica tells us. "He said it would be good to keep everyone out of the house while he tried to figure out what in the hell Jacob was talking about—if anyone was planting cameras and monitoring their home like Jacob said. I was just glad Sabine and I could be okay again. The letter, forgotten. That Carol was with us and we could sit by the pool with our kids. The fireworks..." Her voice drifts.

Carol says, "We didn't know this but he didn't want Sabine coming back to the house on her own."

"I know," I tell her. "I heard him."

Carol turns. "What do you mean, you heard him?"

"At the pool. I overheard you guys talking. Sabine had already left and Mark was sitting with you. He said she got spooked."

I look at Monica. "You said you were all spooked and that you didn't think *they* would try it again."

"I didn't think Jacob would—I hoped he wouldn't and not someone from his group either. I was trying to calm Mark down."

Tish launches forward again. "Jacob wouldn't say that stuff to Mark! He sure as hell didn't go after Sabine like everyone else is saying."

"He made that phone call the night before Sabine disappeared," Monica says. "Mark saw him driving in the neighborhood so of course the cops focused on him. But now they're also considering my stupid drunk letter and thinking I might have hurt her even though I swear I didn't—why in the hell would I?"

"You look pretty guilty to me," Tish says, and Monica sucks in a shocked breath. "Because if Sabine left, she hasn't taken any money. She hasn't done anything to look like she packed any clothes or hopped on a bus. No signs of her at an airport. No wonder the police are considering whether you have a motive."

Monica cries, "It's not true! You have to believe me! The idea she has Erica's passport and could be using it is our only hope."

"Wait," I say, cutting my hands through the air. "You said that Sabine getting a divorce from Mark would never be allowed. She had to do something else."

"Yes, that's right."

"But if you're saying Sabine wanted out of her marriage, that divorcing Mark wasn't an option, then why aren't you just letting her go? If this is really what happened and she's not locked in someone's basement—or something worse—then why not let her take my passport and get out of here? Let the woman leave if that's what she really wants."

Monica meets my eyes. "Because the cops need to follow this up and track her down. If they do that, they can stop trying to pin this on me."

And there it is. My head drops forward in disbelief until all I can do is stare. The best friends showing their true colors. Saving their necks only when push comes to shove.

I stammer. "You guys are horrible. Why didn't you help her?"

"You can't blame me!" Monica screams. "What are we supposed to do?"

"I don't know, protect your friend?"

"You know," Tish says. "I feel sorry for Sabine, thinking she has two best friends when you're nothing of the sort." She grips my arm in solidarity. "Erica has stuck with me through everything. Amanda too. Our friendship is rock solid. But you guys are..." A trembling shake rolls through her voice. "You're horrible, just like Erica said."

But Monica shrieks, "You don't know what it's like to have the police come down on you!"

"The police have talked to us too," Tish tells her.

"But not like this!"

"We just need to figure out where she would go," Carol says. "If we can find out she's safe then there won't be any more suspicions against Monica."

"We have to find her." Monica is tugging at her hair now, her hands ripping at her scalp.

"Maybe she went home," Carol continues. "Maybe she's finding family."

"But wouldn't the police have checked that too?" Tish asks. "They'd make calls, go talk to a few neighbors in Louisiana, find out her parents are dead. There'd be no reason for Sabine to go back to Slidell."

Oh, Tish.

Monica stops. She gives her a strange look. "Wait, how do you know her parents are dead?"

Carol says, "How do you know about Slidell?"

Tish whirls her eyes to me—her face frozen by her blunder. She stammers, "That's just what I heard." But she's clearly horrified she's opened her mouth.

Monica steps forward peering at Tish, then at me. "Wait, how?"

The pause is never-ending. A twenty-five-year decision for Sabine and I to stay out of each other's lives bursting at the seams and coming out in the open.

"From high school," I confess.

And the way Monica is glaring at me, this new information, something sets tight in her jaw, her eyes lasered on mine. I know she isn't going to let this extra detail slip.

CHAPTER 30

I tell Monica and Carol to leave—I insist they go, practically shoving them out the door. I'm still reeling after all that's been said, plus the new specifics they're pushing for, wanting to know about Sabine from St. Mary's and why we're no longer friends. But I don't want to talk to them anymore. They can follow up with their own private investigators and chase down finding Sabine back home in Louisiana *if* that's where she's ended up.

Behind me, Tish sinks against the couch. She looks astonished—speechless. And also apologetic.

"I'm sorry." Her hands rise to her face. "I shouldn't have said anything."

"It's fine," I tell her, but I can't shake the queasy feeling inside my stomach. We've kept quiet for so long and now, of all people, Monica and Carol might start looking into our past. What Sabine has so desperately tried to keep hidden.

Outside my door, Monica's monstrous Escalade roars to life before careening out of my driveway.

"I shouldn't have let it slip you knew each other."

I start to say something to her but a message buzzes on Tish's phone and two seconds later she's leaping from the couch, her eyes stricken with fear. "Erica!"

My stomach leaps to my throat. My God, what *else* is happening?

"A video," she says. "An unknown number. I have no idea who this is, how they got this. How they could—"

I'm struggling to keep up.

She thrusts the phone in my face and presses play.

It's a video of Tish's kitchen. Jacob Andrews is stooping in front of the dishwasher and opening a toolbox as Charlie walks into the frame. The little boy pats Jacob on the shoulder before walking out again. "Bye, buddy," Jacob calls to him. Then Tish appears. She's dressed for meeting me at the pool, sunglasses on her head with several towels in her arms. She gives him a kiss.

The video ends.

What is this?

Tish is in tears. "How did they get that? Is there a camera—is there something hidden inside my house?"

I stare at the screen. The words *Caller Unknown* staring back at me. "Was it Jacob?"

"Why would he hide a camera?"

She snatches back her phone and types, *Who is this??*

But no one answers.

I stare at her. "Was this so he could have more proof?"

"Proof of what?"

"To show he was really at your house?"

"Erica! He doesn't need that! He didn't know what was going to happen to Sabine. How many times do I have to tell you? He didn't plant this camera." She races for the door. "I have to find this thing—I need to know where it is. I'm going home!" Her voice trails outside.

FACEBOOK GROUP POST

Praying for Sabine Miller (Private Facebook Group)

Tamyra Meeks

July 6 at 7:35 p.m.

Who believes what Monica's saying about Sabine taking off and leaving?

> **Carolyn Castillo** I don't believe a word.
>
> **Kerry LeBlanc** Tamyra, don't let this turn into another poll.
>
> **Tamyra Meeks** I'm not. I didn't start the first one. I'm just asking.
>
> **Alexis Redfield** I've heard some of the rumors. There's no way she faked her own kidnapping.
>
> **Scott Wooley** If this was a poll, I'd vote Monica went after Sabine.
>
> **Alice Chin** Me too.
>
> **Anthony Castillo** I agree. This is her way of throwing everyone off her trail.
>
> **Hector Saurez** Less than 24 hours ago some of you were pretty convinced it was Jacob Andrews.
>
> **Carolyn Castillo** New information, Hector. Keep up.

Kerry LeBlanc I hope wherever she is she's healthy and safe.

Anthony Castillo Well there's one vote for Sabine taking off and leaving.

Hillary Danners That's not exactly what I'm saying.

Carolyn Castillo Monica is guilty as hell.

Monica Claiborne If you guys have something to say, why don't you say it to my face?

CHAPTER 31

It takes Tish twenty minutes before she returns to my house winded and hysterical. There's no sign of a video camera. She's thrown open every cabinet and tells me she found zilch. No wires. Nothing hidden in her kitchen or tucked behind a shelf. For good measure, she tore through the rest of her house looking for cameras too.

"I don't understand!" she says. "I couldn't find anything!"

Nothing in the living room. And I shudder—nothing in her bedroom either.

Someone crept back into her house and took it. Or what I'm wondering, Jacob set up the camera in the first place. He placed it there Saturday night wanting the extra insurance for proving his alibi to the police.

He anticipated this…

But if Jacob sent her the video, he doesn't respond to her text. He doesn't deny it either.

*

That evening, a message comes through from Terry.

I feel bad about today. Let me make it up to you?

I'm sitting in bed, exhausted. Tish is resting next to me, one arm flung over her head from the Tylenol PM she's knocked back to get some sleep. Charlie snuggles beside her.

What an insane series of events. And now here is Terry wanting to make up for part of it.

Sure, I text back, thinking I could use a break from this madness.

Are you upset with me?

I sigh. My irritation about our shortened date has long since been eclipsed by everything else that's happening. *No, just have a lot on my mind.*

I didn't mean to cut out so early.

I know you didn't.

What about tomorrow? Want to get together?

I immediately think about how I don't want to return to that same bar.

I get to pick, remember? How about a hike in the morning?

There's no way I'm going to the office tomorrow. The questions from everyone at work will be laser focused on Tish, an onslaught, and made worse when they corner me at my desk and ask directly. Everyone will want to know if I knew about her boyfriend—and I grimace—the very man who may or may not have planted a camera in her kitchen.

A hike is what I need. A chance to get outside, move around. Work off some steam.

That's an interesting idea, Terry says. *I have meetings until ten. How about after that?*

How about 10:30? Meet me near Honeycomb by the lake. It's beautiful there.

I haven't been to this trail since last summer when I went with the kids for a picnic. The lake isn't far from the walking path with plenty of trees for creating shade.

See you tomorrow, he tells me. *I hope I can get your mind off some things.*

*

Entering the parking lot, my car kicks up gray dust near the starting point of the trail. It's not so much a parking lot but a cleared space for maybe three or four cars to pull to one side, a thin layer of gravel spread across its width. At the fence, a sign that reads *Honeycomb* and beside the sign, Terry is standing and waiting for me.

I smile, pleased to see he's arrived early for once. We're the only two people at this spot, his truck splashed with mud where he must have hit the pothole at the curve, the pothole I carefully avoided.

Terry greets me with a kiss on the cheek, another baseball cap on his head, although instead of his usual jeans and polo shirts from work, he's changed into shorts. "I came prepared," he says, motioning at his tennis shoes. And as a peace offering, he adds with that drawn-out Southern twang, "I put my work phone on silent. Scout's honor. You have my undivided attention."

"For how long?"

He gives a sly grin. "An hour, tops. And then I gotta jet."

My heart sinks. *I thought so.*

"It's been a crazy week."

I temper the emotion in my voice. "Well, we'd better get going then."

The trail takes us beneath a hillside canopy, the temperature cooling considerably as we walk beneath the branches of white oaks and pines. On either side of us, the dense forest is filled with yellow buckeye and elm. Further ahead, sugar maples and a cluster of sharp-thorned shrubs, a scattering of wildflowers. The air smells sweet with the scent of dampened leaves from an early morning rainstorm, one of those showers that lasted a minute before drying up quickly again, the sun reappearing from the clouds.

We're silent at first with Terry leading. There's so much I want to tell him, so much I want to share with him about my last few days, but I don't know where to begin. We don't know each other that well yet and I don't want to scare him off.

I start simply with, "Thank you for going hiking with me."

"Sure, no problem. It's a fun idea." He looks to his right, a scurrying in the brush that grabs our attention. Something shoots off through the bushes—a squirrel darting between fallen branches.

The way he's standing and looking out toward the woods, looking so contemplative, I take his picture.

His eyes round at the sight of my phone in my hands. "I'm not very photogenic."

"Sure you are." And I snap another picture.

"It's a beautiful day," I comment, peering up at the sunlight between the trees. "The lighting looks great on you."

He smiles shyly. "Let's keep going."

We lapse into silence with me following in his footsteps as he maneuvers around a patch of wet mud, and then another area of muck.

After a minute, I speak again. "It feels good to get out of the house."

He pulls on a dark green leaf of a sapling and then lets it go so the branch bounces back. Looking at me sincerely, he says, "What's happening in Green Cove sounds like a nightmare."

"An absolute nightmare. Tish has been staying with me."

"How's she doing?"

"Worried. She's decided not to stay home alone."

I monitor him, watching to see if there's any reaction to Tish's name. Surely he's read the news but he doesn't inquire.

"You know," he says, stopping to stare through a patch of trees, a sudden stiffness in his shoulders. "This might sound really creepy but didn't she run through woods like this?"

I balk. "Who? Sabine?"

"Yes."

I follow his gaze. The dense forest. The tangle of tree branches. We're on a cleared path but in Green Cove and especially in those woods behind Sabine's house, she wouldn't have had that same luxury. She would have been forcing her way through thorny bushes and low-hanging vines that—as we found out—tore at her clothes at every turn. That poor woman. My poor friend… someone from so long ago… and now look what's happened.

I pull my arms across my chest. My idea of a hike did *not* involve picturing Sabine running for her life.

I say quietly, "That really is creepy."

He spins around. "I'm so sorry—I didn't mean—" He looks away. "Shoot." His eyes drop to the ground. "Erica, I'm sorry."

"Let's just keep going."

But it's too late. Now I can't stop thinking about Sabine. We're approaching the shore of the lake, the glint of blue-gray water shimmering between the pines, the sight of water just as she may have spotted the lakes around the golf course. Except Sabine was running and I'm able to walk slowly. I can take my time. My heart isn't exploding from my chest.

At the fork in the trail, Terry sidesteps a sticky stretch of mud and motions for me to do the same. He holds out his hand, pressing his warm fingers around mine. And I try calming my jittery nerves. The newness of our relationship. This walk in the woods that I'd intended to calm me. The chance to hold his hand makes my heart beat faster.

We turn west toward the lake, the trail dropping in pitch as we move closer to the water. Through a break in the trees, a cluster of red maples in full bloom is spectacular in the sunlight.

"Can I ask you something? About your tech knowledge?"

"Sure," he says, sounding relieved to hear me talking again.

"What do you know about those Ring doorbell cameras?"

"A lot of people have them. They're good for security, for seeing who's approaching your front door." He lifts his chin over his shoulder. "Isn't that what the cops are using to screen video on Honors Row?"

"Yes, but what about inside people's houses?"

"Why would someone want to install a camera inside their house?"

"I don't know, maybe to catch someone up to something. Teenagers sneaking out. A babysitter. Or maybe there's a room they want blocked off."

"I don't know." He scratches his head. "I guess they could, I reckon."

"But people would see the camera, right? It would be pretty obvious having something like that hanging in the corner?"

He pulls on his mouth, his signature way for patting the sides of his mustache while he's thinking. "Or you could hide it. I suppose you could hide any camera in the air vent or drill a hole in the cabinet. You could hide it on a shelf. Pretty easy stuff." He reaches for a tree trunk and wraps his fingers around it. "Why do you ask?"

"What would you do if you found a camera?"

"Where? Inside my house?" He jolts and turns to me. "Why? Have you found one inside *your* house?"

"No. But I heard about it happening with one of my friends."

His eyes widen. "Someone secretly recording them?"

"Or someone trying to prove they were there."

He grimaces. "Sounds awful."

I've stopped walking at this point, my eyes staring across the water. "What would you do?"

He stops too and shakes his head. "I don't know, but I'd have to find out who it was. And once I did, I'd call the police."

"Would you destroy the video?"

"Depends on what it's catching me doing." My eyes flip to his and he gives a low chuckle. "Relax, hon, I'm kidding." His face turns serious again. "I would definitely call the police."

*

In less than an hour we're backtracking to the parking lot so Terry can return to work. At my car, he gives me a hug and squeezes my hand, almost looking ready to kiss me. But he doesn't. We're there—almost. Maybe the next date.

"I'm glad we could meet up," he says.

Returning home, I find Tish and Charlie still camped in my living room. She's playing a movie for him with the pair cuddling on the couch.

"Terry again?" she says, flashing a weak smile in my direction. Her dating life may have been blown to pieces but she's still happy for me. "Things are starting to pick up between you two."

"Kind of," I say. "Short dates here and there."

"But at least you're talking…" And now her voice drops, so does her gaze. "Still no word from Jacob."

On her shoulder, Charlie rests his head, his eyes glazed over from watching *Peter Rabbit*. She runs her hand along his hair and brushes it from his forehead in soft, steady strokes.

I have to ask.

"Tish, Charlie told me Jacob was always coming over to fix the dishwasher. The same dishwasher, over and over. Is that right?"

Her eyes slide back to me and she gives me a funny look.

Pulling away from Charlie, she whispers to him about getting something to drink which he barely acknowledges, he's so engrossed in the movie. She motions for me to follow her to the kitchen.

"The dishwasher?" I prompt.

"What about it?"

"Was it broken?"

"You saw the video. It was Saturday night."

"But was it really broken? Did he need to come over and fix it?"

"Erica," she says, her face tilting in surprise. "Of course he did."

"But Charlie said—"

Something in her eyes flashes. "He fixed it, okay? Those texts, that video. It shows him there, clear as day."

"But wouldn't he tell you he planted a camera?"

"I have no idea," she says. "But I believe him, I trust him. I need you to do the same."

CHAPTER 32

When my phone lights up with *Caller Unknown*, I don't answer. I'm thinking it's a reporter or it's Monica or Carol, the women rearing their heads again and wanting to ask more questions.

I press end.

But whoever it is calls again. And on the third time, I answer because if it *is* Monica, I'll repeat there's nothing more I have to say. She can talk the cops' ears off about my passport but not to me anymore.

A man's voice identifies himself as Mark Miller.

My pulse quickens. We've never spoken before, not at the Chamber of Commerce or any public event where I'm sitting in the back row and he's at the podium.

"Monica told me you knew Sabine from high school," he says.

My hand tightens around my phone. I knew it was only a matter of time before she told him.

"Can you help me?" His words are short, clipped. Desperate. So unlike how I've heard him at press conferences and campaign speeches. The way he spoke confidently at last year's State of the County address is gone.

This Mark sounds broken, shattered.

But then I remember what Monica told us. About Sabine wanting to leave him. How he would never allow it.

"I have to find my wife," he pleads.

I'm frozen, glued to the spot. I don't know who—or what—to believe anymore. This man who I don't know. What Monica said about Jacob accusing him of misusing campaign funds. Her own story about Sabine wanting to leave their marriage. How that wasn't an option.

But I wouldn't put it past her to make up every one of these lies, any claim to further support her theory Sabine left on her own. Monica wants people to think the Millers have their own secrets and she can appear as the innocent one.

"You knew her before," Mark says. "You know Sabine's past. Is there anything you can tell the police?"

"It was a long time ago..." I begin.

I rise to my feet and cross the living room to the window, willing the anxiety to lower in my chest. How much does he know?

"Was there something she ever told you? Something that could explain what's happening now?"

I peek through the blinds. "High school was twenty-five years ago. We've grown apart since then."

"Please, Erica," he says. "I have no idea what happened to my wife. Every day she's missing... it's intolerable... I don't wish it on anyone." He takes a rattled breath. "I know we've never spoken before and I wish we had, but under much better circumstances. But I need your help. Please, I'm desperately seeking your help."

I squeeze my eyes shut; the pain in his voice is undeniable. I turn from the window.

"I'm sorry, Mark. I don't know what to say."

"I don't know anything about Sabine from when she was a teenager. She doesn't talk about home. She's barely told me anything." He takes another shaken breath, his attempt at not crying, even though I can hear him sniffling through the phone. "Do you know anything about her past? Anything you can share with me?"

"But what would that have to do with her disappearance now?"

"I don't know. Maybe it's something that's come back to haunt her?"

"No, that wouldn't make sense."

"She was always so vague about school," he continues as if not hearing me. "I felt like something happened to her back then but she wouldn't talk about it. She was closed off. Secretive. It was worrying."

Sabine never told him about the abortion, that's painfully obvious. *And of course she wouldn't.* There's a chance he might have judged her. He could have shunned her and they would have never married.

"Nothing happened to her in high school," I assure him.

"Then why does she act like there's some big secret? Something upsetting her. There was never any family to ask, her parents died. She wouldn't talk to me."

"It was pretty traumatic after their accident. I'm sure she doesn't want to relive her past."

"But wouldn't she share that with me? I'm her husband. We're supposed to tell each other everything." His voice cracks. "I wish I could have been there for her."

I grip the phone tighter knowing I can't get involved with this. I'm already caught up in Sabine's disappearance, her recovery, more than I ever imagined, more than I ever thought possible. That damn passport, that one mishap. And then the revelation Sabine and I used to know each other.

And now, even with a crying Mark on the phone, I can't tell him about what happened to Sabine in our senior year. That agonizing time can stay hidden. It's not my secret to share again. She needs to be the one to tell him.

His voice softens. "And why didn't she tell me about you? Why would she hide that you're friends?"

"Again, that was a long time ago."

He doesn't want to let up. "Talk to me," he begs. "What else do I not know about my wife? Why do I feel like you're the one person who can tell me everything?"

CHAPTER 33

I need to get outside. I want to thrash my hands in frustration, the predicament that's growing and has been wrapping its tentacles around me—Tish included—and squeezing so tightly until I can hardly breathe.

I push against the back door and spring forward, the afternoon heat settling upon my head. Kicking off my tennis shoes, the bottoms caked with mud from my hike with Terry, the dry crunchiness of the grass presses against my toes.

Taking in deep calming breaths, I walk the length of the backyard, pacing and cursing silently. *What have we gotten ourselves into?*

Absently, I kick at one of the girls' soccer balls and watch it spin across the grass. It rolls with a thud against my shed, the outdoor project I've been wanting to tackle for months. The shed is nothing elaborate, one of those eight by fifteen mockups on a concrete slab with a single window and a side-entry door large enough for my lawnmower.

I installed air conditioning when the kids were younger and Taylor would come out here and play. We built a reading bench in the corner and she said she didn't mind sitting among the pots and shovels, declaring this as her very own She Shed. But time passed, the girls played on a new trampoline instead, and ultimately the shed filled with junk.

I open the door. A low hum rumbles from the back wall made with aluminum siding, and to my surprise, the air conditioning unit is working again. The air, much cooler than the steady heat of the summer sun.

But the person sitting there is not a surprise.

On the reading bench, with a pillow by her side, is a woman. She looks tired. Haggard. But despite this, her face invokes strength, a mirror of calm. Fierce determination. She'll wait out here for as long as she needs to. For as long as it's humanly possible. As long as it takes.

Her eyes stare back at me, hazel in color. Blonde hair tucked behind her ears. A pair of dangling earrings.

She's content to stay here a little while longer—at least we hope that's the case. Because any day now, the plan will work. *Our* plan. *Our* plan for moving her safely.

The woman smiles and says, "Hello, Erica."

And I smile in return. "Hang in there, Sabine." Sitting beside her, squeezing her hand, I say, "Not much longer now."

PART FOUR:
TWO WEEKS EARLIER

CHAPTER 34

The downtown library is one of my favorite places for bringing the girls, especially Taylor.

In the children's section, she finds a stack of books called *Secret Kingdom* by Rosie Banks and squeals excitedly, "Ella told me about these!" She carries several of them to a table and spreads the glossy paperbacks in front of her. "I'm going to read them too."

"That's great, Taylor." I gaze at the shelf, admiring the twenty or more books left in the collection. "If you're a fan it looks like you've got plenty."

She cracks open the first spine, already entranced, leaving me to wander my way toward the fiction section. "If you need me, I'll be over here." She nods quickly, her eyes not lifting from the page.

I meander through the aisles, selecting a few books and admiring others I make a note to pick up next month. Today, one look at the growing stack in my hands and I'm on a crime thriller kick.

But as I step around the bookshelf, I stop short.

Sabine Miller is standing in the middle of the aisle. She's blocking my path.

She's staring at me, her pink-tinted lips set in a firm line, gold earrings, a long-sleeved blouse covering her thin frame. She blinks once—the lightest touch of mascara on her lashes—before opening her eyes again.

We haven't been this close to each other since that disastrous argument at the auction last year… and now this.

My heart pounds and I step away, thinking this is exactly what we should do. I'll pretend I didn't see her. She'll do the same.

But she does nothing of the sort.

Instead, she reaches out her hand, the firm line of her mouth turning into a tremble. And I'm starting to think she's not surprised to see me here. *She came looking for me.*

"Erica," she says, her voice, an undeniable shake. "I need your help. What happened in the past, let's move on. It's time. Because the truth is," she cries, "I really need you. I've never needed you more in my life."

*

It takes me a long time to come to grips with what she's saying, but after bringing me to the furthest section of the library, a set of chairs in a study hall where we find no other visitors, Sabine proceeds to tell me everything.

Her marriage. The sham she considers her life. What she fears her husband is up to. The numerous affairs. And what I'm struggling with the most: what he does to her behind closed doors when no one is looking.

This can't be right... Her marriage is a disaster. *And Mark is abusing her?* A terror rips through my body.

But she's never let on, she's never told anybody. She says she can't—she can't let anyone know—he would kill her if she did. He would chase her down until she suffered the consequences.

He would also be barred from office. His career, over, and he would never forgive her for this.

This man... I'm sick to my stomach... this man with the dashing good looks and unrelenting dedication to building our community. Everything he said he stood for. He's a monster.

He's hurting Sabine. He's hurting his wife.

Visions of Mark and Sabine smiling to us from billboards flash through my mind. Their images in magazines, the consummate, successful couple. Sabine, looking so happy. Her efforts applauded at the kids' school as she turned and thanked her husband for his support.

Except everything is fake. It's not real—*nothing* about their marriage is real. She is living with a terror. Everything she's projected, what he's projected. It's all lies.

They live in glass castles, I see that now, setting up false pretenses so no one will know the truth. So no one will guess what is really happening behind closed doors. And to think I used to view them as perfect.

I search Sabine's face. This poor, poor woman.

And once upon a time, one of my dearest friends...

"You were right," she tells me. "That night at the auction. When you said nothing in my life is perfect. That I've been pretending." She looks down. "You were right about everything."

She lifts her shirt sleeve and, to my horror, reveals a string of bruises wrapped around her elbow. Another bruise, a deepening shade of black and purple, spreads across her forearm, broken capillaries near her wrist. The pain cuts me as sharply as if someone has shoved against my arm too, twisted it back and done the exact same vicious things, similar bruises now breaking across my skin.

"My God, Sabine..."

She's trying not to cry, but after one look at my face, she winces and lowers her sleeve.

And I want to weep. For everything that's happening to her. The very fact we are speaking again.

"He takes it out on me," she breathes.

An icy fear drops at the back of my throat. "Takes what out on you?"

"That I can't get pregnant."

My heart grinds to a halt.

"I've never been able to get pregnant. After high school... what happened. The doctors think it was botched. It's what you feared."

She's sobbing quietly. "He doesn't know what I did—he can never know. I've never wanted anyone to know!" And my heart aches with the painful memory. "He would have never married me in the first place. A rising politician with someone who's..." And her eyes shoot wide, searching the area where we sit, but no one's in sight. Swinging her head back to me, she whispers, "... had *an abortion.* Can you imagine? As conservative as everyone is here? In the South? I'd be crucified. He'd be crucified. If anyone found out, we'd be shunned. He'd lose every election."

But I'm sick to my stomach with what she's implying. "He beats you *because you can't get pregnant?*"

"He thinks it's my body, my fault. He blames me, and he hates me for it." The lump in my throat hardens. "I'm the politician's wife. I'm supposed to complete this image he has of the perfect family man with the perfect wife and adorable kids. He should be coaching T-ball in front of the cameras or attending dance recitals for our daughter—kids that don't exist. Campaign election posters where I'm standing by his side and he's standing next to me while our children are nestled beside us. But that's never going to happen, Erica. *Never.* I can't give him a child and he's furious." She wraps her arms around herself and squeezes her eyes shut.

My chest heaves. "But Sabine! You can't do this. You can't let him do this to you."

"This is punishment. For what I did..."

"What happened to you in high school *happened*, okay? There's *nothing* to be ashamed of."

"He would never agree."

"But he's hurting you! This is sick. You have to do something. You have to—"

"Leave," she says.

"Yes, leave." This is obvious.

But she shakes her head. "He'll never allow it. He's threatened to kill me if I ask for a divorce." And I gasp, a terrible scream raging inside my ears. "His election plans don't include being a divorcé. Therefore, I'm tied to him. Locked. He plans to run for governor one day."

"Screw what he wants! He can't threaten you. We have to tell the police."

She snorts. "He owns the police."

"What about Monica and Carol?"

"They tell me to suck it up. That this is a small price to pay for being married to the *fabulous Mark Miller*." She scowls. But soon, her scowl turns to more tears. "I thought they were my friends, that they'd want to help. But they're so stuck on what we have. The money. The houses. They tell me not to rock the boat, can you believe that? That I shouldn't mess up how good I have it. How good we all have it. That I just need to make Mark happy." More tears fall. "But I can't take it much longer. I'm worried he'll kill me."

I clench my hands into fists—the anger that's rising in my throat and pulsing in the corners of my eyes—the thought of Sabine's best friends failing her in this way.

She folds her hands over mine, her skin cool to the touch, soft and gentle. And with this gesture, with this tenderness, the emotions rocket right through me. Despite the sadness in her eyes and how worried I am for her, a warmth in my chest spreads to the rest of my face.

Sabine and I, sitting together again. Sharing with one another.

It's been such a long, long time.

This could be her way of forgiving me—the beginning, at least. Maybe I can start forgiving her too.

She clutches my hands tighter. It's not lost on either of us that this is the first time we've sat together since we were eighteen years old. Since before that horrible argument. A lifetime ago and I've never stopped wishing I could go back and change everything—that awful misunderstanding.

I clasp her fingers inside my own and swallow back tears. Something deep inside my heart begins to break. And it's the good kind, coming loose. Breaking free.

Years of pretending and telling myself it didn't matter, that I could get over my heartache of losing Sabine's friendship, and those feelings start tumbling down. All that time I told myself it was okay we were never going to speak again, that it was okay we weren't in each other's lives, and slowly but surely, those reasons are dissipating. Watching her from afar and convincing myself she didn't want to have anything to do with me, that our paths would never cross again and I should learn to be okay with that, and those justifications are slowly fading too. Because here we are.

I miss her. I know this truth more than anything in the world—I miss her incredibly. Twenty-five years later and our friendship suddenly has another chance.

But I'm distraught by what I also know, everything she's told me. How she's been hurting for such a long time and hurting badly. Mark is the one to blame.

I fight the desire to track him down, to wrap my hands around his neck and strangle him. Scream in his face. Tell him to never lay his hands on Sabine again. Call the police. Watch gleefully as he's hauled off to jail.

I rub at her fingers, wanting so badly to protect her and let her know everything is going to be all right. Let her know she can depend on me.

But a question enters my mind.

"Why me?" I ask. "After all this time, why are you telling me now?"

"Because I don't know where else to turn," she says. "And because you also used to be my best friend. I should have never abandoned you."

"You didn't abandon me."

"You were so angry with me last year…"

"We were both drunk and emotional." But then I soften my words. "I love that we're together, don't get me wrong, Sabine. But what's happening? Why are you coming forward with this now?"

"Because I want to make amends," she says. "Tell you I'm sorry. And because I also have a plan." She raises her eyes to meet mine. "I found your passport."

CHAPTER 35

Sabine calls the next day from a burner phone she's recently purchased.

She asks to travel in my name. She's not sure where she will go or when she will go, but she will. The option of divorcing him, even though I try convincing her otherwise, is off the table. "Press charges," I beg of her. "Stand up to him. Make it an ugly divorce." But the only thing she wants at this point is to leave him behind.

She's been saving money, she tells me. Squirreling away cash when Mark isn't looking, when her carefully allocated allowance from him is underspent and he doesn't realize she's pocketing the rest. She'll use this as her nest egg when it's time to cut and run. And with my passport she's thinking she can go somewhere where he can't track her down.

I vow not to betray her again.

"More than twenty years," she says, "and you never told anyone what happened to me when we were teenagers. Not even after we moved here. You're someone I can keep secrets with. This is a secret I know I can trust you with too."

"Absolutely, Sabine," I tell her. "Anything."

"I don't want to go easily," she adds, and the worry rockets through my head. I have no idea what she means until she calls the next day with more details.

"I want it to look like he hurt me."

Her plan: make it appear as if he attacked her. That he harmed her and won't come clean about it, and now she's gone missing. The husband is always one of the main suspects, she reminds me.

She's withdrawing some of her blood.

"You're doing *what?*" I ask, and she explains.

The idea came after her interest in nursing school a few years ago, something she wanted to do after donating time at the hospital. She rallied for the nurses' pay increases and secured funding for them too.

"I thought maybe I could work as a nurse but Mark said no." Her voice picks up. "But I didn't let it go to waste. I learned as much as I could while I volunteered. I learned how to draw blood carefully and can do this to myself in minutes."

It's hard to accept what I'm hearing. "It's like straight out of a thriller book," I whisper.

Her only response: "Where do you think I got the idea from?"

Sabine says she'll spill her blood on the floor and make it look like he attacked her in the kitchen. She'll do it the moment he's returning to the house. Even with most of the police in Mark's back pocket, someone will have to follow this lead. One of the detectives is bound to consider the husband, even if it is the great politician that a large portion of the community supports.

And if he tries coming after her—if Mark somehow figures out she's set him up and fled town—she'll threaten him with what she knows.

The conversations she's overheard—the money he's redirecting from his re-election campaign to pay back investors, the ones that have been steadily breathing down his neck. The money he needs to make up for a company acquisition that tanked. And the investors, one in particular—she hears Mark shouting back at him through the phone—is screaming for his money. Mark has overpromised and he knows it, and he's not sure how to climb out of this hole.

There's a video camera, she tells me. It's hidden on a shelf in Mark's office at home and she planted it there a few days ago to record one of his phone conversations. He demanded someone on his team cover his tracks. *Put the money back. Hide what I've done. Do it now.*

She periodically checks the camera to make sure it's still charged, which means it was recording during the most recent beating. The night they returned from a fundraising event and Mark, drunk and increasingly belligerent, took out his latest frustrations on her. I don't want to hear it—I'm already sick imagining the excruciating details.

"I was checking on the camera. There must have been something he didn't want me to see on his desk because he lost it. Throwing me across the room until I crashed against a wall and blacked out. When I came to, I told myself this was the last time. I wasn't going to do it anymore. Live this life. Put on a front while everyone thinks we're this happy couple. With your passport," Sabine says to me hopefully, "I'm finally going to break free."

"When?" I ask.

"Soon," she says. "I'll let you know."

That afternoon, Sabine sneaks back into his office and while holding the camera, rewinds the video to the night he beats her, and hits play. She checks to make sure the video was rolling, and it was. Images of her standing beside his desk. The moment Mark walks in. The first strike across her face followed by her hard tumble to the floor.

"The bruises will fade, they always do. This video will corroborate that he beats me. It will be impossible to deny that it's him."

"Show this to the police *now*," I plead.

But she says she wants to leave the video as her last resort. She'll hold it over him if he ever tracks her down. She'll threaten to turn everything in to the police if he doesn't leave her alone after she escapes to her new life.

Sabine also explains about her fears he's unfaithful.

"I've never cheated." Her voice is raspy as she breathes into the phone. And at the sound of this, I'm scared for her. The state of Sabine and her emotional wellbeing. Wondering if she's sleeping or if she's lying awake at night, scheming and worrying about how she's going to pull this off. Every day, I wait for phone calls from Sabine, for the time she'll announce she's ready to go. I haven't been sleeping either.

"Not once did I betray him," she tells me. "But he's been messing around. Every chance he gets, a new girl. Someone in DC or someone in Montgomery. Business travel and hotels. There's got to be someone here too. Sometimes I wonder if it's Monica."

I'm not sure if I heard her right. "*Monica?*" But even as I ask, I'm already thinking I know the answer. "She wouldn't do that, would she?"

She says, "Soon, you'll find out Monica only thinks about herself."

CHAPTER 36

"I need to meet with you," Sabine announces.

My pulse races. Since our run-in at the library, she's only called using her burner phone and we've made sure to stay away from each other. Nearly a week has gone by and we've been careful, not wanting anyone to know what we're plotting. Not wanting anyone to know there's a connection between us.

"I'm bringing you the passport and my money. Can I place it in your safekeeping until I go?" Her words are rushed. Panicked. "I can't have him finding anything."

It's Thursday and the kids are home which means I can't risk them seeing Sabine. But she insists on visiting, saying she'll do it at night once the kids are asleep. She won't drive over—that might catch someone's attention—but will cut through the woods behind her house, a track that will bring her past the golf course and over the hill to my section of Green Cove. She won't be seen from the street.

"Was that a mile?" I ask, breathing relief into my lungs the moment she emerges in my backyard. My heart has been in my throat—the minutes ticking by. Waiting. Terrified thoughts of her being out in the dark alone.

But Sabine said she practiced the trek earlier in the day so she would know exactly where to go. So she can try memorizing the path.

"One point two miles," she says, to be exact. "And no one saw me."

On her pants, a scattering of leaves and dirt where she has pushed through brush. Sweat blankets her face turning her blonde hair into darker streaks above her forehead. "It wasn't bad," she says. "Not if you're determined."

She hands me my passport and a large stack of cash. She wants to leave the video camera in his office a few more days. Until she thinks she has enough dirt on him.

And something else, a box of hair dye and gloves for applying the dye. A pair of reading glasses that are in the bag she's carrying, saying she'll wear the glasses to obscure her face when she leaves.

"When it's time, I'll need you to drive me away. Is that okay? Will you do that for me?"

"Of course," I tell her. "I'll do anything."

And I mean it. I really will. I messed up years ago, our friendship disintegrating. I won't let that happen again. With every plan, with every sentence coming out of her mouth, Sabine is making amends by trusting me again too.

Leading her toward the shed, I show her what I've been setting up. The space inside that's been cleared—it's not perfect and there is still plenty of junk to sort through—but to one side, a pile of clothes I've pulled from my closet and placed in the suitcase I promise I'll replace for Tish. Items that are out of the way and now stored on a shelf. The floor swept earlier with the air conditioning unit flipped on.

"Whenever you need it, this is a safe place for you to hide," I tell her. "Anything you want to bring we can store it here."

She steps inside and looks around.

"This will work," she says, her gaze landing on Taylor's old reading bench.

"If he hurts you again… if he tries to beat you…" My throat constricts. "If you need to get away, even if I'm not home, this is somewhere you can come. This will help."

Her eyes soften as she stares at the ground. She grows quiet for a minute. "I didn't mean what I said, you know. That stupid fundraiser."

I touch her arm. "We don't have to talk about it anymore."

"But I want to. I can't stop apologizing. I shouldn't have said what I did, it was hurtful. And I'm sorry."

"I'm sorry too."

"My pride got in the way."

"We were both hurt," I remind her.

"Please forgive me, Erica. For everything."

"I have now. It's going to be okay."

She wraps her arms around me for a hug. "I don't know what I'd do without you."

I hold her tightly, feeling her narrow shoulders pressing against my chest, and let out a sigh. Helping her. Forgiving her. Knowing she's forgiving me too. Telling her she can use the shed. These are things I can do not only to make up for last year, but long ago also. How she thought I betrayed her when I was only trying to help. I only wanted to get her medical attention, to have her parents make her well.

But she hurt me too, all those times she looked away. It's hard to forget—even now, I try shaking them off. I tell myself we can be better now. We can move on.

This time, we can do it right.

I murmur, "Where will you go?" This is something that's been on my mind. It's been hurting, the realization of finally having Sabine back only to lose her again. "Where will you start over?"

She pulls away slowly away. "I don't know but I need to think of something soon. And fast."

"Back home?" I suggest. "Or maybe a large city, somewhere you can get lost?"

"Maybe LA or Chicago." She mulls this over a while.

Sabine lifts her hand and points to a bracelet she's wearing. Blue fire opal. The charm in the shape of Lake Tahoe. The charm that's hanging from her wrist.

I look down. "You still have it..." I breathe.

"I was so young and so stupid, Erica," she tells me. "But it wasn't your fault. It was never your fault. You were only trying to help me. Protect me. I should have known that."

My heart bursts—that's all I ever wanted to do.

On impulse I reach for the charm and feel the smooth surface of the gemstone between my fingers. My memories stir and I'm back in Lake Tahoe. Sabine standing at the shoreline, her long hair whipping behind her like a flag. The boats in the distance. Her parents setting up a picnic lunch as I splash my feet in the cold water. Sabine calling for me to join her, her hand cutting through the wind.

"I never got rid of the bracelet," she says.

And the tears flow from my face. "Neither did I."

Our friendship, thank goodness, is repairing just in the nick of time. But my tears are mournful and aching. Sabine is leaving again, and the pain is something I don't know I can bear.

But she's being so brave, I tell myself again and again. She must save herself. She's found a way and I must help her. And I quiet my tears, knowing I will find a way to be brave for her too.

*

Friday night, Sabine sends a message before Monica, Carol, and their husbands arrive at her home for their July Fourth celebration dinner. It's the night before the fireworks show. She's shopped most of the morning and cooked straight through lunch, telling me, "I want to make it seem like things are on the up and up. Continue playing the role of the happy housewife."

But her text messages hours later are anything but calm. Nothing like the Sabine she's been the last few days: Methodical. Assured. The careful steps and level-headedness she's displayed while we've been concocting this plan.

I slipped to Monica and Carol.

I read her text again and my heart stumbles. *What do you mean you slipped?*

Earlier. They stopped by. Help me! What should I do?

I brace my phone against my head. *What exactly did you tell them?*

That I want to leave. Get away. Travel somewhere. I've been thinking about it. And they told Mark!

What did he say?

He thinks I want to leave him. But I made it sound like it was a vacation. Like I want to go on a trip. But I don't think he believes me.

Her texts are coming in fast and furious, one after the other. Lightning speed as she fires off each one.

The camera! she says. *The USB drive is missing! I think he took it.*

Oh my God. The camera. The proof of what he's done to Sabine, beating her. The recordings of him directing his team to clean up his financial mess. The twist inside my stomach clenches tighter.

I'm scared. Mark is on a tirade. I don't know what to do.

Nothing else. She doesn't send another message. And I can only imagine it's because Mark has entered the room and forced her to drop her phone. Or her friends have returned and it's time for the dinner party.

It's 7 p.m. and I can't sit still. I'm pacing the floor, back and forth, fear gnawing inside my gut. My fear escalating for Sabine. Waiting to hear from her—every minute feeling like an eternity—waiting for any word to let me know she's all right. Hoping to God that Mark isn't going to beat her again. That he isn't going to force everyone to leave his house.

I should call the police. I should drive over there right now and make sure she's okay. But I don't. She wouldn't want me to do that. We'd be ruining the plan.

An hour later, a message from Sabine and I leap to my phone.

The things I know about Mark, what he's up to.

Are you okay? Are you safe?

Someone else is closing in on him, she says. *Bad business deals.*

My fingers jolt with the adrenaline rush. *Who??*

Jacob Andrews.

I stare at the name on my screen. The man who wants so badly to beat Mark and become county commissioner.

Are you okay? I ask again.

But she doesn't answer.

What is happening??

There's no reply.

*

It's the last time I hear from her that night. She doesn't respond the next day. And at the pool, only more confusion. Only more questions. That cryptic look from Sabine as I hold myself back from shrieking across the deep end demanding to know if she's all right. The giant question mark that's hanging in the air because Sabine's not ready to leave yet. We haven't finished the rest of the details. I don't know when she's ready to cut and run.

Because when she walks out that pool gate, I am no longer getting responses to my messages.

PART FIVE: PRESENT

CHAPTER 37

It's Wednesday and the police are marking the fourth day since Sabine Miller went missing with a press conference. They're following up on several leads, they tell the public, but there is still no sign of Sabine or evidence leading to her captor. They are still classifying this as a search and rescue.

I decide to go to the office but only after sending an email to my boss and copying our team that I will not be speaking to anyone about the case or anything they've heard, including Monica's comments that Sabine Miller may have come upon my passport—the odd coincidence, Monica alludes, since we knew each other in high school. Understandably, the press are jumping all over this, the media excited to fill their reports with fresh material.

Damn that woman. Now along with Tish's phone blowing up for interviews, I'm fielding requests from the media too. In the morning, several reporters are camped outside my house. As I reverse from the garage, one of them jogs alongside my car and raps on the window.

I wave him off, mouthing the standard, *No comment*, not wanting him to see the terrified clench to my jaw, how I could burst out of my skin. But he insists.

"Have you tracked down your passport? Is there any credibility Sabine Miller could have used it to escape? Did she talk to you about this?"

I slam on my brakes, deciding the best thing I can do right now to calm my shaking hands and show I have nothing to hide, is to demonstrate everything is on the up and up. Just as Sabine did. I'll make a couple of comments to the reporter and let it rest. I'll face them head on and then get out of here.

Rolling down my window, his eyes widen with zeal, relishing the prospect I might take the time to speak to him. But I draw the boundary and stay behind my window that's cracked only a few inches.

I tell the reporter what I've been practicing in my head. "The tracking service indicates my passport was delivered to my home address on June twenty-third and not to the Millers' residence. There is no indication she has it or has used it. Sabine Miller and I went our separate ways after high school and we live separate lives, anyone can attest to that. But since she's gone missing, I think of her every day just like everyone else. I'm praying she remains safe and well."

None of it lies. All of it can be confirmed.

The tremble in my hands lightens for a moment, long enough for me to roll up my window, finished for now, and cut my eyes away from the reporter's face so I can back out the rest of the driveway. He steps from my car.

A nervous glance in the rearview window as I see him lift a phone to his ear with another reporter running over to find out what I said.

Driving off, I'm reminded of how insane this situation this is, but how calm and collected we must remain. Maintain patience and control with zero chance of slipping up. It's crazy that reporters are *this* close to my house with Tish unknowing, Charlie still inside, and Sabine Miller is hiding only a few yards away inside my shed. Very much alive.

*

At the office, I walk straight past the receptionist's desk. Pam, a badge dangling around her neck, pops up from her chair as soon as she sees me. She wants to call out, slow me down and ask a question, but she doesn't get a chance as a delivery worker blocks her at the counter and asks her to sign for a package. I take the back stairs, avoiding any possible run-ins at the elevator and arrive at the second floor—a few more steps to my office.

Just as Sabine organized her dinner party not wanting those closest to her to suspect anything, I'm going to have to do the same. Continue acting as if everything is okay too. I'll put in a day's work since there is a proposal that needs following up and data calls that are due, although how on earth I'm going to be able to concentrate is beyond me. But I must try. I've sent that email to the staff and am hoping everyone will respect my wishes, Tish's too as she's submitted a request to take off the rest of the week.

I hate that Tish has gone through hell these last few days, but in the beginning, I didn't know—I honestly didn't know what happened to Sabine—and if it involved Jacob Andrews or not. Finding out Tish was dating him came as a total surprise, rocking me completely since she'd kept him a secret. We had no idea—Sabine and I both. That was an element we had not accounted for.

And to make things worse, Sabine had gone radio silent. Not a word from her on Saturday except for that mysterious look at the pool. All I could think was something had occurred at the dinner party and everything was flipped on its head, and I had no clue what was going on. When she went missing, I didn't think she'd run on her own; nothing was what we'd planned. I couldn't ask her if Mark was the one who'd gone after her or if Jacob was the man who'd attacked her either.

She vanished into thin air and I couldn't get through to her on her burner phone. Those next twenty-four hours were some of the darkest times in my life—my worst fears she'd been taken. All of our prep, our actual plan, went to hell on Saturday night after the fireworks show ended and we drove by her house, shivers running up and down my spine to see police in her driveway, my fear something had happened to her and she hadn't been able to leave in time.

It's those same details I'm still unable to share with Tish.

Secured behind my closed office door, thankfully no one comes to see me and I'm able to put in a few hours of work although it's sub-par at best. Fractured. My mind keeps racing and thinking about the last few days. Including the days ahead.

More recently, the food I've been sneaking out to the shed when Tish isn't looking. The air conditioning Sabine only runs at sporadic times so Tish won't notice. The suitcase Tish asked about that I used to store clothes for Sabine. The blue Tahoe bracelet I've returned to my friend when Tish wasn't looking.

It's been five days and we've had no choice but to move to Plan B. Sabine and I must be patient.

A message flashes across my phone. *Can we get together?* It's Terry asking for another date, and I'm surprised. Like Tish said, the pair of us are really on a roll with seeing each other lately. But the timing and the media breathing down my neck is far from best.

I'm at work.

How about tonight?

I tell him no. Not with everything that's happening. Surely he's read the latest reports and knows the new information Monica is trying to link to me. What I should do instead is finish up at the office and go home. Make sure Charlie and Tish and, most of all, Sabine are okay.

Soon, and very soon Sabine told me, she's going to make her move. It's time we move her out of the shed.

Another message: *I'd like to bring you something,* Terry adds. *A gift.*

Well, that's kind of him. And I scratch my wrist knowing I should say no again. I should go straight home.

Can I meet you?

I'm thinking of an excuse when he makes a suggestion.

A parking lot just off the bypass. That old strip mall on your way home.

It'll take five minutes, he says.

*

Flowers. Our cars are parked side by side in the rear of the parking lot. Terry is standing in the space between our vehicles and leaning against his truck as he hands me a bouquet of pink and white roses, most of them in full bloom. They're beautiful. He looks bashful and proud as he places the bouquet in my hands.

"Do you like them?"

I breathe in the sweet rosy scent. "Yes, they're gorgeous." I smile at him. "What's this for?"

"To cheer you up." He shrugs. "It can't be fun having your name in the papers."

I don't say anything in return, only press the flowers close to my chest.

"You okay?" he asks with that Southern twang of his. "You hangin' in there?"

"I think so." And I bite my lip. I'm honestly not sure.

"Any sign of your passport?"

My eyes shoot up. "What? You think Sabine Miller has it too?"

He holds up his hands defensively. "No, that's not what I'm saying. Just been reading the news, that's all."

I go quiet again.

"If I had to guess," he says. "I think you're getting caught up in a whole lot of nothin'. Just a simple mistake." He shoots me a smile. "Some of those people will say just about anything to get out of trouble."

"You mean Monica?"

"Or that Jacob Andrews guy. My bet is they're still going to pin this on him somehow."

I squeeze the flowers tight. "Some people are starting to think it's the husband."

And he snorts. "I suppose that's what everyone wants to think. But something doesn't add up. He wasn't home, he wouldn't want to hurt his wife. He still has my vote come November."

A buzz shakes the console inside my car. It's my phone. I try opening the door to reach it but fumble with the bouquet in my hands. Terry shuffles around me to lift the handle. "Let me help."

"No, I can get it."

Another buzz. He lifts my phone. Another message. "Someone sure wants to get your attention."

"Probably my kids." I jostle the flowers to extend my hand.

His eyes pass over my screen, a quick glance. "Here you go," he says.

I stare hard at the messages—Sabine. The burner phone she's been able to power on again since I brought her a charger.

> *Come home!! Tish tried opening the shed. We need to find that USB drive before it's too late.*

CHAPTER 38

"I thought you said the air conditioning isn't working," Tish tells me when I arrive home.

"Hmm?" I feign ignorance, my cheeks smarting at yet another lie I'm forced to tell my best friend.

"The shed." Tish motions out the window. "When I was outside with Charlie, I could hear it rattling against the wall."

I look out the window. "That's weird."

"The door's locked. And then the whole thing switched off."

My heart hammers hard. "Still doesn't sound like it's working properly." I throw a glance in her direction to see if she's buying it.

Tish frowns. "Call for a service."

"I will." To distract her, I show her the bouquet of roses.

Her face brightens and she's no longer looking out the window. "Who are those from?"

"Terry."

"Wow." A playful smile. "This could really be turning into something."

I pull a vase from the cupboard and add the flowers. My hands separate the stems.

From the couch, a voice pipes up. It's Charlie. "Mom, I'm so bored. There's nothing to do."

Tish rolls her eyes at me. "He's been like this all day. I haven't wanted to go anywhere with the reporters."

Charlie flops onto his back. "How much longer?" he whines. "How much longer are we gonna stay here?"

"Until Mom figures out what to do."

He kicks his feet. "Well, I want to leave. I want something to do."

She sighs heavily, the frustration circling her face.

"I have an idea," I tell him. "What about one of Taylor's movies? She has that one you love, *Trolls*." I give him an excited smile. "Why don't you go watch it?"

His eyes light up and Tish flashes me a *thank you* look. She reaches for Charlie's hand and leads him to Taylor's bedroom.

Once the door shuts, my eyes rip toward the backyard. The shed. I need to talk to Sabine. Her text messages sounding the alarm even as I stand here pretending to be calm.

Moving across the grass, I remove a key from my back pocket and unlock the shed door. She's waiting for me—how she's managing to sit on that bench day after day I can't imagine, a pillow and blanket I've brought to her for added comfort even though it can't be pleasant. But she insists she's okay. She reminds me every chance she gets how determined she is.

At her feet, a large basin of water she's been using to bathe. A stack of towels I've been taking with me to wash.

"Tish came too close," she says as soon as I shut the door.

"I'll figure out a way to encourage her to go home. We can't risk—"

Sabine sets her hands firmly on her knees. "I need to move soon."

I stare at her face. Tish in my house. The reporters that routinely swing by. Neighbors outside.

"But we still need to get that USB drive," she says. "The video is damaging. We need it."

Her eyes widen, and so do mine. It's the one piece of evidence we've been discussing, the one crucial item we haven't recovered. One of the many parts of this ordeal that's been troubling us most:

on Friday night before the dinner party, she checked the camera. But the USB drive was gone.

A noise at the door and I jump—I didn't lock it behind me, didn't think to—and the hinges creak open, the sound of the door rattling closed again. A wave of fear shoots across my body as my eyes lock in on the sight of Sabine's face plummeting. She looks stricken, her cheeks turning ghost white.

I whirl on my feet.

I'll come up with excuses. I'll explain it to Tish. I'll tell her what Sabine is doing here.

But it's not Tish.

Standing in the shed, a mere ten feet away, is Terry.

"What are you doin' in here?" he asks. But then his eyes flick to Sabine. "And what is *she* doing here?"

Sabine rises to her feet and instinctively I move closer to her. But she's shaking—I am too. Her hand trembles as she clutches me.

The shock in Terry's eyes as he stares at Sabine, his gaze turning and roaming the rest of the shed—what is undoubtedly her hiding place.

But then he sneers, a smile stretching across his face until the effect is nearly sadistic.

Chilling.

Like he's caught us in something big and he knows it.

Sabine and I cower back. But this only makes him step closer.

"Hello, Erica," he says to me coolly, and I jerk where I stand—like magic, his Southern accent is gone.

What's replaced it is the voice I've heard a hundred times before. Calm and confident. The man speaking from a podium, the man we're supposed to trust.

His eyes return to Sabine—menacing. A predator who's trapped his prey.

"Hello, my love," he tells her.

Lifting the baseball cap from his head, he smooths one hand along his hair and ruffles the strands into place. With his other hand, he reaches for his mouth and peels the mustache from his skin in one slow excruciating tug. The mustache, golden with flecks of brown—the one I watched him pat absent-mindedly with his fingers while he was thinking, the subtle tic he displayed while speaking to me—is now ripping from his face. He crumples it in his hand.

I can't breathe—the air sucked out of the room. Sabine can't either.

But of course I knew. Sabine did too. We've known for weeks.

Standing in front of us, and far too close for our comfort, the very man we've been trying to get away from, a sickness ratcheting in my throat until my knees threaten to buckle, is... *Mark Miller.*

PART SIX:
TWO WEEKS EARLIER

CHAPTER 39

Sabine

My plan to leave my husband should have worked perfectly. I thought I had it figured out, I really did. I would escape from Mark and nail him in the process.

They always suspect the husband, isn't that what I told Erica? Most of the officers will try to clear his name, but one of those detectives will latch on. They'll have to. I'm banking on it, and I'm hoping to God I'm right.

But if they don't press charges and Mark comes after me, I'll have my backup plan.

Erica's help is a godsend. Our friendship has returned to what it used to be and I'm so thankful to have her once again in my life. Not only because of her passport but for everything else she's doing for me.

Hiding my belongings inside her shed.

Keeping our secret.

And something else: *Dating Terry Prescott when we know he's Mark Miller.*

Because with the many other sordid details about my husband, here is another one: he gets a thrill disguising himself to date other women. He's broken my heart a thousand times. It's sick and enough to make me scream.

His deceit is something I discovered after one of his recent trips to DC. The disguises he keeps in his suitcase. The charges he makes on our credit card for bars located miles from his hotel. The pictures I took of him visiting a rundown bar and grill in Scottsboro, someplace I'd never heard him talk about going before, and somewhere he didn't think I would trail him.

But I did. And my husband—the man who usually dresses neatly in pressed khaki pants, sports coats, and an American flag pinned to his chest—has changed into a T-shirt and jeans, a baseball cap kept low across his forehead.

When he left, the bartender described someone who meets with a different woman every few months. Who the women are the bartender doesn't care. And as for the man, he doesn't care either. Out here and in a different Alabama county, no one, including the bartender, recognizes him as Mark Miller, the great Madison County commissioner.

At this hole-in-the-wall, most of the people couldn't care less about the man's dating life: someone who keeps a low profile, occasionally parking in the lot in an everyday run-of-the-mill truck he uses when no one's looking. He doesn't cause any trouble. And when he leaves, he tips modestly, doing nothing to catch attention. The bartender says he makes a point of keeping out of his customers' business as long as they keep out of his—adding, the man spoke with a heavy Southern accent just like about everyone else out here. "He sounds like my Uncle Joe," he tells me.

But my husband doesn't speak with a strong Southern accent. And he shouldn't be meeting with other women. He sure as hell shouldn't be dating them either.

As Erica now knows, my life is nothing like anyone imagines. Many believe that what I have is remarkable, that I'm so lucky. I would never want to leave. But they couldn't be more wrong.

Mark beats me. He blames me for not bearing children. And he's controlling, forcing me to live in a highly engineered marriage where nothing is of my own choosing. I'm a puppet in his own election campaign. Divorce, he reminds me, is out of the question.

But while I'm faithful and uphold our marriage vows, he can't be bothered to do the same even with as high-profile as he is. It must be the thrill of the game. Something distorted and twisted, a break from the tension and pressures of his life. His job. Alternates for me—women he meets in seedy hotel rooms. Beating me must provide him with the insane power trip he needs.

*

Once Erica granted me permission to travel with her passport, the rest of my plan fell into place. She will be my confidante, someone I can talk to during my final days existing as Sabine Miller. She will help me escape and drive me away, and I'll catch a flight somewhere—anywhere. Anywhere but here.

But before that, Erica will also do something else, something critical. She'll reach out to Mark through a dating app. I found out he goes by the name Terry Prescott to pick up other women and he'll never be able to connect the two of us. I've never mentioned to him Erica's name.

Erica will meet with him and take pictures with her phone. When he's not looking, close-ups of his face. She'll record their conversations too. Further proof Mark Miller is an adulterer.

She'll also sneak into my house. When she knows he's on his way to meet her, she'll come through the back door and use the alarm code I'll share with her. She'll be free of the police and their watching eyes as Mark will make excuses for them to leave. He'll want them to go so he can get out of the house and meet Erica for their dates.

But besides photos of Mark dating Erica, something huge is missing. We still need that USB drive—the critical evidence of Mark beating me. The camera is still in his office where I hid it, but the USB drive is not there and it's not in his desk drawer. Maybe he's crushed it… Maybe he's gotten rid of it… Erica looked everywhere she could but came up empty.

The horror Friday night when I first realized it was missing. It was just before the dinner party started, the rest of the night blowing up in my face too.

Monica and Carol stopped by earlier to check on me. They were dropping off desserts while simultaneously complaining about their marriages, how bored they were, although Carol was thrilled about a trip Ted booked for their anniversary. Monica teased that maybe she could sneak away and meet up with *the concierge boy*, and Carol laughed, saying, "That's exactly something you would do."

What Monica said next made my blood boil. And maybe it was the wine I was drinking while cooking, the wine I'd been sipping all afternoon. My nerves, lately, getting the better of me with everything I'm planning.

Monica said, "You're so lucky, Sabine. At least you have someone who is still gorgeous. I'd sleep with him all the time." And I wanted to scream. The fear I have recently—one of so many—that Mark is reaching out to Monica behind my back, that he's wanting to rekindle their relationship from college. The two of them always flirting, but to make matters worse, my belief she's been actually reciprocating.

"He's so perfect," she told me.

And I snapped, the rage rushing through my lungs. "But he hurts me! You know this. You can't think he's a good person."

They only stared at in disbelief. They didn't want to hear me tell them… again.

Carol looked away, muttering softly, "It's not true."

Monica insisted, "He wouldn't do that to you, Sabine."

And I was back to having no one believe me. My two supposed best friends not wanting to think Mark could ever hurt another person, least of all his wife.

Describing Mark's violent ways was something I'd shared with them once before, but they hadn't supported me. Without proof, Carol made excuses and thought we both got carried away in our argument, both of us at fault. Monica reminded me of how much pressure he was under. “It’s a small price to pay for being with the men we’ve married,” she’d say.

I couldn’t believe what was coming out of their mouths—the shock wave racing its way through my stomach until my cries stayed trapped inside my throat. Their sickening dismissal. Their very defense of Mark, and even their own marriages.

What do *they* put up with? I wondered. Their marriages to Ted and Frank. They’ve never told me, and truth is, I shouldn’t have been afraid to ask. The nausea spread through my stomach.

But before the dinner party, here was a chance for me to show them proof about Mark. The bruises from the last beating had faded, but there was something I could do—I could show them the video. Proof their beloved Mark Miller was a monster and lashes out at me.

I led Monica and Carol to his office and reached high on the shelf where I knew the camera was hidden, the device still charging. But when I cradled the camera in my hands and pressed play, nothing showed. No video. The women stared blankly. When I checked for the USB drive, it was gone.

A pulsating fear pumped through my chest—I’ll never in my life forget that feeling. Terror raced up and down my spine as I could only imagine what happened: *Mark. He found it. He’s on to me.*

Monica and Carol didn’t understand. “What video? Why would you hide a camera? He doesn’t hurt you. You’re under a lot of stress too. You should relax—”

I was trembling all over. “But he has, and he does. And if I don’t leave soon, I’ll regret it.” Spinning from the door, I was beyond freaking out, the words spewing from my mouth. “I should leave this place. Get away.”

Monica’s eyes narrowed. “You can’t go anywhere.”

“Not while he’s running for election,” Carol said. “You know this. Not while you have engagements scheduled for months.”

"A vacation. Later." I tried to recover, but Monica watched me carefully. She crossed her arms and stared at me pointedly.

An alarm went off, a hideously loud shriek, and our heads whipped in the direction of the kitchen. It was another second before I realized it was the oven going off.

I broke free from the women and moved quickly down the hall, hoping—praying—they would ignore my random mumbling. But Monica did not. Once again, she betrayed me. She went in search of Mark and told him everything I said.

*

With the table set, every single one of us moved steadily through bottle after bottle. The mood so tense that several times Monica and Carol's husbands darted their eyes around the dining room asking if everything was all right. Mark could hardly look at me, and when he did, he only asked me to bring more wine. But his words came out as a bark.

I jumped—Carol did too—but another glance at my friend and she was changing tack, plastering a reassuring smile on her face and commenting to Ted about the delicious beef tenderloin. Anything to distract him, and herself I imagine. For Carol, it's better to pretend everything is going to be fine. Sweep it under a rug. She only wants to get through this evening, and so do I.

I poured my husband another glass of pinot noir. Turning to Monica, I asked her if she'd like more too but what I really wanted to do was fill up her glass so I could throw it in her face.

She didn't answer, and I continued standing, letting the bottle hover as I glared at her.

Frank, Monica's husband, broke the silence. "What the hell is going on between you two?" His eyes zipped around the table. "With everyone?"

No one answered. No one knew quite where to start.

But after a moment, Mark brought his glass to his lips. "We're fine," he answered him. "Just figuring out our allegiances."

"*Allegiances?*"

Mark looked coolly at Frank. "How much do you trust your wife?"

The question was abrupt, startling Frank. He turned to his wife. "I trust Monica more than anything."

Mark rewarded him with a calculated smile. "Interesting," he said. And then added, "I do too. She *is* loyal."

I clenched my hands around the bottle, silencing a voice inside my head that was screaming. My cheeks burned. Monica cracked a smile, basking in their attention. She had yet to meet my eyes.

"A one-of-a-kind wife," Mark continued. "You're so lucky."

"She is, isn't she?" Frank exhaled and reached for her hand.

But I laughed. "You can't possibly trust *her*." The bottle swayed in my hands—I was certifiably drunk, drunker than this afternoon. Angry and hurt. The fight with Mark still ringing in my ears after he accused me about the video camera.

Frank turned to me. Monica's eyes swiveled to me next.

"She only looks out for herself."

"Sabine, that's enough!" Mark shouted.

But I didn't flinch—not this time.

Through drunken lips, I said, "No, you started it. Talking about Monica and how amazing she is. *How loyal*." I laughed again. "If you only knew, Frank. If you only knew how much she doesn't love you anymore. The men she's sleeping with behind your back—"

"*Sabine!*" Carol shrieked.

Monica frantically turned to her husband. "She doesn't know what she's saying."

Another laugh. "You guys want to talk about allegiances…" I stared hard at Monica. "How you can cheat on your husband with…" I let my eyes trail to Mark, and at the last second, let them slip away. "… with these men… and *you're* the one who's called loyal." I pressed a finger against my chest. "*I'm* the one who's loyal. *I'm* the one who's been putting up with everything." I glared at Mark. "I've been nothing but a good wife to you and you know it."

Mark slammed his hands on the table, every plate and glass rattling, one of the wine glasses spilling red. "But now you're the one who's talking about leaving. Getting out of here." He pursed his lips. "You can't leave. And if I find out you've been up to something—"

"Up to what? I've never cheated on you!"

"Your own little surveillance..." He let his sentence drift.

My heart pummeled in my throat.

The silence broke when Mark's cell phone rang. It was coming from inside his pocket and he ignored it at first, only continued to stare, the moment lasting painfully long until everyone in the room looked ready to jump from their skin.

The ringing stopped, and what was left was silence.

Until it started up again.

"Answer it!" Ted pleaded, and Carol jumped, this time gripping her husband's arm.

With a yank, Mark pulled the phone from his pocket. He looked ready to hit end but after taking another look at the caller ID, his jaw set, some sort of surprised recognition, and he moved the phone slowly to his ear. "Mark Miller speaking." A steady crease streaked across his forehead. Whatever the person was saying to him grabbed his full attention until he stood from his chair.

"Jacob, what are you talking about? Don't you dare threaten me!" The color in Mark's face drained from his forehead to his neck. "I would never do anything like that. Campaign funds—no, absolutely not. You've got it all wrong." A glance at the rest of us before he marched to the other room.

I excused myself and ran for the hall. Hands shaking, I felt Monica's eyes on me while everyone else craned their necks listening to what Mark was shouting into the phone.

I bolted straight for the bathroom. With the door closed, I tried shutting out the noise. Holding my hands against my ribcage, I leaned against the wall and took several deep breaths.

This was not how I wanted tonight to go. Not when I was this close to escaping. Me, drunk and stupid and thinking I could show Monica and Carol the camera and they wouldn't run and tell on me. My stupid self blabbing and talking about leaving.

My mind whirled again—Monica is nothing but a backstabbing friend. Carol will always take her side. My husband is a cold maniacal bastard and—

I kicked the wall—dammit, he will try to destroy that video, I just know it. He'll think he's gained one over me. He's furious, but he'll rest assured the moment he's wiped the tape clean. He'll be furious I tried setting him up in the first place which means more hell will be coming my way when everyone leaves this evening.

But then I think of what I heard Mark saying on the phone—talking to Jacob which can only mean it was Jacob Andrews. Questions about Mark's campaign funds. Mark desperately refuting them. What did Jacob know? Was he closing in on my husband too?

When I returned to the dining room, Mark appeared also. He was quiet and looking sick to his stomach and I remember thinking, *good. Someone else knows what a scumbag you've become.* They might also have evidence.

Everything about that night seemingly went from bad to worse—a vicious fight between Frank and Monica. Frank demanding to know who she'd been sleeping with before demanding the rest of us tell him. Monica swallowing another glass of wine until a screaming fight broke out between us too.

Mark sat at the head of the table and clutched a glass of whiskey in his hand. He didn't say much but was clearly shaken by what Jacob said. The net closing in. At one point, he shattered his glass. Frank slumped beside him as Carol and Ted gathered their things and headed for the door. Monica pleaded with Frank not to listen to me, that she only loved him.

And when they left, Monica's hateful letter—the words I read in one fell swoop, my eyes swimming with tears, before balling up the letter and throwing it in the trash. Her hurtful threats, how she wanted me to die. Our friendship, ruined. Although I knew it was ruined a long time before. I just didn't think she'd put it in writing.

I reminded myself, only a few more days and then I'll be rid of them. All of them. A new life. A chance at starting over. I'll let Erica know when it's time to pull the trigger. But not yet… we're getting close but not yet…

Except nothing ever goes to script, I should have known that. No plan is ever solid. Changes are made, surprises come up. Some of them so frightening I never saw them coming.

And we've been making up for it ever since, Erica and myself. Scrambling to catch up. We're not sure what will happen next.

Because what happened Saturday night after the pool caught us both by surprise.

PART SEVEN: PRESENT

CHAPTER 40

The heat in the shed is overwhelming. Even though Sabine ran the air conditioning earlier, the cooler air is gone—all of it sucked from the room when the door opened and we found ourselves standing face to face with… Mark Miller.

How did he find us? How did he know we were here?

But here he is, menacing and towering over us. Standing in the shed. Blocking our path with absolutely no indication he's backing down. Veins pulsing in his neck. A frightful tightening around his eyes.

He's trapped us and he knows it.

Daggers of fear rip through my heart.

"You thought you could get away with this," he says, clenching the baseball cap in his hands.

Sabine falters against me, almost fainting, and I reach one arm to lift her, my other arm crossing in front of her body as a shield. But that only makes him sneer.

"What? You think that's going to help any?" He snorts in my direction before his eyes worm their way back to Sabine. He takes a long, good look at her. "Here you are, sweetheart. Safe and sound. And to think I feared you'd been kidnapped. Hurt. *Killed.* The crazy idea you might have already fled. When all along, you've been right here. You've been hiding…" He shakes his head but the look on his face is nothing but bone-chilling. "You've been hiding in plain sight."

I see it in his eyes: the once-familiar look he gave me across the table at the bar sitting as Terry Prescott, the eyes that turned away and pretended to be shy when I snapped a picture of him during our hike. Those eyes as Mark Miller, the consummate politician who once appeared so warm and welcoming—*trusting*—and promising transparency for a better tomorrow, for every time we would reward him with our votes. Those eyes are now nothing but cold and full of foreboding.

His stare roams the length of each of our bodies until my skin crawls.

Turning to me, he says, "You. Pretending to date me when you're really only helping my wife." He cocks his eyebrow, a strange form of amusement curling his lips. "It was clever, I'll give you that. I didn't suspect it at first, didn't think. Not until Monica said she found out about your link to Sabine as teenagers. When we went hiking, your questions about hiding video cameras." He jeers. "You were just trying to rattle me, weren't you? Get me thinking about"—he points at Sabine—"that camera you hid."

Mark lifts his hand, and roughly, he pushes aside a gardening shovel, then tips over a box of nails, the sound of hard metal clanging to the floor, each nail slamming against concrete and setting my teeth on edge. Sabine lets out a small whimper.

He checks behind the shelf. He looks beside a bag of mulch, but nothing. And I know what he's looking for: Sabine's getaway bag and my passport, the items that are tucked beneath the reading bench. A stack of cash that will help Sabine start her life over. Everything, I'm painfully aware, that is hidden inches from our feet.

I hold my breath. The temperature in the room is stifling.

Mark knocks over a bottle of fertilizer. He shoves against the lawnmower, shaking it, as he looms closer. He's narrowed the distance to five feet.

Sweat beads across his upper lip. His jaw tightens and more sweat trickles down his neck. On my own skin, a clamminess that spreads the width of my back. The constant banging of my heart against my ribcage.

Mark glares at me. "Your phone. I saw it today. I brought you flowers as a bullshit excuse since I wanted to get near you and confirm that you're really this Erica person from high school, Sabine's long-ago friend." He laughs and turns his eyes at his wife. "Your messages couldn't have come at a better time, my love. My God, it was perfect." He mimics her voice. "*Tish tried opening the shed. We need to find that USB drive.* And I thought, no way. Could it be that easy? Is that really you sending those texts? You're hiding at *her house*?"

He rakes a hand through his hair, pausing to let his words sink in. We've been so careful. We've tried to be so methodical, and yet, Sabine's panicked messages came at the most awful time. How could she have known?

Every part of me is shaking to my core. Sabine's body bristles against my arm, the dampness of her skin pressed against mine.

"And, honey," he says, his words dripping with sarcasm. "Here I was thinking something bad really happened to you. That you'd been taken. There was even a poll about whether you were alive or dead. Did you see it? So many guessed you were long gone. Dead in a ditch somewhere..." He curls his lips upward. "I had no idea I'd get that many answers."

My breath rockets from my lungs. "*You* created that poll? *You're* Trevor Blankenship?"

He provides a ruthless grin. "Guilty."

"You sick son-of-a-bitch," Sabine whispers.

"I was just feeling the pulse of my constituents," he says. "Always a good idea to get poll numbers, right?" He tilts his head at Sabine. "But you had us fooled. You really had me worried."

"You *should* be worried!" Sabine spits out. "You should be—"

But Mark holds up a hand. "Tell me how you did it. I'm stunned, I really am." He says this with an eerie chuckle. "I'd love to know."

"I left."

Mark rolls his eyes. "No shit you left. But how? What happened? After a hell of a Friday night, you managed to go to the pool with your friends. Everything seemed okay."

She doesn't answer, and I'm wondering if she's trying to figure out what to tell him—or how much she wants to tell him.

Mark prompts. "You made up with Monica and Carol..." Still no word from Sabine and he tries again. "Which surprised the hell out of me after that letter... wow... something so spiteful. But all three of you hugged and said you'd forgive each other." He rubs his chin. "I had no idea you're such a great liar and could lie to my face too. And who knew how much that letter would come in handy? Taking the investigation off me for a little while with big thanks to Monica."

Sabine jumps. "You found it in the trash, didn't you? You wanted to show it to the police and pin it on her."

He smiles. "Like I said, it came in handy."

Her voice breaks. "Monica has always had this sick loyalty to you, choosing you over me I don't know how many times even when..." She trembles. "... even when it meant sleeping with you. Sneaking behind my back. How could you do that to me? To her? After all she's done, this is how you repay her? You keep using her? You use everyone!"

Mark says dismissively, "She makes her own choices." He eyeballs her once again. "But back to Saturday, all that nonsense about making up and not just with Monica, but with me too, it was all just for show, wasn't it? You wanted us to move on and think we were moving past our fight. Everyone's fights. The girls said you were managing."

"They fell for it," Sabine tells him.

"Yes, they certainly did. It turns out you had us all fooled."

"Well, so did you." Her voice goes cold.

"Saturday afternoon," he begins. "You went to the pool. A couple of hours later you told the girls you were running home for a few minutes... and then what? You smashed in the back door? The police have been trying to figure out who broke in and attacked you, but it was *you* who staged it, wasn't it?" His face once again contorts. Amused disbelief. "You broke the glass—"

"I'm not the one who smashed it."

His eyes flare. "I don't understand."

"The door was smashed by the time I got there."

A hiccup in his voice. "What?"

No longer needing my protection, Sabine pushes against my arm and lets it drop gently. "There must be someone who's really gunning for you," she tells him. "Someone who's dangerous and coming after you like Jacob warned."

A nerve below Mark's eye twitches.

"It scared the hell out of me," Sabine says. "Someone breaking into our house. It had to be a threat. A warning for whatever mess you've gotten yourself into. And I wasn't going to stick around and wait for them to try something again. That door, when I saw it, it sped up my whole plan. Everything I was going to do accelerated in minutes because I wasn't planning to go away so soon. It wasn't supposed to happen that night, but it did."

Sabine continues, "When I saw the back door broken, I told myself to take advantage of it. This was one extra detail where I wouldn't have to break the door myself. I drew blood"—his eyes bulge—"something I've done before, something I've practiced many times, and dripped it on the floor. Made it look like someone attacked me, make them think it was *you* who attacked me. I needed to call Erica and let her know the plan had been ramped up, that it was go-time. But my phone was dead." She pulls the burner phone from her pocket and flashes it in his face. "My link to Erica, except"—she frowns—"I didn't have it charged. A horrible mistake."

My heart pounds viciously, Sabine recreating this tale for her husband while I listen. She's trying to keep him talking. But I'm also staring at the door, our only exit. Calculating our chances for escape. A steady glance at the window we might be able to break through. The tools I could use to beat Mark's head in if only the shovel was in arm's reach. I need to get past him. Distract him, figure something out—

"I thought I had more time," Sabine says. "I thought I could find the charger and quickly send Erica a message. But then you came home. I heard your car pulling into the garage and so I ran."

"Through the woods?"

"Of course. I cut through those woods like a pro. It wasn't exactly how I'd practiced but it was close enough, tearing off a piece of my coverup and drenching it with blood. Breaking my bracelet and leaving it on a part of the golf course that would make it look like I went in the opposite direction. No one saw me. Most everyone, it turned out perfectly, was waiting for the fireworks and I cut my way back to Erica's house, to this shed. To where I could wait here and rest and was safe."

Mark stares blankly at her. It's what he asked for, the details, but his look soon turns into a heinous grin, his wheels turning. "Bravo, my girl. I had no idea you were this capable." His eyes laser back at me. "And you found her out here? You've been hiding her ever since?"

My mouth opens, and to my dismay, my voice comes out as a croak. "Yes."

But the truth is, I didn't know at first. Sabine had stopped answering my messages. All I knew was she feared Mark had swiped the USB drive from the camera and her last text to me was about Jacob Andrews.

When I saw her at the pool, it was a relief knowing everything was okay. A fight with Mark the night before hadn't escalated with another beating since she was lying out in the sun and sipping a cocktail. I assumed she was laughing at the pool with her friends as another part of her ruse, another way to make things look like they were fine. But I sure wished she would have answered my texts.

But then there was that look—the look that left me stumped, not knowing what was going on inside her head. She wasn't supposed to leave yet. It wasn't supposed to happen for a few more days. And I sat at the pool, waiting for her to return. I found her bracelet by the gate—the Lake Tahoe charm that means so much—and my heart fell, wondering what this meant. A sign? A clue? Was she leaving her bracelet in my safekeeping? But she never returned to the pool.

And then the police cars. The details about the smashed back door and Sabine's blood trailing along the grass. Mark claiming to see Jacob Andrews driving near their home.

And what was I to think? Without Sabine answering her phone, I was terrified something really had happened—someone bad had gone after her. My first thought was Jacob Andrews or someone who wanted their money badly enough had gone after Mark but hurt Sabine instead.

Hours went by with Tish and Amanda at my house, the panic rising through me with every minute of the search, and I know I should have checked the shed sooner. I should have thought to go outside and look. But it was the next day before I finally did—my intuition grabbing hold of me and forcing me to look just in case. It was the one place I'd told Sabine to hide if she ever needed to, the safe space where we kept everything hidden.

And there she was, curled up on the bench, my heart bursting at the sight of finding her safe. She was nervous, disheveled, and shaking, but most importantly, unharmed.

But now, new challenges. I had no choice but to keep Sabine hidden until she recovered. And inside my home, the pressures of comforting Tish and sorting through the ongoing revelations about her dating Jacob. Was Jacob the one who'd smashed in Sabine's back door? Was Tish also dating a monster?

And then to make matters worse, the part about my passport slipped. Amanda only meant well but it was too late and Monica was shouting it from the rooftops to clear her own name. Sabine couldn't travel using my document anymore and I could no longer take her to an airport. The new plan: I would rent a car and she'd hit the road.

But not until I dug up a little more evidence first—about Mark Miller disguising himself as Terry Prescott. Sabine insisted that we needed more of a backup plan, an insurance policy to keep Mark from coming after her and making it public about where she was hiding in the future.

I met up with Terry and took pictures of him on the sly, especially that moment his phone rang and he made up excuses about leaving for work. The whole time, the sickness swirling in my stomach I was sitting with Mark Miller, that he would have the audacity to take another woman to lunch when his own wife was missing. Letting tears fall at the press conference. And not far from that restaurant, a full-blown search for Sabine.

I met up with Terry/Mark again during that hike. I listened to that son-of-a-bitch talk about Sabine running through the woods and it was everything I could do not to shove him down the hill and hope the lake waters sucked him under.

But prior to me pulling up to the trail, there was something else Sabine and I had planned. Something to help her. The reason I asked him to leave the house and go hiking with me in the first place.

Another trick up our sleeves. Another way for getting back at Mark.

CHAPTER 41

Mark clicks his teeth, a sickening sound. Taking another step forward, he's within arm's length of us in the shed. I swallow the bile rising at the back of my throat.

"And now here we are," he says, a low snarl. "What's next?"

"You're going to let me go," Sabine tells him.

Mark roars with laughter. "You can't be serious."

"You'll turn away from here and let me leave."

His eyes flash hard and cold. "Absolutely not. You're coming home."

"I won't—"

"You're coming home!" he shouts. "We'll tell everyone it's been a big misunderstanding. We'll come up with a formal statement." He thrusts a finger at me. "And you'll keep your mouth shut and not say a word."

"I'm never going home with you!" she cries.

"Oh yes you will. I won't take the chance of being considered a suspect for my wife's disappearance when you're standing right here *in front of my face*. I won't let you drag me down."

"I have proof! They'll find out how much you hurt me. What you've been doing with that campaign money."

Mark smiles again. "That money nonsense? I've figured a way out of it. We've destroyed all the documents. Every trail. And that little video camera you set up? That USB drive is long gone, my sweet. The files destroyed." His eyes travel the length of her body. "And as for you, you don't seem to have come to any harm. I haven't hurt you. You look perfectly fine and healthy."

"You *abused* me, Mark. You've been beating me for years. Cheating on me too. Meeting with these other women. You won't get away with it."

He pops out his hands. "You don't have anything to prove it."

"We have Erica's testimony. The man she's been seeing—*you*. Proof of you running around in some sick disguise. We'll track down the other women and get them to talk."

"Seriously, Sabine? You against me? My attorneys will get me out of everything, you know they will. They always do. We'll tell everyone you suffered a psychological break. We'll claim Erica's a liar. You just need to come home so we can provide you with proper medical care."

"We planted a new camera," Sabine says abruptly.

Mark jolts.

"You'd better rethink your plan," she tells him. "There's no way I'm going home with you so you can turn around and send me to some hospital."

But Mark barely hears her. He's only focused on one thing. "What new camera?"

"You thought we'd only have the one?"

Mark falters, lips parting.

"Another reason Erica dated you was to know when you'd be out of the house, when you'd send the police away so you could leave the house too." Sabine casts me a conspiratorial look. "She used the alarm code and snuck in. She hid another camera in your office to catch you saying everything else. The additional orders you've been directing to your team to get rid of your files. Cover up the money trail. The lies you've been spinning to everyone. We've got it all."

Mark's upper lip twitches.

"You didn't think there'd be more video, did you, Mark? A new camera?" She grips my hand in hers and squeezes tight. "We played you together, Mark. How's that for justice?"

Her words send chills up and down my spine, a rush of adrenaline that shoots to my fingertips. The satisfaction we've pulled one over him. *We're getting to him.*

Again, no movement from Mark. But behind his eyes, a terrorized flicker—his brain racing to conjure what's been caught on that video.

"The file is waiting for us to hit send," Sabine says. "Recordings of you telling your team to hide the cash. Do whatever it takes to cover up the truth. I may not be able to get you for abuse, but I can sure as hell hold this over you instead. We'll send it to every media outlet. The police. Everything is prepared." She squeezes my hand again. "You'd think us idiots not to have another plan in place."

Another twitch above his jaw, a steady grind of his teeth.

"Your career will be ruined, Mark. Your attorneys can try to get you out of this but not when there's video of you plain as day authorizing your scheme. Everything, captured in your very own words." She laughs. "You won't be able to dodge this."

Dumbfounded, Mark stares into space. Then he turns and says simply, "You got me, Sabine."

And I'm thinking, that's it? But I should have known better. He's flying forward, his face twisting as he fires his hand across her face—the movement so explosive, so quick, a rush of air barrels past my cheeks until Sabine is launched backwards, a vicious blow to her head as she slams against the wall, her body crumpling against the bench. Her phone drops from her hand.

"Sabine!" I scream and reach for her shoulders, scooping her in my arms as she lets out a hollow moan.

A blow strikes my head next, a firework of stars, a scattering of pain erupting behind my eyes. I'm crashing against the wall too, a searing ache to my skull followed by the sensation of falling. Sliding. My body collapsing until all I want to do is squeeze my eyes shut against the throbbing. But I can't. I must grab hold of Sabine and rescue her.

My arms swing out, but something stops me—a pocketknife. Inches from my face. The blade brandished from Mark's back pocket and glinting in the light.

He jabs at us both. We're crumpled on the floor. "I'm not going to let you get away with this!" He grabs hold of Sabine's arms and drags her as she's kicking and flailing.

I throw an arm on the bench, hoping I can use it to push myself up. But I can't see—something thick and warm is oozing down my face and dripping into my eyes, blinding me. The distinct smell of something tangy fills my nose.

Drawing my hand down my face, I feel blood. It's coating my fingers and I wince, the dizziness shaking me.

Sabine stretches across the floor to reach me. She yanks on my legs, desperately clinging to heave herself up, another hand swinging to grab hold of my elbow next. I push against the reading bench and lunge forward to help, but Mark tugs her away again. Sabine is shrieking.

"You're coming home with me!" he screams.

Swiping to clear my eyes of blood, I blink rapidly until I can see. But when I step forward, I fumble into the back of Sabine.

The knife swoops close to my face again—the rush of air inches from my nose. He's stabbing at me, the pointed end of the knife terrifyingly close. My God, he's going to slice me open. He's going to plunge that blade right into my neck.

He's going to stab Sabine…

A hideous cry from my friend. The vicious sound of her hair ripping.

She kicks something in the shed, a large bang, her body flailing until she's skidding over the nails that are scattered across the floor.

Mark hurls Sabine up by the waist as I thrust my arms forward. He hoists a foot and catapults me backwards, the air knocked from my lungs, his boot slamming against my chest until I'm afraid he's cracked my ribs. I can't breathe. A choked moan escapes my mouth. A labored gasp for air.

But a loud *whack* strikes against the side of Mark's head. It comes from above and I wrench my eyes up.

His body flings sideways as he fights to remain on his feet. But thankfully, it's enough of a blow he lets go of Sabine and sways, ready to crash against the shed. I watch him fall.

Sabine whirls around to see who it is. I do too.

I never would have thought, but thank God they're here—

CHAPTER 42

A shovel smashes down again on Mark's face, metal with sharp edges. He cowers with an *oomph*.

Our savior reaches up, her arms lifting once again, preparing to thrash at him repeatedly. *Yes, thank God! Someone is rescuing us!*

My eyes land on my best friend's face. *Tish.*

"You bastard!" she screams, her eyes filling with rage. "Don't you dare touch them!" And she strikes again with the shovel.

Mark crumples to one side and hollers with pain, his hands cradling his bloodied head.

Tish towers above him. "Leave them alone!" She grits her teeth, fear and anger pulsing from her body with every powerful swing.

I lock eyes with my friend, the hair that is falling across her face, her breath coming out in sporadic bursts as she turns to hustle us to our feet. "You guys need to get out of here," she breathes.

Dizzy, I try standing up. Sabine does too but she is knocked down again. Mark is yanking at her legs.

"*No!*" she cries.

He flips her over. Holding the knife to her throat, he presses hard against her chest and pins her down. Tears streak her face, her eyes wide open and unblinking, and I crumple to my knees. I can't shriek even though everything in my brain feels as if it's setting on fire.

I brace for what will happen next. The slice of the knife. The spill of her blood. He'll stab her first before stabbing the rest of us too.

Sabine chokes hysterically on her sobs.

But Tish isn't ready to give up. She's charging toward Mark but he rears back and throws an elbow against her ribs. With a fist, he barrels against her shoulder and Tish staggers against the shed howling with pain. He throws himself once again at Sabine, tools and flowerpots crashing from the shelf, a loud screech of metal as the lawnmower bangs against the wall. There's not enough space. Everyone is toppling over one another and crammed in the shed with no chance of escape.

I look at my friend, Sabine's hair covered with dirt as her blonde strands are splayed against the floor.

She's out of reach—Mark is in my way. The path to the one and only door is blocked. *We're going to die in here…*

But Tish is raining down with that shovel once again, a strength I've never seen in her before as every bit of rage and horror from the past few days culminates in this very moment. She's been wanting to bash against something—and at someone—for days.

She whacks the shovel hard across his back, his shoulders juddering as he lets go of the knife, the blade ricocheting out of reach and skittering across the floor.

I leap across his shoulders and hold him down. Tish drops on top of him too, the pair of us using our body weight for as long as we can, as much as we can muster. But we're not strong enough. Keeping Mark restrained isn't going to last long.

"*Run!*" I scream to Sabine, but her mouth forms a terrified *O*. "Get out of here! *Hurry!*"

Tish pulls a set of car keys from her pocket and tosses them at her. She catches them with a startled jerk. "Take my car! Get away as fast as you can!"

Beneath us, Mark is moving. His back is bucking as his groan gets louder.

Sabine clutches the keys. She's hesitating—she doesn't want to leave us behind.

"Go!" I plead. "*Now!*"

Tears spring to her eyes. She looks at me one last time—a terror and a thousand apologies scrawled across her face—before she bolts from the shed, the door slamming behind her.

Mark shifts and with a giant heave he pushes against us. Tish falls to one side and I nearly do too but manage to slam a knee into his kidneys. *Take that, you asshole.* Another groan as he crumples into a ball. My eyes race across the floor. I'm hoping this will buy me enough time to find the knife. I'll use it if I have to. I'll stab him if it comes down to that.

I spot the blade—it's in the corner and wedged beneath the shelf.

I scurry to one side and reach for it but Mark throws back an arm, whacking me hard. Blood bursts from my lips. He stiff-arms Tish before scrambling to his feet. He's unsteady but moving and heaving himself out of the shed. He's going after Sabine.

I watch in slow motion, the terrifying sight of him lumbering into the sunlight. We need to chase after him. *We must stop—*

But stars return to my eyes. Everything hurts.

Tish is injured too, her pale face dripping with sweat at her temples. The wind has been knocked out of her and she grimaces terribly. But she throws out her hand. "Come on! We've got to go."

My eyes tear toward the door. Mark will be approaching Sabine by now. He'll be chasing her in the driveway. We don't have a second to lose.

If we wait too long—our worst fear—he'll catch her.

CHAPTER 43

Sabine is gone. Tish's car is no longer parked out front.

By the time we stumble from the shed, she's nowhere to be found. Mark's car is missing too.

A race from the driveway is what we imagine as Sabine used Tish's car to escape. *Please* let that be the case. Please let her have eluded him.

But the sound of another set of tires squealing moments earlier flares worry inside my chest—Mark peeling out of my driveway and going after her.

Will he close in?

Did she get enough of a head start?

Or will he ram his car into the back of hers until she grinds to a stop and he drags her home? Will he do everything he threatened?

Wincing, I raise my hands to my eyes and shield them against the sun. Leaning against Tish, we hobble a few more steps before she stops and sinks against my shoulder. We're crying, the pair of us out of breath and peering into the distance, terror ripping through our minds wondering what is happening down the street. Visions of both cars hurtling out of the neighborhood with Sabine careening onto the bypass before flooring it—we hope—her heart in her throat but gaining some distance. Every muscle in her body gripping the steering wheel and slamming on the gas, willing for her to get the hell out of there.

She's getting away, that's what I tell myself. She's losing Mark. And within hours, she'll find a way to message us. She'll notify us she's safe. She found a back road instead of taking the interstate. Or she ducked behind a strip mall and pulled around to where he couldn't see her. When the coast was clear, she turned the car and went the other way.

Bloodied and bruised, Mark will decide not to call the police. He won't make any demands they search for Tish's car because how will he explain it? How will he tell them why he's so beaten up?

But sheer panic seizes my heart. With every passing minute, thoughts rage of what will happen if he *does* catch up with her.

I should call the police, I know I should. I should tell them what's happening. They can go after them and stop Mark. They can prevent a fiery crash from taking place before it's too late.

But if I notify the cops, they'll know about Sabine. She won't be able to escape undetected like she planned. If there's a chance she's losing Mark in her rearview mirror—that she's outsmarting him and he's eventually giving up and pulling over—me calling the police will ruin everything we've tried to do. The last weeks of Sabine's planning will be wasted. Her time holed up in my shed for nothing.

So I wait. I don't make the call, and it's excruciating.

Worse, there are no calls from Sabine either. Her burner phone was kicked out of her hands during the horrible fight in the shed and she hasn't gotten a new one. She doesn't send a message. No texts. No calls from a pay phone. Which means…

Only radio silence and it runs the blood in my body cold.

Sabine is missing. But this time she's missing from me too.

*

In the evening, Mark's camp releases a statement I don't want to hear. To my horror, they can't find him either and they're announcing an additional search for Mark Miller as he hasn't arrived home.

What's happened? Did he really catch up? Did she abandon the car and take off through the woods?

I'm reeling with every possible scenario, every nauseous gut-punch that is coursing through my mind. Paralyzing thoughts he found her. What he did when he grabbed her arm and yanked her hair. He ran her off the road, dragged her into a remote area, and dumped her body.

Or they both crashed. They didn't brake in time and plunged off a bridge. Mark rammed into the back of her until both cars tumbled into the river, their vehicles taking in water at ferocious speed before tipping below the surface. Mark and Sabine trapped inside their cars with no one to witness the accident and no indication the pair of them are now buried underwater.

I can't sit—won't sit. It's only Tish who tries comforting me. She's the one who tends to my busted lip and bloodied head. She checks the rest of my body too and my ribs aren't broken, thank goodness, but my chest hurts every time I breathe, a rattled intake of air, pain soaring through my lungs as I cry. Mostly, I cry for Sabine.

The rumor mill goes wild about Mark. His wife is missing, and now, so is he.

Does Mark know something? Has he found her?

Someone went after them both.

Jacob Andrews orchestrated the whole thing.

I delete Facebook from my phone and so does Tish. Accusations tear through our group texts too, a renewed fervor that Jacob Andrews is the one who's taken the Millers down. First, he went after Sabine. Now, Mark. But no one wants to imagine the real culprit. So many of our neighbors will never suspect Mark since he's their golden boy. They have no clue as to the monstrous lengths the man will go to—the real person behind his fake image, the way Tish and I now know him. The knife swinging in our faces. What he's done to Sabine. Jacob Andrews having nothing to do with their disappearances.

With Mark missing, our neighbors worry obsessively for his safe return. Tish and I silence each group text and continue to ignore reporter calls.

I keep waiting for Jacob to divulge whatever evidence he has against Mark. Why won't he tell them what he knows? That Friday night, those phone calls he made when he turned up the heat and said people were watching Mark's every move, was that all just for show? Empty threats and political bullying just as Monica described? I'm starting to think he doesn't have anything concrete against the man, which is agony in itself. We need more proof. It's only Sabine and I who have the extra video.

Except everything she told Mark? What she said about the file that's ready to send to every media outlet and police station? Not quite. *We weren't ready.* We didn't think Mark was going to spring on us like that—not in the backyard and bursting in on us when nothing had been finalized yet. When he did show up, she told him those things to scare him to death, to urge him to back off. Because there is only the one copy—the one and only USB drive that remains. No files are loaded on my hard drive ready to be attached to a hundred emails. We were hoping for a few more days before launching everything.

And the USB drive? It's not in her bag. When we told her to run, Sabine shot out of that shed with no time to grab her belongings, everything she'd stockpiled—leaving behind her money and my passport. But the thumb drive isn't among the items—trust me, we looked. We tore through everything in that shed hoping we'd find the drive and show the police. The whole time I kept thinking, while the cops are out searching for their glorious saint of Mark, if he really does cause harm to Sabine, we'll show them what he's been up to.

But the drive is gone, and all I can think is Sabine has it. The evidence so important she kept it in her pocket at all times. She drove off with it. And if Mark chased her down, our video evidence disappeared along with her.

When I snuck back into the Millers' house and removed the thumb drive, I should have made copies—I'm kicking myself about that now. I should have insisted on immediately downloading the file and creating a backup. But Sabine said we had time. That was until Tish nearly stumbled upon her in the shed.

Tish is sitting with me at the kitchen table now. In tears, I explain everything to her and apologize profusely, especially for that first night when Sabine went missing and I had no idea she was hiding in my shed. I sincerely thought something happened to her and didn't know if someone had taken her like everyone was saying. Her last text messages had been so cryptic, her mention of Jacob too. The onslaught of accusations that Jacob hurt her especially when Mark said he saw him driving in the neighborhood. How was I supposed to know she'd bolted early—days before we planned for her to?

But I also tell Tish *thank you*—I say it again and again, unable to find the right words to thank her for saving us. For coming in right when we needed her and stopping Mark. She says she didn't think twice about getting us out of that shed.

She also says she understands about Jacob, why I had reason to fear. It still hurts that I questioned him in the beginning but over the last few days her heart has hardened to him. She's wised up and become increasingly concerned about the man she's been seeing. As for everything else, she tells me she would have done the same thing: helping one of us escape a monster like Mark. She didn't realize what he was capable of and says I'm brave for hiding Sabine, I'm a good friend for protecting her… but that I should have told her sooner. She could have helped. We didn't have to wait until Mark had us cornered with a knife.

It's hard for me to hear her words, the part about being brave. Because right now, bruised and sore with no idea what's happened to Sabine, I'm not sure if I've done enough—if I've done the right thing. Because *nothing* worked. Nothing I did helped anyway.

Despite all our planning and Sabine's ruthless scheming, nothing appears to have helped her get away from Mark. We came so close but he still found her in the end. He tracked her to the shed. Even with threats of the extra video, he's chased her and taken her down.

And it hurts so much—paralyzing, really—no clue as to what's happened. Calls from her, non-existent. Any chance of her reaching out to me, cold and silent. Snuffed out. The same fate I'm praying hasn't also happened to her.

The police demand to know Mark's whereabouts but there is no information. Monica tells reporters she's still clinging to the idea Sabine left on her own. She believes Mark is out looking for her and we'll know something soon.

Looking for her, *not quite*. More like hunting her.

Twenty-four hours go by and I'm becoming increasingly sick. The pit of my stomach is in turmoil as I double over unable to breathe. A hollowness inside my chest that won't go away because I need to know. I need to know she's safe. I refuse to believe he's gotten to her.

I can't eat, can't sleep. Tish paces in my living room; she can't stop wringing her hands either. She makes up a story to Charlie that I was hurt in a bicycle accident, that I'm shaken up but getting better. He's careful not to hug me in case I cry out in pain.

I clutch my phone hoping that at any moment there will be a call. I sit at the table and stare out the window to the shed where I managed to keep Sabine safe for a few days. But now I don't know any longer.

But I keep the faith. Any second, a call will come through and I'll know she's okay.

But there's still no word.

And it's what I fear most—what's already happened. Mark got to her first.

CHAPTER 44

Tonight, the county commissioner reappears. It's a ghostly sight. While everyone is cheering, audibly relieved, Tish and I are seconds away from collapsing.

Mark is on the evening news and Tish releases a hair-raising, blood-curdling scream that makes me freeze in front of the television.

Standing on his front porch, he's talking to a crowd of reporters, a whole slew of them shoving microphones in his face and lobbing questions: *Where have you been? What can you tell us?*

And all I can think is: *what have you done to Sabine?*

Tish frantically pulls on me to join her on the couch. In tortured disbelief, we stare at the screen, the very sight of that monster standing in front of his house as if the last twenty-four hours never happened.

But he's returned home, and more chillingly, he doesn't have Sabine. He makes a generic statement about her disappearance, with Tish and I being the only ones who know every word is a lie. He's covering up what he's done to his wife for good.

Gray rings streak beneath his eyes. A baseball cap covers what we know are large contusions across his head. Knotted flesh and bruises for every instance Tish whaled on him with the shovel. But he's not showing the reporters any of that; he won't want anyone to see.

The rings beneath his eyes will be mistaken for genuine anguish about his wife. The baseball cap will be interpreted as someone who's too grief-stricken to dress properly in front of the cameras, especially when he's recently returned from medical care.

Because that's what Mark is claiming. He took leave to attend to his mental health, his fears for Sabine's whereabouts and safety and the last week of searching for her proving to be too much. *He is lost without her*, he says tearfully and looks directly into the cameras. He tells them this with a straight face. He doesn't know how to exist without knowing what's happened to his wife so he went away seeking therapy. I can almost hear the reporters murmuring their deepest sympathies.

Of course, not a word about finding her. Nothing about chasing her down.

"*It's bullshit!*" I scream. "You're a liar! A liar and a murderer!" And I burst into sobs.

Tish wraps her arms around my shoulders and holds me tight. "We have to tell the police. It's time. I'm so sorry, Erica, but I don't think Sabine found her way out of this."

I rub at my face, the tears that keep coming. I don't want to believe this is true, but haven't I been preparing myself the last twenty-four hours, telling myself we'll go to the police the moment we don't think she's pulled through?

"You have those pictures," Tish reminds me. "From your lunch date and hiking. Show them to the police and we'll tell them what Mark has been doing."

I sit up—I can show these photos, the ones of Mark in disguise. They should count for something, right? Tish and I can describe in our own words about the way he attacked us. How he chased Sabine.

My phone rings. Leaping from the couch, I stare at the screen. *Please let it be her. Please let me know she's safe.*

Caller Unknown flashes and with shaking fingers I press answer, hope surging within my chest, my eyes squeezing shut. With every fiber of my being, I wait to hear her voice, for her to say those golden words: *I've made it.* She successfully escaped Mark. His appearance on TV is a sham, it's only a way for him to explain why he went AWOL. She lost him and she's going to be okay.

But it's not Sabine… it's Mark.

My eyes race back to the television. The press conference is over and the newscast is already showing the anchors on set, but Mark has stepped away from the cameras. He has the gall to turn his back to the reporters so he can call me from his front porch.

"She's gone," he says.

Every hair on my body jerks to attention. My words burn inside my throat. "*What did you do to her?*"

"You don't need to worry about that."

I raise a hand to my chest as Tish rushes to my side.

"Where is she? Tell me she's okay," I cry.

His voice comes in low and even. "Erica, if you know what's good for you, you'll stay away from me. You won't tell a soul about what's happened—or else."

My eyes remain frozen to the TV, the news report that's transitioning to a smiling photo of the impressive couple, the Millers. An image of Mark and Sabine at his last campaign fundraiser, the pair of them leaning together close as Mark clutches her waist.

No one had any idea…

His breath whispers in my ear, menacing. What I fear he's done to Sabine. The realization I will never see her beautiful face again. The paralyzing terror at seeing his face on the news while he threatens me on the other end of the line

"Don't come near me," he warns. "Don't say a word or I'll put an end to you too. Your children, Tish and her son. No one is safe."

Something hollow bursts in my chest. I drop my phone and sink to the floor.

*

We lie to Amanda when she asks to come over. I tell her I'm sick, Tish too, since we can't have her seeing my busted lip or the way I'm hobbling as I walk. The welt on my head hasn't gone down yet but I refuse to go to the hospital. I don't want to bring any attention especially after what Mark told me and there could be too many questions from a nurse. It could get back to Mark and I can't stop shaking.

If Amanda arrives, she'll also ask about Tish's car. She'll want to know why it's missing and we're not sure how to explain that one yet. We'll have to replace her car soon but there are too many things to worry about first.

I'm grieving for Sabine and barely leave my bed. Tish sits by my side while Charlie stays in the living room, the little boy's eyes round with confusion since he still doesn't understand what's happening. But I curl into a ball and suffer our loss, not wanting Tish to know the full extent of what Mark threatened to me over the phone either. But she knows. At the doorway to my bedroom, she hugs her son close. She locks the doors and double-checks them at night.

I throw my head against the pillow. How do I seek vengeance? What do I do? I want so desperately to tell the police, to tell them how Mark killed Sabine, what he's willing to cover up for the rest of his life—but what if that plan backfires? What if he comes through with his threats and hurts our families?

By morning, new developments are emerging in the case, but they're about Jacob Andrews. Interestingly, and despite Mark remaining steadfast his opponent is the culprit and despite Mark having a hundred friends in the police force, all it takes is one detective to remain unconvinced it was Jacob who broke down the Millers' door. He's not the reason Sabine cut and run that night, and the Buick caught on camera isn't the one Jacob rented. Furthermore, the detective asserts, he has that alibi with Tish. Which means whoever broke into the Millers' house is still a mystery.

Jacob makes it known there are plenty of people who would go after Mark since he says the man owes quite a few people money. With this latest statement, the press are in a frenzy and they badger Jacob about why he would come up with such an allegation. No one has accused Mark Miller of wrongdoing before.

As for Tish, she eventually hears from Jacob, which is too little and too late in my opinion. A phone call in the afternoon with an apology about cutting her off and not reaching out sooner or more sincerely, but Tish doesn't have much to say. He's no longer someone she can trust. After all, what he was doing—the disguises, the lies, sneaking around to see her—is exactly what Mark was doing and it makes her ill. The understanding she was a part of something like that and was too blind to see and she tells Jacob to never call her again. This time, she doesn't cry. She's been through a lot but she knows it's nothing like what Sabine experienced. She can remove herself from a dangerous person before her own situation escalates.

As for Monica, the police continue to grill her about the hate letter. Her intentions, that she had motivation especially if she's secretly in love with Mark, is enough to keep her at the top of their list. But she also has an alibi. She was at the pool watching fireworks along with so many others, us too. I'm wondering when the police will drop her as a suspect.

And I cry. I cry for the loss of my friend Sabine. The words I wish I could have said to her in the end. If I'd known that was going to be my last time seeing her, I would have told her I loved her. I would have hugged her before I screamed for her to run. I would have said something more meaningful. But you never know in the moment, do you? Neither of us could have imagined. Even the best plans can get ruined.

CHAPTER 45

It's hard to move on but I try. I force myself to return to work even though I can't concentrate in a single meeting and my co-workers hover in my door and worry I'm losing weight, losing sleep. They have no idea how hard I'm crying inside, or why.

On Sunday, my ex-husband returns the girls and simply seeing their faces is enough to lift my spirits. I squeeze back my tears and hug them close, telling my daughters I'll never let anything happen to them. I'll do everything I can.

Only Taylor pulls away and blissfully skips ahead to her room while Lydia stands back and watches me cautiously. She knows something is wrong but can't put her finger on it—how could she? How could my child know what we're going through? How could she imagine the lengths people will go to so we can protect each other's secrets?

I turn my head and try my best not to show her I'm petrified. But I am. With every phone call that comes in, I've given up on it being Sabine. Instead, the shrill sound of the phone sets my teeth on edge; it makes me want to jump right out of my skin—and I worry that it's Mark. He's calling to check up on me. He's wondering who I've told, if we've contacted the police. He'll sneer something into the phone about going after my children.

Tish and Charlie return to their home. She's having an alarm installed in case Mark tries to come near them; I know she's scared too. I continue setting my own alarm, locking every window at night and checking the doors religiously. I monitor the street.

The reporters are no longer swinging by my house but they periodically camp outside Tish's front porch waiting for her to make a comment. But she doesn't give them the satisfaction. She also doesn't want Mark to think she might be talking.

With my driveway clear—no sign of reporters or Monica's Escalade screeching to a stop, or worse, Mark leaping at me from the garage—I step quickly to the mailbox. If I spot a neighbor, I'll backtrack. I'll duck inside and avoid small talk.

But the coast is clear and I reach for my mail. It's been days since I checked and inside are a ton of bills. Among the pile, several envelopes, a couple of catalogs, and something else that sticks out in the middle. Glossy card stock looking different from everything else in the stack.

A postcard.

On the front, a glorious image of Lake Tahoe. My breath catches in my throat.

It's a photo of Lake Tahoe, captured in all its splendor. White firs lining the shore with tall sugar pines and their long, pendulous cones hanging from branches. At the center, shimmering blue water—the gorgeous lake that's as deep in color as the blue opal charm I'm once again wearing on my wrist. The bracelets we purchased so long ago. The jewelry I'm wearing to remember Sabine.

I turn the postcard over but there are no words. No message. Just a single letter: *S*.

My heart hammers against my chest.

Sabine.

Is this her? Is this her way of telling me she's all right?

Did she really get away? Mark made it sound like he killed her but she's traveled to Lake Tahoe. She's safe. She sent me a postcard of the one place we loved, a picture of the lake so I would know it's her.

Memories of us standing together on the shoreline rush to my head. Wonderful times we shared with her parents.

I can't believe it—she's returned. She's made it. I press the postcard against my chest and inhale a huge, consuming breath.

Sabine can take refuge there. She can remember her parents and take the time needed to heal from memories of when she was a teenager, what happened to her. She can recover from a marriage that nearly ended her life.

I lift the postcard to my face and let my finger run across the picture. I hope she's found the same lake house, the chalet retreat with its quaint red door and alpine roof and endless views of the water. The house she said she wanted us to return to as adults.

My heart blooms until I feel it could burst, a warmth and a happiness spreading to my cheeks.

This postcard means everything. I can rest again. It's Sabine's way of telling me *she's alive.*

But something catches my attention—the tiniest of scribbles in the bottom right corner. Two words she's written, so small that I almost overlooked them. A message for only me to see.

I read her message.

Got him, she says.

*

Mark is arrested. I'm still standing in the driveway when Tish calls, shrieking into the phone for me to turn on the news. I rush back inside, discarding the stack of mail and tossing it to the floor. Sabine's postcard, however, I keep crushed against my chest.

A gasp as I see the breaking news alert flash across the screen. The sight of Mark Miller—*the man in handcuffs.* Being led away by the police.

The reporter says someone who wants to remain anonymous sent them a video—the same video they've already turned over to the police. It shows Mark in his home office where he's directing members of his team to cover up the money trail. Instructions for them to hide every dollar he's stolen. A flippant comment from Mark that no one will catch him.

My breath is coming out shallow but steady. On the other end of the line, Tish is whooping for joy and crying while I keep my eyes locked on the screen, hot tears streaking down my face.

This is really happening. Mark Miller is going away for good.

She got him. We both did.

A LETTER FROM GEORGINA

Thank you so much for reading *The Missing Woman.* Inspired by a neighborhood where I used to live, I've highly exaggerated the situation, thinking what fun it would be to create a suspenseful story between two neighbors who have nothing in common, at least at surface-level, but end up sharing a mysterious look. I wanted to explore how that solitary moment could carry so much weight between two women and explode into a gripping storyline. I hope you enjoyed the twists and turns as much as I enjoyed writing them.

If you'd like to keep up to date with all my latest releases, please sign up at the following link. Your email address will never be shared and you can unsubscribe at any time.

www.bookouture.com/georgina-cross

One of the best parts about writing comes from hearing the reactions from readers. Did you work out the next twist? Did you figure out what happened to Sabine? Did you enjoy the story of friendship, the power of forgiveness, of people coming together and protecting each other during times of need? If you did, I would absolutely love it if you could leave a short review. Getting feedback from readers is amazing and it also helps to persuade other readers to pick up one of my books for the first time.

Thank you so much for reading!
With much appreciation,
Georgina

Georgina-Cross-Author.com

GeorginaCrossAuthor

@GCrossAuthor

GeorginaCrossAuthor

ACKNOWLEDGMENTS

It was a dream to publish my first book and now to be able to launch my second book into the world is very special. I am forever thankful.

Thank you to Rachel Beck, my agent with Liza Dawson Associates, for your attention to detail and endless support. I believe it's a testament to you that so many of your clients are now friends. We call you *The Best Agent Ever*!

To my editor, Maisie Lawrence at Bookouture, your edits and critical eye are propelling my writing forward in such important ways. I'm truly growing as an author in big thanks to your hard work and fabulous collaborations with me. Thank you.

To all my friends and family who bought my first book, *The Stepdaughter*, and are now eagerly reading my second, you guys are the best and you continue to blow me away with your support. Thank you for your kind words and for taking the time to read my work. Your excitement is what encourages me to keep writing.

Thank you to all my newfound readers near and far. It's astonishing to write something and know that people are picking up copies of my book around the world. I went from being pleased if a next-door neighbor read a few pages to absolute delight that others are discovering my words too. Thank you for your support and for leaving such fantastic reviews!

The author support groups I've found online and the friends I've made in writing, thank you for being an incredible source of camaraderie, knowledge, and shared experiences. We are learning from one another, and more importantly, cheering on each other. These groups include the 2020 Debuts, 2021 Debuts, Bookouture Authors Lounge, Women's Fiction Writers Association, On Submission, Agent Rachel Beck and her crew, especially authors Rea Frey (your emails and messages mean so much) and Nicole Angeleen (your friendship is special plus your gift for making edits and early suggestions are truly game-changers for improving my work), and a shout-out to the original group from back in the day: Writing Bootcamp Buds. We've been together since the beginning.

To my beloved Susie, I think you knew I always wanted to keep writing but I wasn't sure how I was going to do it with two small boys. When you passed away and I wrote about that experience, something healed inside. My endearing letter to you. Writing that short story is also what reignited a passion for me to write again, a catharsis and a distraction, and I thank you for that gift (although I'd much rather be sitting with you and sharing a beer). I miss you and love you, Susie-Q.

To my parents, Kelvin and Cecilia, my sister Davinia, my gorgeous nephews Leo and Elliot, my Aunties Rosie, Liz, and Beryl in England, my E-E Grace and dozens of aunts and uncles and cousins in Malaysia, and my best friends from Alabama and Louisiana, I love you! You are the original support team. The ones who know me best and the crew that keeps shouting about my books from the rooftops. Thank you all! I couldn't do this without you.

To my husband, David, thank you for supporting me from the first day I sat down to write and the day I called announcing the first book deal. Champagne and cake! Thank you for every kiss on my forehead every time you check on me as I type.

And to our sons, Reece, Liam, Andrew, and Matthew, you are the reasons why your dad and I do what we do. You are our everything. We have big dreams for each of you. Thank you for continuing to tolerate my cooking, for remembering to hang up your bath towels, and especially for the day Reece said to me while I worked, "Mom, I respect the grind." I hope all of you achieve everything you work hard to accomplish too.

CPSIA information can be obtained
at www.ICGtesting.com
Printed in the USA
LVHW020335240321
682229LV00005BA/1269